the perfect image

(a jessie hunt psychological suspense—book 16)

blake pierce

Blake Pierce

Blake Pierce is the USA Today bestselling author of the RILEY PAGE mystery series, which includes seventeen books. Blake Pierce is also the author of the MACKENZIE WHITE mystery series, comprising fourteen books; of the AVERY BLACK mystery series, comprising six books; of the KERI LOCKE mystery series, comprising five books; of the MAKING OF RILEY PAIGE mystery series, comprising six books; of the KATE WISE mystery series, comprising seven books; of the CHLOE FINE psychological suspense mystery, comprising six books; of the JESSE HUNT psychological suspense thriller series, comprising nineteen books; of the AU PAIR psychological suspense thriller series, comprising three books; of the ZOE PRIME mystery series, comprising six books; of the ADELE SHARP mystery series, comprising thirteen books, of the EUROPEAN VOYAGE cozy mystery series, comprising six books (and counting); of the new LAURA FROST FBI suspense thriller, comprising four books (and counting); of the new ELLA DARK FBI suspense thriller, comprising six books (and counting); of the A YEAR IN EUROPE cozy mystery series, comprising nine books, of the AVA GOLD mystery series, comprising three books (and counting); and of the RACHEL GIFT mystery series, comprising three books (and counting).

An avid reader and lifelong fan of the mystery and thriller genres, Blake loves to hear from you, so please feel free to visit www.blakepierceauthor.com to learn more and stay in touch.

ISBN: 978-1-0943-7508-3

BOOKS BY BLAKE PIERCE

RACHEL GIFT MYSTERY SERIES
HER LAST WISH (Book #1)
HER LAST CHANCE (Book #2)
HER LAST HOPE (Book #3)

AVA GOLD MYSTERY SERIES
CITY OF PREY (Book #1)
CITY OF FEAR (Book #2)
CITY OF BONES (Book #3)

A YEAR IN EUROPE
A MURDER IN PARIS (Book #1)
DEATH IN FLORENCE (Book #2)
VENGEANCE IN VIENNA (Book #3)
A FATALITY IN SPAIN (Book #4)
SCANDAL IN LONDON (Book #5)
AN IMPOSTOR IN DUBLIN (Book #6)
SEDUCTION IN BORDEAUX (Book #7)
JEALOUSY IN SWITZERLAND (Book #8)
A DEBACLE IN PRAGUE (Book #9)

ELLA DARK FBI SUSPENSE THRILLER
GIRL, ALONE (Book #1)
GIRL, TAKEN (Book #2)
GIRL, HUNTED (Book #3)
GIRL, SILENCED (Book #4)
GIRL, VANISHED (Book 5)
GIRL ERASED (Book #6)

LAURA FROST FBI SUSPENSE THRILLER
ALREADY GONE (Book #1)
ALREADY SEEN (Book #2)
ALREADY TRAPPED (Book #3)
ALREADY MISSING (Book #4)
ALREADY DEAD (Book #5)

EUROPEAN VOYAGE COZY MYSTERY SERIES
MURDER (AND BAKLAVA) (Book #1)
DEATH (AND APPLE STRUDEL) (Book #2)
CRIME (AND LAGER) (Book #3)
MISFORTUNE (AND GOUDA) (Book #4)
CALAMITY (AND A DANISH) (Book #5)
MAYHEM (AND HERRING) (Book #6)

ADELE SHARP MYSTERY SERIES
LEFT TO DIE (Book #1)
LEFT TO RUN (Book #2)
LEFT TO HIDE (Book #3)
LEFT TO KILL (Book #4)
LEFT TO MURDER (Book #5)
LEFT TO ENVY (Book #6)
LEFT TO LAPSE (Book #7)
LEFT TO VANISH (Book #8)
LEFT TO HUNT (Book #9)
LEFT TO FEAR (Book #10)
LEFT TO PREY (Book #11)
LEFT TO LURE (Book #12)
LEFT TO CRAVE (Book #13)

THE AU PAIR SERIES
ALMOST GONE (Book#1)
ALMOST LOST (Book #2)
ALMOST DEAD (Book #3)

ZOE PRIME MYSTERY SERIES
FACE OF DEATH (Book#1)
FACE OF MURDER (Book #2)
FACE OF FEAR (Book #3)
FACE OF MADNESS (Book #4)
FACE OF FURY (Book #5)
FACE OF DARKNESS (Book #6)

A JESSIE HUNT PSYCHOLOGICAL SUSPENSE SERIES
THE PERFECT WIFE (Book #1)
THE PERFECT BLOCK (Book #2)
THE PERFECT HOUSE (Book #3)

THE PERFECT SMILE (Book #4)
THE PERFECT LIE (Book #5)
THE PERFECT LOOK (Book #6)
THE PERFECT AFFAIR (Book #7)
THE PERFECT ALIBI (Book #8)
THE PERFECT NEIGHBOR (Book #9)
THE PERFECT DISGUISE (Book #10)
THE PERFECT SECRET (Book #11)
THE PERFECT FAÇADE (Book #12)
THE PERFECT IMPRESSION (Book #13)
THE PERFECT DECEIT (Book #14)
THE PERFECT MISTRESS (Book #15)
THE PERFECT IMAGE (Book #16)
THE PERFECT VEIL (Book #17)
THE PERFECT INDISCRETION (Book #18)
THE PERFECT RUMOR (Book #19)

CHLOE FINE PSYCHOLOGICAL SUSPENSE SERIES
NEXT DOOR (Book #1)
A NEIGHBOR'S LIE (Book #2)
CUL DE SAC (Book #3)
SILENT NEIGHBOR (Book #4)
HOMECOMING (Book #5)
TINTED WINDOWS (Book #6)

KATE WISE MYSTERY SERIES
IF SHE KNEW (Book #1)
IF SHE SAW (Book #2)
IF SHE RAN (Book #3)
IF SHE HID (Book #4)
IF SHE FLED (Book #5)
IF SHE FEARED (Book #6)
IF SHE HEARD (Book #7)

THE MAKING OF RILEY PAIGE SERIES
WATCHING (Book #1)
WAITING (Book #2)
LURING (Book #3)
TAKING (Book #4)
STALKING (Book #5)

KILLING (Book #6)

RILEY PAIGE MYSTERY SERIES

ONCE GONE (Book #1)
ONCE TAKEN (Book #2)
ONCE CRAVED (Book #3)
ONCE LURED (Book #4)
ONCE HUNTED (Book #5)
ONCE PINED (Book #6)
ONCE FORSAKEN (Book #7)
ONCE COLD (Book #8)
ONCE STALKED (Book #9)
ONCE LOST (Book #10)
ONCE BURIED (Book #11)
ONCE BOUND (Book #12)
ONCE TRAPPED (Book #13)
ONCE DORMANT (Book #14)
ONCE SHUNNED (Book #15)
ONCE MISSED (Book #16)
ONCE CHOSEN (Book #17)

MACKENZIE WHITE MYSTERY SERIES

BEFORE HE KILLS (Book #1)
BEFORE HE SEES (Book #2)
BEFORE HE COVETS (Book #3)
BEFORE HE TAKES (Book #4)
BEFORE HE NEEDS (Book #5)
BEFORE HE FEELS (Book #6)
BEFORE HE SINS (Book #7)
BEFORE HE HUNTS (Book #8)
BEFORE HE PREYS (Book #9)
BEFORE HE LONGS (Book #10)
BEFORE HE LAPSES (Book #11)
BEFORE HE ENVIES (Book #12)
BEFORE HE STALKS (Book #13)
BEFORE HE HARMS (Book #14)

AVERY BLACK MYSTERY SERIES

CAUSE TO KILL (Book #1)
CAUSE TO RUN (Book #2)

CAUSE TO HIDE (Book #3)
CAUSE TO FEAR (Book #4)
CAUSE TO SAVE (Book #5)
CAUSE TO DREAD (Book #6)

KERI LOCKE MYSTERY SERIES
A TRACE OF DEATH (Book #1)
A TRACE OF MURDER (Book #2)
A TRACE OF VICE (Book #3)
A TRACE OF CRIME (Book #4)
A TRACE OF HOPE (Book #5)

PROLOGUE

"Jessie, will you marry me?"

Her jaw dropped at the question.

Was Ryan Hernandez really proposing to her? As she looked down at him, kneeling in the snow in the small California mountain town of Wildpines, her brain could barely process what was going on.

When she went to bed last night, she was just happy that she, Ryan, and her sister, Hannah, were alive after facing off with the notorious serial killer called the Night Hunter. And that confrontation had happened only hours after uncovering who had been murdering local female entrepreneurs. Now her boyfriend was on his knee on a chilly mountain morning holding out a ring in a small black box, asking her to spend the rest of her life with him.

"Jessie," he repeated nervously, "will you?"

She realized that she'd been staring silently at the ring for longer than might be considered customary. She blinked hard, snapping herself out of it.

"Yes!" she exclaimed with tears in her eyes. "Of course I will."

Ryan's face cracked into a wide smile. He stood up and put the ring on her finger before giving her a long kiss. She returned it with equal enthusiasm.

"You had me worried there for a second," he said quietly.

"I'm sorry," she replied excitedly, the impact of what had just happened finally hitting her for real. "I was just momentarily stunned. I didn't see this coming, certainly not after the day we just had. I'm just trying to wrap my brain around it. Give me a minute and I'll turn into a bowl of giddy Jell-O."

"You guys coming?" Sam shouted from the cabin. "The breakfast is getting cold."

For a second Jessie had forgotten that they had visitors. In addition to Hannah, who was still asleep inside, they had been joined last night by U.S. marshals Samuel Mason and Thomas Anderson. Both men were sent up to escort them back to L.A. today. After that, she and her family would lose federal protection; not that they needed it now that the Night Hunter was dead.

Jessie had a brief flash of just how the Night Hunter had died, before forcefully pushing it out of her head. That wasn't what she wanted to be thinking of in a moment like this.

"We'll be right there," she yelled to Sam before turning her attention back to Ryan. "This is amazing. It really is. But can I make a weird request?"

"Considering the one I just made, that seems fair," Ryan said.

"Do you mind if we keep this a secret for now?" she asked. Seeing his face falter slightly she pressed on. "I get that you want to shout it to the world and I do too. But you know that we're going to have tons of department debriefs and media interviews over the next few days. If people see a ring on my finger, that's only going to add to the complicated questions. At least for a little while, I'd like for this to just be ours, something no one else can have. What do you think?"

His frown softened once he understood her reasoning, or at least the reasoning she was willing to provide to him right now.

"Of course," he said. "I get it. We can tell people once all this madness settles down."

"Thank you," she replied, relieved.

"I guess you better do what I've been doing for the last week."

"What's that?" she wondered.

"Hide it," he said, closing the box and handing it over to her. "Hopefully you won't be as nervous with it as I was."

"Big strong Ryan Hernandez was nervous holding a little tiny box?" she replied playfully. "How sweet!"

"I guess that's your first time officially teasing me as my fiancée."

"Trust me," she assured him, "it won't be the last."

*

Marshal Sam Mason drove them back in the Service's large, black SUV while Marshal Tom Anderson followed behind in their rental car. Hannah, who had to be threatened with having water poured on her to get out of bed, had fallen asleep almost as soon as the SUV started down the winding mountain road from Wildpines back to the freeway.

Sam had the radio on, listening to some L.A. smooth jazz station. During a news break, the anchor came on to read the latest updates. The first story was about the president's current international trip. The second story hit closer to home.

"In local news, renowned criminal profiler Jessie Hunt has done it again. Last night in the small Riverside County town of Wildpines, she and LAPD Detective Ryan Hernandez took down one of the most infamous serial killers in American history. The true identity of the man, known to most as the Night Hunter, has yet to be determined and may never be. Sources say that the killer burned off his fingerprints and replaced his own teeth. The Night Hunter won't be shedding any light on his real name, as he was killed during his apprehension."

The anchor continued but Jessie tuned him out. Saying that "he was killed during his apprehension" was technically true but didn't accurately describe what transpired last night. The truth was that her half-sister, Hannah Dorsey, shot the Night Hunter in cold blood, when he was unarmed and had already been handcuffed. Just as bad, she didn't seem to have any remorse about it.

The old woman whom the Night Hunter had taken hostage—a shopkeeper named Maude—had covered for Hannah, saying the shooting was in self-defense. No one had contradicted her and the police seemed satisfied with that explanation. But that didn't make it true. Her sister had committed murder. They would have to deal with that fact and whatever repercussions came with it.

With that hanging over her head, Jessie couldn't help but wonder if she'd made a mistake in accepting Ryan's proposal. Was this the right time? Hannah was in a precarious psychological situation, if not a legal one. Ryan himself was still recovering both physically and emotionally from the attack that left him in a coma last summer. And the frenzy she would have to deal with in the aftermath of the Night Hunter case would be crushing for all of them. Maybe this wasn't the ideal time to get engaged.

She turned to Ryan, wondering how she could broach the topic delicately later, and was surprised to find that he was asleep too. Suddenly she felt tired as well. The weight of the last few days had been enormous and now that at least some of it was lifted, she found that she couldn't maintain the level of adrenalized alertness that had helped her push through until now.

She allowed her eyes to close. A sharp curve in the road made her open them, though it took some effort. But within seconds, they were closed again and she drifted off.

CHAPTER ONE

Ten Days Later

Everyone had gone to bed; everyone except Gillian, of course.

As usual, while the rest of her family slept, Gillian Fahey puttered around the house, waiting to get tired. It was after 1 a.m. but she still felt wide awake. Watching TV hadn't helped. Nor had reading or knitting.

Despite therapy, meditation, and pills, she still struggled with insomnia. Oftentimes, she wouldn't drift off until 2 or 3 a.m., only to have to wake up again at six to get everyone ready for the day. It had been this way for months now. It was worse than usual tonight because her husband, Simon, was away on a business trip.

Gillian wandered from the sitting room, where she'd been looking at a collection of framed family photos, through the game room, the music room, and the family room, until she reached the kitchen. She wasn't especially hungry but thought that maybe hunting through the fridge for expired food or leftovers that had turned bad would keep her busy for a while. Perhaps she'd even reorganize the small pantry.

She was just grabbing a few suspicious-looking Tupperware containers out of the fridge when she heard something. She immediately recognized the noise. The rope chain for one of the back deck table umbrellas was banging against the umbrella pole, making an annoying clanging sound.

She put the containers down on the center island in front of the knife block and headed in that direction, trying to keep her frustration in check. How many times had she asked people to properly tie off those chains for just this reason? It was almost as bad as nails on a chalkboard. When she had events on the deck, preventing the "chain clang," as she called it, was essential in order to keep guests from going inside to escape the irritation.

When she got to the sliding back door, she turned on the deck light. Sure enough, the chain on the middle of the three tables was loose and clanging away. She hurried out to tie it down. It took longer than usual, as the chain ducked and parried in the howling wind. Luckily, she was wearing cozy sweats and her long black hair was tied back in a ponytail.

When she finally got the chain secured, she returned inside and locked the sliding glass door. Now there was no way she could get to sleep anytime soon, so she returned to the kitchen, resigned to an hour of pantry reorganization.

But as she reentered the kitchen, she noticed something odd. The Tupperware containers were no longer where she thought she'd left them: on the island, in front of the knife block. Or had she moved them and forgotten? Maybe the lack of sleep was playing tricks on her. Even though she was only thirty-one years old, she'd read that sleep deprivation could have all kinds of psychological effects, including hallucinations.

Not wanting to go down that road, she pushed the thought from her head and headed back to the smaller pantry to get started on the boring task. She decided to begin with the shelves and settled on the top one in the back, where all the canned goods were. The first step was to determine what had expired.

She had just stepped into the pantry when she felt a hard shove in her back. The force slammed her into the back wall and several cans toppled down on top of her. Turning around, she saw that she wasn't alone. Someone wearing a face-covering watch cap with small slits for the eyes, nose, and mouth closed the door and stared icily at her. The trespasser was holding a long carving knife that looked to be hers.

It took a second for shock and confusion to give way to fear. But when it did, she opened her mouth to scream. The large intruder was already slicing at her neck. When the sound came out, it was more of a hoarse hiss than a scream. She felt a stinging sensation, then a burning one. She reached her hands up to her throat and saw that blood was shooting out the side of her neck, drenching the nearby cereal boxes. Yet somehow she was conscious. Somewhere behind the tower of fear that suddenly dwarfed her, a thought emerged. It occurred to her that the attacker had cut her vocal cords.

The attacker advanced on her and something in her brain told her it was a man. She extended her arms to defend herself but he swatted them down with unexpected force. She thought he was going to come at her neck again but instead, he swung the knife at her left thigh, just below the groin. Again she tried to scream as the pain ricocheted through her but no sound came out.

She stumbled to the right, where she slammed against another shelf and crumpled to the floor. Several more packages tumbled down on her, but she barely noticed. Her neck was burning and her leg, with blood spewing out of it, was throbbing. She didn't know which hurt worse.

She fought to remain conscious as the man in the mask moved toward her. Her disorientation again made way for terror. She tried to open her mouth to try to scream again but found that her body wasn't responding to commands. Desperate, she attempted to reach out and grab a large soup can in the hopes of slamming it down on the top of the assailant's shoe. But her fingers wouldn't grasp the thing.

She managed to loll her head up at the man standing over her. He removed his mask. She did her best to focus on him but it was difficult. He leaned in closer, gazing into her eyes intently. And then, in her last conscious thought before she died, she realized something.

I recognize him.

CHAPTER TWO

Jessie sat down at window three in the visitor area and waited. The plastic chair was bolted to the floor. Attached to the wall near the window was a corded telephone.

On the other side of the glass were two deputies. One stood by the door on the inmate side. The other repeatedly walked back and forth behind the inmates, his eyes constantly moving as he watched for any unexpected activity. Jessie glanced to her left and right, trying to get a peek at the inmates on either side, but the dividers were about six feet high, making it impossible. She was left to stare at the door and wait for the inmate's arrival.

She'd been to the Twin Towers Correctional Facility many times before. But this was her first visit to the Medical Services Building and its infamous Female Forensic In-Patient Psychiatric Unit. She wasn't happy to be here but she had no choice. A woman being held in this psychiatric prison had seemingly inside knowledge of the movements and plans of a serial killer on the outside, one whom the inmate had never met. If Jessie wanted to learn how, she'd have to talk to her, even if that woman, Andrea "Andy" Robinson, had once tried to kill her.

As she waited for her to arrive, her thoughts drifted to how the last ten days had gone. In order to get her head straight after the Night Hunter confrontation, she had taken a brief leave from UCLA, where she taught a weekly seminar in criminal profiling. She also informed the LAPD that she wouldn't be available for consulting work for the same reason. That leave ended today.

She could have used more time but wasn't sure how much difference it would have made. Hannah, despite having multiple teletherapy sessions with Dr. Lemmon in recent days, still hadn't said a word about gunning down the serial killer up in Wildpines.

Ryan seemed to be doing better than her, but Jessie still got the sense that he was struggling a little. Even though he'd been instrumental in taking down the Night Hunter, she knew he still blamed himself for several deaths that occurred because he froze the first time he had a chance to stop him.

Jessie felt like she was in a comparatively good place, but she didn't want to delude herself. If she was really doing so great, why had it taken her a week and a half to come here, to finally speak to the person she should have visited the day she got back from the mountains? Maybe she wasn't doing as well as she liked to think.

But then she caught a glimpse of herself in the glass. Considering everything she'd been through lately, she thought she didn't look too bad for someone approaching her thirty-first birthday. Her brown hair settled just below her shoulders. Her green eyes were bright and alert. And she'd used much of her paid leave from UCLA to work out, hoping to keep her five-foot-ten, athletic build from falling apart.

The door opened and she snapped to attention. A guard came in, followed by someone she couldn't see. Then the guard moved to the side and she had a clear view. It was Andy.

For a brief moment, Jessie was overwhelmed by panic. After all, this was the woman who had poisoned her during a girls' movie night at her Hancock Park mansion. And this was the first time they'd been in such close proximity since she'd testified at Andy's trial.

She knew that with four deputies in spitting distance and a physical barrier between them, she was safe. But the apprehension was there all the same. Still, she needed to know what Andy knew, so she ignored the intense desire to just get up and leave. Instead she took a deep breath and did her best to hide her anxiety by looking as bored as possible.

Andy projected the untroubled calm that Jessie was trying to manufacture. She wore the assigned uniform for inmates with a mental health issue designation: a yellow shirt and blue, loose-fitting pants. Her blonde hair was slightly longer than it had been when they'd had a video chat seven months earlier but still much shorter than it had been on the outside. She wore no makeup but since she didn't wear much back in her country club days, the difference wasn't noticeable. In fact, despite celebrating her thirty-fourth birthday behind bars, she looked shockingly put-together.

She was good-looking in an understated way that had helped her seem unthreatening when they'd first met. With one exception, all her features were pleasant but unmemorable. That exception was her eyes. Bright blue, they gleamed with what Jessie had originally interpreted as charming playfulness. But in reality, that twinkle suggested something much darker, a malicious intent that Jessie foolishly missed in their earlier, friendly interactions.

Andy sat down across from her and smiled like she didn't have a care in the world; as if she was settling in for coffee and chit-chat with an old pal. She picked up the phone on her side of the wall and waited.

Once more, Jessie was tempted to just get up and leave. But she swallowed the urge with a gulp and grabbed the phone beside her.

"I wasn't sure you'd come," Andy said.

"I wasn't going to," Jessie told her. "But I thought I should give you the opportunity to explain."

"Explain what exactly?"

Jessie saw that the woman wasn't going to make this easy.

"Explain how you knew that the Night Hunter would try to use Katherine Gentry to get to me," Jessie said, though she had no doubt that Andy already knew this.

Kat Gentry, a private investigator and Jessie's best friend, had received a collect call from Andy the evening before the Night Hunter's attack, warning that he would manipulate her to get to Jessie. She had been right.

"Let's just call it women's intuition," Andy said with a thin smile. Jessie refused to play this game.

"I see," she replied. "Well, I suppose now I can go back to Captain Decker and tell him I did my due diligence, but all I have for him is women's intuition. So I guess we're done here."

Andy nodded knowingly.

"Ah yes, how is Roy Decker doing these days?" she asked. "I'd imagine pretty well after the department bumped up his budget for the Homicide Special Section unit."

Jessie pretended she wasn't surprised by how much Andy seemed to know about the inner workings of the LAPD budgetary process and attempted to redirect the conversation.

"Apparently you're well-versed in how things are going with HSS. Care to share where you got that information?"

"Happy to," Andy replied. "But first, how are you doing? My understanding is that things got a little sketchy during your final encounter with the Night Hunter. Sleeping okay? No major emotional or physical fallout, I hope?"

"I'm not here for chit-chat, Andy," Jessie said, her tone more measured than her thoughts. "If you don't have anything useful to offer other than your intuition, I'll be on my way. I've got a lot on my plate."

"So I hear," Andy said, clearly amused. "Between raising a teenage girl, taking care of your injured beau, and juggling teaching and consulting gigs, it's a wonder that you're functional at all."

"I knew this was a waste of time," Jessie said, starting to stand up.

"Hold on," Andy said, slightly more animated than before. "I promise to tell you. I was just hoping we could catch up a little before getting down to business."

"I'm not telling you anything about my life," Jessie insisted, still standing.

"Fine. Then will you humor me briefly by letting me tell you a little about mine? I feel like what I have to share will make more sense if it's in context."

Jessie knew that Andrea Robinson, an admitted narcissist, would eventually demand to tell her tale of woe behind bars. It had always just been a matter of time. She suspected that it was the real reason she'd called Kat to tip her off about the Night Hunter; that her cryptic warning was simply bait to get Jessie face to face with her. But the only way to be sure was to let this play out a little.

"Go ahead," she said, sitting down again. "You have two minutes. Then you start spilling or I walk out that door."

"A whole life reduced to two minutes," Andy said, theatrically simulating deep sorrow. "I guess that's what it's come to."

"No one to blame but yourself," Jessie reminded her. "Besides, you seem to be getting by in here. I don't see any visible scars."

Andy smiled patronizingly, as if Jessie couldn't possibly understand the unseen scars she had.

"That's true," she conceded. "And it's part of what I wanted to discuss with you. You see, one of the major reasons I've managed to get by in this place is oddly counterintuitive. I've convinced the psychos in here that I'm crazier than they are. I periodically scream bloody murder for no reason. I took on the most violent inmate on the floor—beat her senseless with a plastic lunch tray—to make sure no one messed with me. She didn't do anything to prompt it but I knew that if I told the guards she attacked me and I was acting out of self-defense, they'd believe me over her, which they did."

"Sounds like you've adapted quite well to your new environment," Jessie noted, both impressed and troubled.

"I'm getting by as well as I can," Andy corrected. "I make a point to never alienate the guards. I attend all my required therapy sessions. I take all my prescribed medications. The doctors say I'm doing great."

"But are you *really* doing great?" Jessie challenged. "It seems like you're playing a role to me."

"Of course I'm playing a role. But can you blame me for that? I have to survive in this facility any way I can. If that means making the other inmates a little scared of me, that's what I'll do. There are multiple women in here who get in shouting matches with imaginary enemies, sometimes with imaginary friends. One inmate started ripping out another's hair, claiming it was covered in snakes. I have to protect myself, Jessie. Besides, I may be working the other prisoners but I'm not working the guards or medical personnel. I doubt you'd do things any differently if you were on the other side of this glass."

Jessie pretended not to be appalled at the description of daily life in this place. She didn't want to give Andy the edge that came from knowing she'd shocked her.

"You'll forgive me if I have a little skepticism about how forthcoming you're being with the people treating you," she said blandly. "I've seen how good you are at manipulating people, even those trained to be on the lookout for it."

It pained her to admit out loud that she'd been so easily deceived, but it was a preemptive move. Acknowledging how Andy had played her back in the day removed it as something that could be lorded over her. Andy gave the hint of a smile, as if she was impressed by the humility.

"That gets me to the other part of why I asked you here," she said, "beyond merely describing the woes of incarceration."

"And the other shoe drops," Jessie proclaimed, sensing that Andrea Robinson was finally getting where she intended to end up all along.

Andy looked mildly irked by her sarcasm as her eyes flashed briefly. But she quickly regained control. Jessie made a mental note of it.

"I was just going to say," Andy said calmly, 'that if you think I'm snowing the doctors here, maybe I should be placed at a facility where they're more practiced in dealing with folks like me."

Jessie studied her through narrowed eyes.

"What are you saying exactly?" she asked. "Stop playing games and just spit it out."

"Okay, cards on the table," Andy replied. "This place is supposed to be for short-term incarceration of inmates with mental illness; *short-term*, as in no more than a year. They cycle in new women every day, often on misdemeanor charges, then medicate them enough to release them once they've served their time, and send them back out into society. But not me—I've been in here well over a year with no sign that a transfer is imminent."

"Maybe accommodating a murderer isn't their top priority," Jessie pointed out.

"Maybe not," Andy allowed. "But I'm not looking to get my sentence reduced or go to some country club prison. There are multiple, high-security, lockdown facilities that I'm eligible for. I'm talking about places where the inmates don't throw their own feces at each other, or if they do, it's cleaned up more often than every twenty-four hours. I don't think that's an unreasonable ask, Jessie. And I'm hoping that they'd consider the request, if it was accompanied by a good word from the woman I allegedly poisoned."

"It's not alleged, Andy. You were convicted."

"Touché," Andy said. "So what do you say?"

Jessie knew that the bartering had begun. Andrea Robinson didn't expect her to support a prison transfer out of the kindness of her heart. She would have to offer something valuable in exchange. That's the reason this conversation was happening in the first place.

"I'm still confused," Jessie said. "Are you offering me anything worthwhile to get my support for a transfer to a different facility?"

"If I were," Andy wondered, "what would you say?"

"I'd say it depends."

"On what?" Andy asked with a wry smile, fully aware that her bait was generating interest.

"On how secure the alternate facility is and, more importantly, on what you have to offer."

Andy's smile grew wider.

"Then I guess we're at an impasse for now," she said. "Maybe you just need to sit a little with the idea of helping me secure that transfer. If you give me your word that you'll provide that, I promise to share information far more valuable than how I knew what the Night Hunter was up to."

Jessie stared at the woman, fully aware that she was being maneuvered. Still, she couldn't deny that Andy had somehow managed to predict that the serial killer would attempt to specifically manipulate Kat rather than anyone else. Maybe finding out how she knew was worth writing a letter in support of her transfer.

"Let me be straight with you," she said firmly. "If I write a letter for you, I will only submit it if I deem the information you share worthwhile. And a letter from me doesn't guarantee that a transfer will happen. I don't make those decisions. Are we clear on that?"

"Crystal," Andy said, beaming. "I will await your decision with bated breath."

She hung up without another word, stood, and indicated to the guard that she was ready to return to her cell. As she was escorted from the room, Jessie was left staring at the empty space behind the glass barrier, wondering if she'd just made a terrible mistake.

She decided to talk to the one person who might know the answer to that.

CHAPTER THREE

Kat was already waiting.

When Jessie walked into the downtown coffeehouse where they so often met, her friend was seated in a back corner table, far from prying ears. She saw Jessie, waved, and held up the drink she'd bought for her.

Jessie headed in that direction, passing by the mid-morning crowd, which consisted mostly of people sitting alone at tables, hunched over laptops. Kat stood to greet her in her normal work uniform—jeans, a casual shirt, and a brown leather jacket.

As usual, her dirty blonde hair was in a ponytail. Unless other customers took notice of the IED-induced long, vertical scar under her left eye, other customers wouldn't have any hint that they were in the presence of a former Army Ranger who had served in Afghanistan.

As she walked over, Jessie could hardly believe that less than two years ago, back when Kat headed up security at a psychiatric prison for men, the two of them had constantly been at odds. Now they were best friends, despite some recent, very rough spots.

"What do I owe you for the drink?" Jessie asked as she sat down.

"It's on me," Kat said. "I got a nice retainer this morning so I'm flush."

"Thanks," Jessie said. "What's the case that got you so freewheeling with your cash?"

"It's pretty boring actually. The owner of an accounting firm discovered about thirty-seven grand missing. He thinks one of his employees may be siphoning off small amounts from client payments, but he has no idea who it is so he can't trust anyone there to investigate. Enter Katherine Gentry, private investigator. He provided me with a mountain of documents that may have the answer in them."

"I didn't know you took on forensic accounting cases," Jessie said. "When did you start doing that?"

"This morning when I heard what he was offering as a retainer. I figure I'll learn as I go along."

Jessie couldn't help but laugh.

"I hope that works out for you."

"I have every confidence," Kat said without much confidence. "But that's not why we're here. You said you wanted to talk to me about Andy Robinson. What has she done now?"

"Nothing actually," Jessie replied, taking a sip of her coffee. "She made me an offer I'm not sure I can refuse."

"What's that?"

"Remember how you told me she called you out of the blue that night to warn you that the Night Hunter would use you to get to me?"

"Of course," Kat said, "And that's exactly what he did when he planted a piece of paper with an address written on it in a vehicle at a car dealership, where he was sure it would eventually be found. He knew I'd go to the address, discover the building across the street with the dead body, and call you. That's why he planted those listening devices in there. And like an idiot, I did exactly that, which led him to where you guys were hiding."

"Don't beat yourself up over that," Jessie replied. "Anyone would have fallen for it. I'm more interested in *how* she knew. She promised she'd tell me if I wrote a letter supporting a transfer to a different facility."

"You're not going to do it, are you?" Kat asked incredulously.

"I'm thinking about it," Jessie admitted. "If she has a pipeline to information that could be valuable, I can't just ignore that. Besides, any facility she goes to will be as secure, if not more so, as Twin Towers."

Kat nodded in understanding but it was clear she was skeptical.

"Do you really want to open yourself back up to communication with this woman? I mean, she did try to kill you. And from the way she talked to me that night, it sounds like she's fixated on you in a less than healthy way. With everything going on with both Hannah's and Ryan's recoveries, it seems like an unnecessary burden."

Kat had a point. Kat didn't even know about Hannah shooting the Night Hunter and she thought the kid was a handful. And even though Ryan was doing better physically, he was still struggling emotionally.

"It is a lot," she conceded, "and that doesn't even include the engageme—"

She stopped mid-word, realizing that she wasn't supposed to mention Ryan's proposal; that she was the one who'd insisted on secrecy. Feeling her face redden and her heart start to pound, she desperately tried to think of some other word to replace the one she'd started to say. Looking at Kat, she knew it was useless. Her friend's eyes were wide and her jaw was open.

"You're engaged?" she demanded.

"I didn't say that I was—"

"You absolutely did," Kat countered gleefully. "Don't try to walk it back. You're a frickin' engaged person."

"Lower your voice," Jessie whispered, feeling weirdly panicked. "Yes, I'm engaged. But it's supposed to be a secret. Ryan will lose it if he finds out I told someone and he can't."

"Why can't he tell anyone?" Kat asked, perplexed.

Jessie sighed in embarrassed frustration.

"Because I asked him not to."

"Why?" Kat asked, flabbergasted.

"I…I just wanted some zone of privacy. He proposed the morning after the Night Hunter confrontation. I was worried about Hannah. I was worried about him. And I knew that if I walked into our debriefs and media hits with a ring on my finger, it would be what everyone focused on. So I made him promise not to say anything until all this madness settles down."

"Hasn't it settled down yet?" Kat asked.

"Yes, somewhat. But you know how it is with us—nothing ever settles down completely. And I've started to wonder if it's such a great idea to pile a wedding on top of all the chaos in our lives right now."

"So are you saying you're having second thoughts?" Kat asked.

"No. Not about him. Not about us. It's just that I'm all turned around these days. I wonder if maybe this just isn't the right time."

They both sat quietly for a few moments, sipping their drinks.

"Is it at least okay for me to offer you congratulations?" Kat asked. "Your stud of a boyfriend—make that fiancé—wants to grow old with you. That seems congratulations-worthy all on its own."

"Of course. Yes. Thank you," Jessie said. "Just please don't breathe a word of it to anyone; not until I'm ready."

"My lips are sealed," Kat said, miming that action before leaning close and whispering, "Can I at least see the ring?"

Jessie cracked a smile despite herself. The ring should have been in the safe at home but for whatever reason, she'd been taking it with her everywhere. She pulled the box out of her pocket and opened it.

"That's beautiful," Kat admired. "Considering that he's on a cop's salary, it's pretty impressive. Put it on."

Jessie did so with less reluctance than she thought appropriate. She had to admit it looked, and felt, good. Kat fixed her with a stern stare.

"I hope you two work this out soon," she said, "because people need to see that rock on your finger. It'd be a disgrace to keep it in the dark."

"I'll see what I can do," Jessie said, blushing yet again.

Before Kat could pepper her with any other questions, Jessie's phone rang. It was Captain Decker.

"I thought you were on leave," Kat said, looking at the screen.

"It ended today," Jessie said. "I guess he held off as long as he could."

She answered the phone. Before she could even get in a word, Decker started in.

"Hunt, it's a good thing you're back on the clock," he said urgently. "We need you."

CHAPTER FOUR

Jessie was at LAPD's downtown Central Station ten minutes later.

Ryan was waiting for her when she pulled into the underground parking lot. As he walked over, she noted that his coma-induced limp from last summer was almost gone. Standing at his full six feet, he had regained some of his imposing stature. And while he wasn't back to his pre-hospitalization 200 pounds of muscle, with intense daily workouts, he was getting there. Luckily, his familiar black hair and kind, brown eyes had never changed.

"What's wrong?" he asked anxiously as soon as she got out of the car.

"Nothing," she lied. "Why?"

"When you texted me asking to meet down here before we talked to Decker, I started to worry."

"Sorry," she said. "I didn't mean to freak you out. I just wanted to go over how we're handling things on the engagement front before we go up there."

"Seems pretty straightforward to me," he said with a shrug. "We just act like nothing has changed. I don't see why it would come up."

Though he sounded amenable, Jessie got the sense that keeping it a secret was starting to wear on him. As much as she understood, especially now that she'd accidentally let it slip to Kat, she held firm.

"Okay, sounds good."

Ryan tilted his head curiously.

"You didn't need me to come down here for that. Secrecy was already standard operating procedure. What's the real reason I'm down here, Jessie Hunt?"

She chuckled despite her nervousness. He really did know her well.

"I'm just not sure if I should accept whatever this case is. Did Decker tell you anything about it?"

"Nope—just that it's big. He thinks that it's an ideal case to jumpstart the bigger, better HSS. Why wouldn't you accept?"

Jessie tried to think of the best way to broach what she knew would be an uncomfortable subject.

"There's just a lot going on," she finally said. "I already cancelled one seminar at UCLA because of my leave. I'm really concerned about

Hannah. She still hasn't told Dr. Lemmon about what really happened up in Wildpines. And I realize that you're on the mend and back on active duty, but we both know you're still struggling with what happened to Trembley. It's like you have some invisible anvil on your back that you refuse to throw off."

Ryan gave her a bittersweet smile. She could tell he was doing his best to hide how much he still blamed himself for the death of Detective Alan Trembley, who had died at the Night Hunter's hands while the two men were partnered up.

"I love that you're worried about me," he said soothingly. "But trust me, I'm working through it. I'll be okay. And I understand your apprehensions about taking a case with Hannah's situation. But the world can't just stop because things are hard right now. Of course I'll support you in whatever you want to do, but I think taking a big case might actually do you some good right now."

Jessie knew he really would support whatever decision she made. But she could tell that he was champing at the bit to dive into something big. He was literally bouncing on the balls of his feet as he spoke.

"I guess we better get up there then," she said.

"Great," he replied, leaning over to give her a kiss. "Just one thing."

"What?" she asked.

"If you want to keep our engagement a secret, you might want to take off that ring."

*

The second Jessie saw Captain Decker, she noticed a change in him.

When they walked into his office, he was standing up to greet them. His face was still more wrinkled than any sixty-one-year-old man's should be and his few tufts of white hair still jutted out wildly as if he'd just been in a wind tunnel. But his normally stooped posture seemed slightly straighter and there was a brightness in his eyes, a jauntiness in his step, that was unusual for him. It was obvious why.

Since the recent run of solved cases, including the murder of a social media star and the end of the decades-long serial-killing spree of the Night Hunter, the world was his oyster. Media attention was glowing. Headquarters had expanded his unit's budget and his staff.

The unit—Homicide Special Section—specialized in cases that had high profiles or intense media scrutiny, often involving multiple victims or serial killers. Now HSS had carte blanche to investigate any high-profile case in the city limits that Decker deemed part of their purview, regardless of whether the crime took place in downtown Los Angeles, the San Fernando Valley, or as far away as Pacific Palisades.

"You seem chipper today, Captain," Ryan said, noting the same positive energy that Jessie had picked up on.

"Things have been worse," Decker conceded, apparently constitutionally unable to actually describe himself as happy. "I'm glad to see you two. As I mentioned, I've got a hot case for you."

"Do you ever give us any other kind?" Jessie asked.

"Now that you mention it, I guess not," Decker replied. "But this one is hotter than most. Do you know who Simon Fahey is?"

"The name is familiar," Ryan said.

"It should be," Decker told him. "Fahey is one of the wealthiest men in Los Angeles. He started Pacific Advisory, a lobbying firm that advocates for Southern California businesses in D.C. It goes without saying that he's plugged in politically all over town."

"What did he do?" Jessie asked.

"It's not him. It's his wife, Gillian—thirty-one years old; two kids; worked as an executive at a tech firm in Playa Vista. She was murdered last night in their house in Santa Monica; sliced up with one of her own knives. The housekeeper found her this morning in their pantry. Thank god the kids weren't awake yet."

"How old are they?" Jessie asked as pity twisted her insides.

"I'm not sure," Decker admitted. "I was only told they're little."

"The husband's not a suspect?" Ryan asked skeptically.

"Not based on what we know so far. He was in Washington for a business roundtable with several senators. My understanding is that he caught a private plane back the second he heard. He'll be landing soon. From what I've been told, he's saying and doing all the right things so far. In fact, he was the one who requested HSS take on the case after it had already been assigned to detectives at Santa Monica PD. They obliged, of course."

"Great," Ryan said, "so we'll be investigating on someone else's turf, right after their own detectives were pulled. I'm sure there won't be any animosity from the folks there."

Decker ignored his sarcasm.

"You've dealt with tougher situations," he said unsympathetically. "Besides, HSS didn't request the case, the victim's husband did. You're in the clear."

"Officially, sure," Jessie agreed. "But why do I suspect that you would have fought for the case even if it hadn't fallen in your lap?"

"I might have," Decker admitted, "but not for the reason you think. Gillian Fahey isn't the only victim. Another woman was murdered in much the same way about a week and a half ago."

"What?" Ryan exclaimed. "Why don't I know about it?"

"Because we only made the connection today," Decker said. "Until now, there was no reason to think the first murder was anything worthy of HSS. Besides, it took place right around the time you guys were up in the mountains and everyone else in the unit was searching for the Night Hunter. It probably would have stayed off our radar if there wasn't this second murder."

"Who's the other victim?" Jessie wanted to know.

"Her name is Siobhan Pierson. She's a bit older than Gillian Fahey, forty-two. She was a socialite, married into money. Her husband, Ian, is an heir to the Pierson Farms fortune."

"Never heard of it," Ryan said.

"They're based in the Central Valley," Decker explained. "They grow something like one-sixth of the entire country's almonds."

"What makes you think the cases are connected?" Jessie asked.

"Pierson lived in the same part of town. She was also killed in her home, at night, with one of her own knives. Like Fahey, the attack was precise; no wild stabbing everywhere. There were just a few deep cuts near major arteries. Her husband found her later that night when he got home from visiting Pierson Farms headquarters in Bakersfield."

"So that's another husband off the hook?" Jessie asked.

"I believe that's what the initial investigation found but you'll want to revisit that," Decker instructed.

"And she's from Santa Monica too?" Ryan assumed.

"Actually, no—they live in Brentwood, but their house is only a few minutes from the Faheys'. Still, that's one less bureaucratic hassle for you since Brentwood is LAPD territory."

"That doesn't mean they'll be happy that we're taking over," Ryan countered.

"No, but it smooths things over a little bit," Decker offered. "Anyway, you two will be primary on the case but feel free to make use of other detectives you might need. Nettles and Valentine are doing required training today but Reid and Bray are in between cases, so they're available if you need them."

"I'm sorry," Jessie said. "Who's Valentine?"

Ryan and Decker exchanged a knowing look.

"I guess when you're just a consultant and don't show up every day like I do, you miss out on the office scuttlebutt," Ryan teased.

She was about to reply in kind, but Decker was too quick.

"Susannah Valentine is my first hire since they upped the budget," he said without Ryan's snark. "She worked patrol here for half a decade before taking a detective slot up in Santa Barbara. She was there for two years but her mom got sick and she wanted to move back to L.A. so she put in for the open position."

"I gather she's pretty good, if you picked her over LAPD candidates," Jessie observed.

"She closed seventy-eight percent of her cases as a detective, including busting up a local drug ring that targeted her for assassination after she started making things difficult for them, all before she turned thirty. I think you'll like her, Hunt."

"Why is that?" Jessie asked.

"She's almost as stubborn as you."

Jessie had to fight the intense urge to stick her tongue out at the captain of LAPD Central Station.

"Where are the files on Fahey and Pierson?" she asked, showing what she considered admirable restraint.

"On Hernandez's desk," he said. "You'll have to review them on the way out there. They're expecting you in Santa Monica within the hour. So get your asses in gear."

CHAPTER FIVE

The bullpen looked different.

Since the last time Jessie had been at the station for her debriefs more than a week ago, the set-up had been reconfigured to make room for Jim Nettles and Susannah Valentine. She couldn't help but notice that she no longer had her own desk. It had been reassigned to Valentine, who didn't appear to be around at the moment.

Jessie tried not to take offense at the change. After all, Valentine had to sit somewhere and Jessie only came in on special occasions, when Decker really needed her and it didn't conflict with her teaching schedule. But it still smarted a bit.

Her wounded pride was forgotten as soon as she saw the collection of happy HSS faces as she and Ryan approached. She realized that she hadn't seen everyone together since before the trip up to Wildpines, back when she, Ryan, and Hannah were under U.S. Marshal Service protection because of the threat from the Night Hunter.

"Long time, no see!" bellowed Detective Callum Reid.

Despite his cheerful demeanor, Reid looked tired. Jessie wasn't surprised. In a rare moment of vulnerability a few weeks ago, he'd confided that he had a serious heart condition and intended to retire as soon as he felt that HSS was back on its feet. No one else in the department was aware of his plans and though Jessie suspected the decision was imminent, she wasn't going to mention it if he wasn't ready.

Other than his weary bearing, Reid looked the same as usual. In his mid-forties, he had a bit of a belly. His brown hair was beginning to recede and he wore black-framed glasses that wouldn't have looked out of place on *Dragnet*. He gave her a big hug, and then did the same with Ryan.

Next to him, Detective Karen Bray looked equally pleased to see them, if far more healthy than Reid. Approaching forty, Karen had dirty-blonde hair pulled back in her now-standard ponytail. She was still the petite, eminently professional cop Jessie remembered.

But unlike when they first partnered together on the case of a murdered actress, there were no heavy bags under her eyes or food on her blouse. Maybe that was because her child was no longer waking her up in the middle of the night. But Jessie suspected it was also due to working in a friendlier job environment than the Hollywood Division she'd recently transferred from.

Jim Nettles, a longtime beat cop recently upped to detective, waved warmly despite looking generally apprehensive. Jessie assumed the nervousness was because of the training he and Valentine had today. She wanted to tell him not to worry; that his years of experience would more than compensate for his relative newness to being a detective. But since that might embarrass him, she said nothing. At thirty-seven, he was a walking callus of a man who'd spent fifteen years patrolling downtown streets. He didn't need a pep talk.

The biggest surprise was the presence of Jamil Winslow, who normally stayed in his research cave all day. Jamil was a brilliant investigator who operated a computer like Beethoven played a piano, able to uncover connections and details that slipped past far more experienced people. Small and fragile-looking, the twenty-four-year-old was indefatigable, often staying at work long after his colleagues were asleep in bed. He was also abidingly polite. Jessie had never even heard him curse.

But according to Kat, he'd grown restless at being perceived as just the research guy. Because of that, he'd accompanied her and Nettles into the field while they were searching for the Night Hunter. It was lucky that he had, because he was the one who found the listening devices the killer had set up to try to uncover Jessie's location. As they approached now, he broke into a big, confident grin.

"What's got you so giddy?" she asked him.

"Oh, didn't you hear?" Reid told her before Jamil could reply. "Winslow here has been promoted. He's not just a research grunt anymore. He's the official lead research grunt assigned exclusively to HSS. No more side gigs for the Vice or Gang units."

"Not only that," Karen added teasingly, "Decker is letting him hire his own assistant grunt. He's going to be a supervisor at the tender age of fifteen."

"I'm twenty-four," Jamil reminded her, though he didn't seem all that annoyed.

"I guess it's not that impressive then," Karen poked.

"Congratulations, Jamil," Jessie said with complete sincerity. "You really deserve this."

"Thank you, Ms. Hunt," Jamil said, blushing and averting his gaze.

Ryan looked about to add his well-wishes when someone spoke up from behind them.

"What did I miss?" a female voice asked.

Jessie turned around to find herself face to face with one of the most striking women she'd ever seen. About five foot six with long, black hair, olive skin, and sparkling hazel eyes, she had a lithe, athletic frame and a confident stance that suggested she knew how to use her body as a weapon in a pinch. Jessie knew who she was before the introductions were made.

"Jessie, this is Detective Susannah Valentine, the newest addition to HSS," Ryan said. "Susannah, meet Jessie Hunt, our consulting criminal profiler."

"Nice to meet you," Jessie said, extending her hand.

"It's an honor," Valentine replied, shaking vigorously. "I've been watching your exploits from my little township with fascination. Every time I think you can't top yourself, you go out and do it. You're a real star."

"Thanks," Jessie said, though she couldn't help but notice that Valentine was describing her more like a tabloid celebrity than a criminal profiler. She tried to give her the benefit of the doubt, adding, "Anything I can do to ease your transition, just let me know."

"Now that you mention it," Valentine said, pulling open one of the drawers in what used to be Jessie's desk and taking out a large Ziploc bag, "I collected some stuff of yours I found. I've been saving it for you so it wouldn't get tossed out."

She handed it over with a saccharine smile but her intent seemed clear. Jessie got the distinct impression that she was really saying "This is my territory now. Pack your stuff and get out of my way."

"That's so sweet," Jessie said, refusing to let Valentine see her irritation.

Ryan seemed to sense the unspoken tension and stepped into the breach.

"We'd love to catch up with everyone," he said quickly. "But we're just here to grab the case files and go. We can talk more later."

Jessie wasn't entirely sure she wanted to chat with everyone but held her tongue.

"Sounds good," Reid said. "We'll get out of your hair."

"Actually, Reid," Ryan replied, "Decker said you and Bray might be able to help us out. The case he assigned us has two connected murders. He has us headed to Santa Monica to investigate the most recent one from last night. Are you able to look into the older killing in Brentwood?"

"No problem," both detectives said simultaneously.

"Thanks," Ryan replied. "Here's the file on that one. Can you send us a copy while we drive? We're already late."

"You got it," Karen assured him.

Ryan grabbed the Santa Monica file and he and Jessie headed for the door. Once they were out of earshot, he leaned over to her and whispered, "Valentine's not usually that much of a bitch."

Jessie looked over at him skeptically.

"If you say so."

CHAPTER SIX

It looked more like a boutique hotel than a single-family home.

In fact, when Ryan and Jessie first pulled up at the Fahey residence, that's initially what she thought it was. Located on 2nd Street, just north of the Fairmont Miramar Hotel, the huge house faced west, near a cliff overlooking the Pacific Ocean. It was surrounded by small hotels and large, fancy apartment complexes. The California Incline Foot Path, which led down to the beach and Pacific Coast Highway, was within walking distance.

They got out and headed up the path to the place, a Spanish-style mansion protected by a ten-foot stucco wall that circled around the entire property. Glancing over at Ryan, Jessie again observed that his limp was barely perceptible anymore. In fact, he was walking faster than she was. As they got closer to the security gate she noticed, to her surprise, that there was no police presence on the street.

"Where's the SMPD?" she asked. "Did they bail the second we were assigned to the case?"

Ryan shook his head.

"My understanding is that they were going to stick around to update us," he said. "I'm guessing they parked around back to keep a low profile. The murder hasn't broken on the news yet and I bet Simon Fahey prefers it that way."

They reached a large metal gated entrance at the end of the walkway. Ryan buzzed the call button. After a few seconds they got a staticky response.

"Residence," said an admirably unflustered-sounding woman.

"Hello," Ryan replied. "I'm Detective Ryan Hernandez with LAPD's Homicide Special Section, along with Jessie Hunt. We're here about the investigation."

"One moment, please," the voice said.

It didn't take long for the gate lock to click open.

"Someone will meet you at the front door," the voice promised.

They stepped inside, pulled the gate closed, and headed toward the house. With the high wall no longer blocking their view, Jessie got a better look at it. It wasn't on a large lot, but it made up for the lack of lateral space with four stories. In fact, it was taller than the hotel next door.

The exterior was a mix of additional stucco and sandstone wall cladding. There were multiple ivy-strewn balconies on each floor. A small Koi pond surrounded by flowering cacti sat just to the left of the entrance. The place even had what appeared to be a bell tower.

As they stepped onto the front porch, the front door opened to reveal a fastidious-looking woman in her late forties. She wore business attire and her gray hair was tied up in a bun. She looked like she'd been crying recently.

"Hello," she said quietly. "I'm Ann Roth, the Faheys' house manager. Thank you for coming. Mr. Fahey is just upstairs showering now that he finished his interview with the other detectives. He'll be back down soon. In the interim, I can take you to meet your colleagues from the Santa Monica Police."

"That sounds good," Ryan said, matching her hushed tone.

They followed Ann down the central hallway past a wide set of floating stairs that Jessie had to crane her neck to see the top of. After passing through several rooms seemingly intended solely to house historic furniture, they came to a more modern-looking living room with a couch that seemed like people actually sat on it.

Standing at the far end of the room, speaking to each other in low voices, were two men. One was a skinny, youngish-looking uniformed SMPD officer. The other man, in his mid-thirties, with a deep tan and slicked-back black hair, wore a nice suit and shiny shoes. Jessie guessed he was a detective. He looked over when they entered the room.

"Ah, I see the cavalry has arrived," he said with the very disdain that Ryan had been worried they'd encounter.

"Ryan Hernandez," he said evenly, pretending not to notice the other man's tone. "This is Jessie Hunt."

"The legendary profiler in the flesh," the man in the fancy suit said with something less than admiration. "What an honor it is to have you here. I'm Detective Clarke Gore. This is Officer Butler. We're on messenger duty."

"Has everyone else already left?" Jessie asked, unable to hide her surprise as she and Ryan walked over.

"Yep," Gore replied, sounding bored. "The deputy medical examiner and the crime scene unit cleared out about an hour ago. The rest of our guys took off a half hour later. We've been waiting for you; expected you at ten a.m. It's closer to eleven."

"Sorry," Ryan said, keeping his cool. "We only found out we were assigned to this an hour ago. With traffic, it took a while."

"Well, let's not waste any more time," Gore replied irritably. "I can brief you on what we know. We already talked to the husband but I assume you'll want to re-interview him. He should be down in a few minutes."

"Sure," Ryan said. "Maybe you can start by giving your impressions of Fahey—his credibility and such."

Gore shrugged.

"He seemed pretty dazed to me," he said, finally easing up on the sarcasm, "like he was having trouble processing the reality of the situation. Hard to know if that's legit but verifiable data backs up his alibi. We've already got footage of him dining at some D.C. restaurant last night with a couple of celebrities who went on the lobbying junket with him. A cable news crew caught him going into Senator Black's office this morning. He agreed to share his phone data so we can verify his other movements. I guess that's something you two will have to follow up on."

Jessie got the distinct impression that Gore was fed up with being here and would do almost anything to end this briefing. She wasn't inclined to accommodate him.

"I guess so," she said. "So what can you tell us about the crime scene?"

"Follow me," Gore replied curtly.

He led them into the adjoining kitchen. It was massive, with a huge, metal center island. Above it was a collection of hanging pots and pans. There were two refrigerators, an eight-burner stove, and a three-level oven. Jessie noticed that one slot in the knife block was conspicuously empty.

"Was that the murder weapon?" she asked, pointing in that direction.

Gore nodded.

"It's already bagged and back at the main station on Olympic Boulevard. The chief medical examiner still has to confirm for sure but on visual inspection, the wounds match the blade."

"Was there any sign of forced entry?" Ryan asked. "Anything reported stolen?"

"Not that we could find. We're still checking for missing items but nothing so far. And according to Belinda, the housekeeper who found her this morning, all the doors were locked. Everything seemed normal. She arrived at six a.m.; said she usually cleans downstairs for a while until the family comes down around seven. The thing that finally got her attention was seeing blood leaking out from the other side of a pantry door, which was locked. The M.E.'s preliminary estimate is that she'd been dead for five to seven hours."

"Locked exterior doors," Jessie noted. "No sign of forced entry. Attack occurs in a confined space. It all happens when the husband is out of town. This doesn't feel like a crime of passion to me. It looks planned, deliberate."

Everyone was quiet for a moment as that disquieting possibility settled in.

"When did the house manager, Ann Roth, get here?" Ryan asked, breaking the silence.

"She usually arrives around eight," Gore explained. "But she said that Belinda called her in hysterics as soon as she discovered the body. Apparently she wasn't sure what to do, especially with the kids in the house. She didn't know if they'd been killed too and was afraid to go upstairs to find out."

"So it was Roth that called you guys?" Jessie asked.

"Correct," Gore said. "She called it in while driving over here; said she got here just before seven. Our first unit, including Officer Butler here, arrived just minutes later."

"That's right," Butler said nervously when Gore nodded for him to take over. "We went upstairs with Ms. Roth to check on the kids—Quentin is four and Cicely is two. They were both still asleep. She called Mr. Fahey in D.C. to tell him what happened, and then stayed upstairs with the little ones while the CSU folks did their work downstairs."

"Where are the children now?" Jessie asked.

"When they woke up, Roth had Belinda get them dressed and take them out a side door far from this area. They went for breakfast and then to a park. I think that's where they are now. When he arrived, Mr. Fahey insisted that they not come back until the crime scene was cleaned up and all of us were gone."

"Speaking of the crime scene, can you show us the pantry?" Jessie asked.

"There are actually three," Officer Butler said as he motioned for them to follow him. "Mrs. Fahey was found in what Belinda called 'the small one.'"

He directed them to the open pantry. Jessie thought that for a "small" pantry, it was pretty big, certainly larger than anything she'd ever had. It was completely empty and there was no sign that a person had been killed inside.

"Everything's been taken to the station as evidence," Gore said. "We're testing every soup can and cereal box in the hope that something pops—fingerprint, DNA, whatever. We're also checking some partial shoe prints we found in the blood. There are photos of everything, including the body as it was originally found. I can AirDrop you the data file that we've developed so far."

"That would be great," Ryan said.

Gore pulled out his phone and sent the file. Jessie's phone had just buzzed to indicate she got it when a voice spoke from behind them.

"I want to see those photos too."

They all turned around to see who it was. Jessie recognized him immediately from the web search she'd done on the way over. Standing before them in only boxer shorts and a white T-shirt was Simon Fahey.

CHAPTER SEVEN

He didn't look good.

In addition to apparently forgetting to get completely dressed, Fahey seemed stunned, as if he'd been hit over the head and had only just regained consciousness. His eyes were red and cloudy, and his brown hair was damp and disheveled. Though he looked to be tall—well over six feet—he appeared to be sagging in on himself.

"I don't think that's a great idea, Mr. Fahey," said Detective Gore, who was the first among them to recover from the sight of the man. "This is the sort of thing you can never unsee. That's not how you want to remember your wife."

"I deserve to know what was done to her," he insisted, his voice cracking. He looked on the verge of collapsing. Jessie hurried over to him and gently took his forearm.

"Let's sit down, Mr. Fahey," she said, leading him to the nearby breakfast nook.

"Who are you?" he asked as he settled onto a bench. Jessie took the bench across the table from him.

"My name is Jessie Hunt," she said, feigning ignorance that he'd specifically requested her unit. "I'm a criminal profiling consultant for a special unit of the LAPD called Homicide Special Section. This is Ryan Hernandez, the lead detective for the unit."

"Right," Fahey said vaguely. "I remember you now. I requested you guys. You were on the news a few weeks ago, caught that Night Hunter guy; killed him."

Jessie didn't contradict him. This wasn't the time to address any inaccuracies in his version of events.

"That's us," she said. "And we're to help you, but Detective Gore is right. Seeing those images right now would only make things worse. There will be lots of time to review them when your wife's killer is on trial. But for now, I don't recommend it."

"Okay," he said weakly, "if you say so."

He lowered his head forlornly, as if it was too heavy for his neck to support. Despite her natural inclination to be suspicious, Jessie was overcome with compassion. Assuming he was innocent, this man's whole world had just been blown up. His wife was dead. His children were motherless. No matter how many times she dealt with situations like this, it never got any easier, especially when there were kids involved. She could only imagine the frenzied heartbreak he must have felt on his cross-country flight this morning, unable to do anything to make it better. He was still undoubtedly a suspect, but at least in this moment, sympathy won out over scrutiny.

"I think it would be best," she reiterated before moving on. "But let me tell you what *could* help. I know you've already been interviewed, but Detective Hernandez and I have a few quick questions, if you don't mind."

"Okay," he said, lifting his eyes and attempting to make eye contact.

"Thank you," she said, leaning in closer to him. "First, Detective Gore tells us you're sharing all your phone data with us, correct?"

Fahey nodded numbly.

"Great. That will help us a lot," she said before moving on to a question she already suspected the answer to. "Now I noticed that you have a security system with cameras set up in various locations. Have you provided the login information yet?"

"He has," Gore said, answering for Fahey. "We've already looked at it and the attacker scrupulously avoided getting in the frame of any of them."

Jessie did her best to hide her frustration. She already assumed that was the case or else Gore would have told her right away. The question was intended to get Fahey talking and the detective had stepped on that effort. She tried again.

"Thank you, Detective," she said, and then turned her attention back to Fahey. "Can you think of anyone who might have wanted to hurt Gillian? Anyone who threatened her—a friend she had a falling out with or a co-worker?"

Fahey shook his head vigorously.

"No. Gilly almost never got into it with folks. The worst stuff she ever talked about were things like someone parking over the line into her space at work so she couldn't get into it or a PTA mom not showing up for a fundraiser. I don't remember her ever being truly worried about someone she dealt with."

"Is there someone else she might have discussed a concern like that with?" Ryan followed up. "Maybe someone in HR at work or a female friend she was close to?"

"I guess it's possible," Fahey conceded, "but I doubt it. She always asked me to look over any potentially sensitive work correspondence before she sent it out to make sure it was okay, so I doubt she'd have addressed a work issue without talking to me first. As to female friends she'd confide in, I don't even know who that would be. Gilly was friendly with lots of women but I wouldn't say she was tight with any one person in particular."

Fahey seemed like he might say more but then he seemed to lose his focus. Jessie wasn't sure what more could be gleaned from the guy in his current state. She looked over at Ryan to see if he felt differently. He shook his head that he didn't.

"Okay, Mr. Fahey," she said, starting to stand up. "That's all we have for you for now. We'll let you know if that changes."

Fahey nodded meekly.

"One more thing," Ryan added as if it was an afterthought. "We know that you have to travel to D.C. often for your work. But I'd ask that until we get resolution on this, please don't leave the state without authorization."

"Of course not. I would never leave the kids," he said before having some kind of realization. "Oh god—how am going to tell my children that their mother is dead?"

Jessie was stunned at the question. Hadn't he been asking himself that the entire flight back to L.A.? Before she could think of a diplomatic reply, his phone rang.

"It's our housekeeper, Belinda," he said, ashen-faced. "What do I do?"

"Answer it," Ryan told him without hesitation. "You need to go to your children and tell them the truth in whatever way you think they'll understand. Don't lie to them and suggest that Mommy is coming back. Your job is to be there to support your kids. Our job is to find out who did this and catch them. We'll do ours. You just focus on making your little ones feel safe. Got it?"

Fahey nodded and answered the phone. The rest of them filed out of the room to give him some privacy. As she walked away, Jessie attempted to focus exclusively on what needed to happen next: getting to the Santa Monica police station to see Gillian Fahey's body and review the case file. But no matter how hard she tried, it was impossible to ignore the sound of Simon Fahey breaking down on the phone as he tried to speak.

CHAPTER EIGHT

As always, the morgue was freezing.

Ryan pretended not to notice while he waited for the medical examiner to remove the sheet from Gillian Fahey's body. Though he'd seen hundreds of dead bodies over the years, he always found it best to steel himself for what was to come.

It was just the three of them in the frigid, antiseptic room—him, Jessie, and the M.E. That was because, after showing them to a small conference room where they could set up shop and pointing to the elevator that would lead them to the basement morgue, Detective Gore had unceremoniously abandoned them.

"Good luck," he had told them with clear relief on his face that his responsibility to them was complete. He was gone before they could reply.

Ryan studied the M.E., a small, bald man in his fifties whose office door placard read *Dr. Morris E. Orzabal, Chief Medical Examiner.* Orzabal had a dour expression that Ryan thought seemed appropriate for the task at hand and he wasn't especially chatty, which was fine. It always felt unseemly to engage in small talk in the presence of someone who'd had her life violently snuffed out.

"You ready?" Orzabal asked.

He and Jessie both nodded. The M.E. pulled back the sheet to reveal Fahey's naked body. Her sagging flesh pressed down on the metal table below her. Her eyes were closed and her hair had been pulled to the sides of her head so it didn't bunch up under her. It was thickly matted with dried blood.

Other than two deep cuts—one on her neck and another on her upper thigh—there was no indication of further assault. No bruising to speak of. No superficial cuts that might have suggested she'd tried to evade the killer while they swiped at her with the knife. Of course, where could she go? She'd been cornered in that pantry.

There was blood all down her front where it had gushed out from her neck. Similarly, her entire left leg was stained red. But setting that aside, Ryan found himself agreeing with Jessie's earlier theory that this murder was well planned and not spur of the moment, especially in light of how the killer managed to avoid all the home security cameras.

"The cuts are very clean," he noted. "I don't see any sign of hesitation or sloppiness."

"I agree," Orzabal said. "Whoever did this was very precise. He or she knew exactly where to use the knife to kill without getting messy. The wounds occurred only at the carotid and femoral arteries. She would have bled out, probably lost consciousness within thirty seconds, and died in under a minute, if not less. I obviously haven't begun the autopsy yet but barring some shocking revelation, I think the cause of death is clear."

Ryan couldn't disagree.

"I don't see any obvious signs of struggle, no defensive wounds," Jessie noted. "Have you had a chance to test under her fingernails yet?"

"No," Orzabal answered. "I will do that momentarily, but I'm skeptical that it will reveal much."

"Me too," Ryan said. "This whole thing looks professional. The killer struck fast, knew exactly where to attack to get maximum impact with minimal effort."

Jessie sighed softly. Ryan looked over at her. After all their time together, he knew that sound. It meant his secret fiancée had come to some conclusion, usually one that surprised herself. He loved that they could read each other so well, but was apprehensive about what ugly realization she had come to.

"What?" he asked expectantly.

"It's weird to say this," she began, "but this murder almost feels…considerate. Her death wouldn't have been painless but it would have been quick. It wasn't sadistic or intended as cruel. It's almost clinical, as if the killer was testing their skills, to see if they could complete the goal they'd set out to accomplish. It feels like some kind of experiment."

Ryan didn't know whether that prospect made the killing somehow better. He was inclined to think it was worse. If the person who did this was testing themselves, how many times would they need to take the exam before they felt they passed it?

*

The conference room that Gore had put them in was stiflingly hot.

As they started reviewing the files on both murders, Jessie compared the details of Gillian Fahey's death with that of Siobhan Pierson in Brentwood a week and a half earlier. They were remarkably similar. Both were cut in almost exactly the same places with similar knives from the victims' own homes.

"I'm going to see if I can find a fan," Ryan said, breaking her concentration. "There's no way I can spend hours in this room without any circulation. I'd just as soon go to the Pierson house to see things in person than sit around here."

"That would be a waste of time since Reid and Karen are handling it," Jessie reminded him. "Let's just wait and see what they have to say."

"Shouldn't they be done over there by now?" Ryan asked. "How long did they leave after we headed out?"

Just then, Jessie's phone rang. It was Karen Bray.

"Speak of the devil," she said, answering the call and putting it on speaker. "Hey, Karen, we were just talking about you guys. Are your ears burning?"

"Jessie," Karen said, her tone immediately suggesting that something was very wrong. "I'm sorry I couldn't call until now but I haven't had time."

"What is it?" Jessie asked, instantly focused.

"Reid had a heart attack."

"What?" Ryan demanded.

Jessie's heart sank. She found that she was unable to speak.

"He's alive," Karen said quickly. "The doctor said it was mild and that he should be okay."

"When did this happen?" Jessie finally managed to ask.

"We were on our way to the Pierson house in Brentwood when he started complaining of chest pain. I was driving and we were only five minutes from Providence Saint John's Health Center so I drove straight over. That's where we are now. The doctor said that even though it wasn't the most severe attack, it was good that we were so close."

"Is he conscious?" Ryan asked.

"No," Karen said. "The doctors just finished putting in a stent. He's zonked out in recovery right now. They said they want to monitor him so they're keeping him here for at least a few days."

"Should we come over?" Jessie wanted to know.

"No," Karen insisted. "There's nothing to do right now. His wife is on her way. I'm staying at least until she arrives. Depending on how she's doing, I might stick around. I've already called Decker so he's making arrangements for Callum to take an extended leave."

Hearing that last comment, Jessie had a brief moment of guilt as she questioned whether she should have said something. If she had gone to

Decker with what she knew about Reid's heart problems, would he be in a different position right now?

She dismissed the thought. Reid had confided in her and she swore to keep his secret. She had to respect his wishes. Still, when he and Decker finally got a chance to speak, she suspected their conversation wouldn't be about a leave of absence so much as retirement. Callum Reid had only been holding off on it until HSS was in better shape. It clearly was. There was no reason for him to stick around now.

"But we obviously won't be able to go to Brentwood," Karen added, snapping Jessie out of her internal debate. "I did just get a text from Susannah Valentine offering to postpone her training and go in our place. Should I tell her to do it?"

"No," Jessie said more firmly than she'd intended. She tried to calibrate her next words better. "Tell her thanks, but I would hate for her to have reschedule the training. Besides, we're already right here. It's silly for her to drive all the way from downtown when we can be there in ten minutes."

She could feel Ryan's probing eyes on her but refused to look in his direction.

"Okay. I'll let her know," Karen said. "Oh, the nurse is waving at me. I think Reid may be waking up. I've got to go."

She hung up. Jessie gathered the case file, hoping Ryan wouldn't say anything about how she shut down the offer of help from Valentine. He didn't.

She did feel a little ashamed of how definitive she had been. She wasn't sure exactly why she was so opposed to the new detective participating in the case, though she had to admit that it was likely tied up in their earlier, tense interaction. Was there more to it? Was she jealous of the new girl?

Those were questions she probably needed to explore, but not right now. Right now she was going to investigate a murder in Brentwood and satisfyingly, the new girl was not.

CHAPTER NINE

"I need to start an almond farm."

Jessie couldn't help but laugh at Ryan's words. He was right. If being the heir to an almond farm fortune meant living where the Piersons did, she was on board too.

After a quick drive over from the station, they got buzzed in. Once the automatic gate opened, they drove up to the Pierson Estate. And that's what it was—an estate. They lived just a few miles north of the Faheys' mansion, on a quiet residential street off Montana Avenue, near the Brentwood Country Club. The Pierson place lacked one thing the Faheys had: an ocean view. But they made up for it.

Unlike the Fahey home, whose lot butted right up to hotels and condo buildings on all sides, the Piersons didn't live within fifty yards of their closest neighbors. Their property was surrounded by a metal gate that actually had pointed spikes at the top. The structure was barely visible behind the veritable forest that lined the driveway.

"Better almonds than peanuts," she said. "Remember, I'm allergic to those."

"How could I forget," Ryan replied. "Isn't peanut oil what Andrea Robinson slipped into your drink that night to poison you? Speaking of which, how did your chat with her go?"

"Not great," Jessie told him, frowning at the memory of the visit. "She wants me to support moving her to a different facility. She made vague promises about telling me where she gets her inside info if I do."

"Are you going to?" Ryan asked.

"I haven't decided," Jessie said curtly. "I've been a little busy since we met so it's not at the top of my priority list. Should we go introduce ourselves?"

Ryan must have sensed that she didn't want to discuss it further because he didn't pursue it.

"Sure," he said. "Let's see how an almond heir lives."

*

Pretty well as it turned out.

The Piersons' home wasn't as many stories tall as the Faheys'—it had only three. But it had actual wings separated by a central portico section. Its design seemed to be modeled on the White House, which suggested something about how the Piersons thought of themselves. As Ryan was parking, they got simultaneous texts.

"It's from Jamil," Jessie said. "So far he's coming up empty on that search of the victims' social media that I asked him to do. He says there are no obvious connections between Gillian Fahey and Siobhan Pierson. No online friends in common. No shared groups. No indications of any feuds of any kind. He's going to dig deeper but that might be a dead end."

"That's surprising," Ryan said as they got out of the car. "I would have thought that with all Simon Fahey's political connections, he would have interacted with a family as powerful as the Piersons."

"He may have," Jessie replied. "But it's just not showing up in their social feeds."

"Maybe they're connected through their kids?" Ryan suggested.

Jessie shook her head.

"The Piersons didn't have any."

"Okay then, wasn't Siobhan Pierson a socialite?" Ryan pressed as they approached the massive front doors to the house. "It seems like there would have been some overlap there. Hey, wasn't Andy Robinson a socialite too?"

Apparently Jessie's earlier assumption that he wasn't going to push her about their Twin Towers meeting was premature. He had just been biding his time. Jessie pressed the doorbell and turned to him.

"Are you trying to piss me off, Hernandez?" she demanded. "Because you're doing a great job of it."

He looked amused at her irritation.

"I thought this was how a good fiancée was supposed to behave. It's my job to tease you."

Jessie was immediately chastened. She realized that she'd forgotten all about the engagement. Looking down at her naked ring finger, she felt a surge of heat along the back of her neck. How much longer would they need to keep this a secret and at what point would Ryan start to balk? Before she could reply, the door opened.

A pale young woman with red hair stood before them. She couldn't have been more than twenty-five but looked wiped out.

"You're the detectives?" she confirmed politely.

"I'm Ryan Hernandez. This is Jessie Hunt."

"Please come in," the woman said, stepping to the side. "My name is Kelly Hoffs. I'm the Piersons' personal assistant. Mr. Pierson is in the game room. I'll take you to him."

As they followed her through the massive entrance hall, Jessie could hear her shoes echo with each step. Kelly moved quickly, passing through multiple elaborate dining rooms, one with a chandelier the size of a small car. Eventually they reached a more casual section of the house. Jessie saw a kitchen, a full bar, a breakfast room, and a living room that looked like people actually used it. Kelly stopped suddenly outside a huge, closed oak door. Beyond it, a TV was on at high volume.

"I need to let you know that Mr. Pierson is not in a great place right now," Kelly whispered to them.

"In what way?" Jessie asked quietly, leaning in. Ryan did the same.

"Ever since Mrs. Pierson's death, he's been understandably struggling," Kelly said. "He held up pretty well for a while, when he had things to keep him busy like planning the funeral, dealing with her will, coordinating with the foundation boards she served on. But now that all that's taken care of, he doesn't know what to do with his time. He's taken to listening to music they liked or watching old videos of them, usually while drinking—a lot. He's already well on his way today. He's not at his best. I just wanted you to be prepared."

"Thank you," Ryan said. "Where's the rest of the staff during all this?"

"Most are on temporary leave," Kelly said, "although I'm worried he might make it permanent. The vast majority of folks who worked at the estate were part of Mrs. Pierson's team. She did her foundation work out of her home office."

"That's where she was killed, correct?" Ryan confirmed. "The report said she died between eight and midnight."

"Uh-huh," Kelly answered with a wince. "Mr. Pierson found her when he got back from Bakersfield around one in the morning."

"No one else was here?" Jessie asked.

"Not at that hour. The only people who are regularly here outside of business hours are me and Patty, the housekeeper. But like we told the other detectives, we were both gone by six that night. And nowadays, she and I are the only people still working here on a regular basis. I pay the bills and schedule maintenance and deliveries. She keeps the place from falling apart. To be honest, I wouldn't be surprised if he lets us go too. He doesn't seem to care about much of anything anymore."

It occurred to Jessie that his stagnation might actually be a mark in his favor as a suspect. Unless it was part of an impressive long con, it didn't logically follow that someone who killed his wife as part of some involved plan would fall into a torpid malaise afterward.

"Okay, thanks for the heads-up, Kelly," Jessie said. "Can you let him know we're here?"

Kelly knocked loudly on the big door and didn't wait for a response before opening it. She poked her head in.

"Mr. Pierson, those detectives I mentioned would be coming by are here. They'd like to speak with you now."

A gruff male voice said something unintelligible to Jessie. But Kelly seemed to understand and waved for them to enter. Once inside, Jessie took in her surroundings. The room was dark, with deep wood paneling. There appeared to be a large window in the center of the room but it was hidden by a thick curtain. The only light came from the dimmed overhead lights and the television.

It may have been called the game room but that seemed to reference just two games. There was a pool table at one end of the room and a nearby dartboard. Other than that, there was just the TV, several couches, and a small bar in the far corner. Most of the bottles were empty.

Ian Pierson was sprawled out on one of the couches. A half full glass of something golden rested on the coffee table in front of him. Kelly hadn't been kidding. The man looked terrible.

Jessie had reviewed the case file on the way over and had been expecting the strong-jawed man in a tailored suit from the photos she had flipped through. But that man was almost unrecognizable as this one.

The Ian Pierson before them now was in a long robe. Underneath it, he wore a gray sweatshirt and sweat pants. His dirty-blond hair was a bird's nest and he had at least five days' growth of beard. His eyes were red and watery, and the skin around them was puffy. She knew he was forty-four but he looked at least a decade older than that.

When he saw them, he made a clumsy, half-hearted attempt to sit up straight. After fumbling with the remote control for a moment, he muted the TV. Kelly stepped forward.

"Mr. Pierson, please meet Jessie Hunt and Ryan Hernandez. They're with the LAPD," she said crisply as if everything was normal. "This is Ian Pierson."

"Thank you, Kelly," Ryan said. "We'll take it from here."

She nodded and left without another word. Ryan and Jessie walked over and sat on the couch adjacent to Pierson's. The man followed their movements with sluggish eyes but made no attempt to speak.

"Mr. Pierson," Ryan began, "thank you for meeting with us. First, we want to express our condolences for your loss. We know this is a difficult time and that you've already been interviewed by prior detectives. But Ms. Hunt and I work for a unit that specializes in cases like this and we were hoping to ask you a few additional questions."

"Cases like this?" Pierson mumbled in a bitter, gravelly voice. "You mean rich women murdered in their own home offices, bleeding out, knowing they were about to die but unable to do anything about it—those kinds of cases?"

Jessie knew he was being sarcastic but he wasn't far off. Nonetheless, she answered diplomatically.

"Our unit, called Homicide Special Section, typically handles cases that are well-publicized or have high-profile victims. We also deal with cases that involve more than one victim. Your wife falls into several of those categories, as does the other victim."

"What other victim?" Pierson demanded hotly. "No one mentioned anything about that to me."

"There's no reason you would be aware," Ryan told him. "The second victim, a woman named Gillian Fahey, was killed last night."

Pierson looked genuinely stunned.

"She was killed…the same way?" he finally asked.

"That's correct," Ryan said. "Just like your wife, she was killed in her own home by an unknown intruder. Like your wife, she was cut with one of her own kitchen knives in specific areas of the body near major arteries. Just like the case file for your wife's death indicates, the perpetrator in this second attack was able to avoid cameras around the home. We suspect the murders are connected. But we're here so long after your wife's death because we only made the connection this morning."

Pierson, his face a cocktail of confusion and pain, tried to push himself fully upright. It took a great deal of effort. When he settled into a position where he seemed unlikely to topple over, he lifted his head and blinked. Though he was still a little unsteady, he did his best to focus in on Jessie

"Okay," Pierson said, slurring slightly, rubbing his hair aggressively as if that would give him some extra cognitive edge, "ask your questions. I want to help."

Jessie thought that, despite what had just happened, he seemed to be making a good faith effort to fight through his drunkenness. She decided to press on.

"Thank you, sir," she said softly. She started with information they already knew from the case file, to ease him in. "Our understanding is that you were up in Bakersfield the night of your wife's death. Is that correct?"

"Yes," he said very deliberately, so as to get each word right, "I had an executive board meeting."

"And where were you last night?" she asked as casually as she could when trying to pin down a potential suspect's alibi.

He thought for a second before the cloud lifted from his eyes.

"I was here, doing this," he answered, extending his arm to indicate the drink, the couch, and the television.

"To be clear, you were getting drunk and watching TV?" Jessie asked.

"That's right," Pierson said almost proudly, "same as every day for the last…the last while."

"Can anyone confirm that?" Ryan asked.

"Nope," he replied with amazing nonchalance. "The maid, Patty, doesn't work Sundays. Kelly came by to check on me at…some point but I don't remember exactly when. She could probably tell you. I know it was daytime. But once she was sure that I was still breathing and hadn't soiled myself, she took her leave."

He said that last line with an elaborate arm flourish. Jessie was about to ask her next question when a light seemed to go off for him.

"Hold on, are you asking me that because you think I might have killed this Gilly woman?"

Jessie, her eyes narrowed, was about to follow up when Ryan beat her to it.

"It's just a routine question," Ryan assured him. "The cases appear to be connected so we would be remiss not to ask you. Would you be willing to share your phone data to verify your whereabouts last night?"

"Sure. Do I need to hand it over?"

"No," Ryan said. "Now that we have your authorization, we can get what we need on our own."

"Mr. Pierson," Jessie said, holding out a photo on her phone for him to see, "did you or your wife know either of the Faheys?"

Pierson studied the picture for several seconds before looking at her.

"I already knew Simon Fahey by reputation," he said, measuring each word carefully. "I definitely recognize him and maybe her too. But I'm not sure if that's from seeing them in news stories or actually meeting them in person. To be honest, I'm not all that clear-headed right now."

His response was perfectly reasonable, but something about the way he answered felt off to Jessie. She couldn't quite put her finger on why. Instead of fixating on it, she decided to let it go for now. She found that if she allowed these things to percolate, something worthwhile usually rose to the surface. She moved on to another question.

"Did Siobhan ever say that she felt threatened by anyone?" she asked.

From his quick response and fairly streamlined speech, Jessie knew he'd been asked that before.

"People were always mad at her. She influenced the budgets of several charitable foundations and had final say on her own. People tend not to like it when they don't get the money they ask for. Sometimes they're pretty blunt about it. But she never mentioned being worried about her safety and none of those disputes sounded like the kind of thing that would lead someone to come into our home and kill her!"

By the end, Pierson had worked himself up to the point that he was yelling.

"Are you—?" Jessie began before he cut her off.

"Besides, how could they even get in? You saw the gate outside. Someone could get impaled on those spikes. Am I supposed to believe that some old biddy that runs a homeless shelter in Santa Monica is going to pole vault over our gate because she didn't get her desired donation? Come on!"

Ryan looked at Jessie and she knew what he was thinking: Pierson was too agitated to be of much use to them at this point. She nodded in silent agreement. They both stood up.

"I think we have all we need for now, Mr. Pierson," Ryan said. "Thank you for being so generous with your time. We'll reach out to Kelly if we have any further questions. And again, we're very sorry for your loss."

The anger having petered out of him, Pierson muttered something mostly incomprehensible, though Jessie thought she heard the word "biddy" again. They saw themselves out, doing their best not to get lost.

"What do you think?" Ryan asked as they walked down the cavernous hallway that they hoped led to the front door.

"I think that man gave me an itch but I don't know where to scratch," she said, thinking back to their exchange about whether he knew the Faheys.

"What do you mean?" Ryan asked just as the hallway gave way to the central foyer where they originally entered the house.

Jessie was about to explain when she got a text. It was from Callum Reid. The message read: *Recovering. But the plan I mentioned to you privately is a sure thing now. Keep it to yourself. I want to tell everyone myself.*

As soon as she saw it, she realized she'd made a mistake by looking. Ryan would ask what it was. And in order to honor her promise to Reid, she'd have to lie.

"Who was that?" Ryan asked almost immediately.

Trying to think on her feet, she did her best to keep her deception to a minimum.

"Reid—he said he's doing okay."

"That's it?" Ryan asked, surprised. "No more details?"

"Not really," she lied. "I could ask him but I get the sense that he's wiped out. It was probably a chore just to text at all. Why don't I just wish him the best from both of us? We can interrogate him later."

"Okay," Ryan agreed, though he looked slightly put out.

She hurriedly typed her reply: *Of course. Talk later. Wishing you the best.*

She shoved the phone in her pocket and quickly changed the subject.

"Besides, right now, there's someone else I need to interrogate."

"Who?" Ryan asked.

"My sister."

CHAPTER TEN

Watching unobtrusively from behind a window, he saw the police leave the estate and smiled to himself as he snapped photos of them. Neither of them seemed to have a clue.

The woman was talking on her phone and appeared agitated. The man next to her had a concerned look on his face. These didn't seem like people who had made some kind of investigative breakthrough.

And how could they? He had planned these killings for months, gaming them out carefully, considering every variable. And so far at least, they had gone like clockwork, just as he knew they would.

He was aware that cockiness was a risk, one that was common in his profession. But he also knew that the same meticulous approach he took to his work would continue to serve him well in this far more important endeavor.

After watching them disappear into the distance, he returned his attention to the task at hand. He had planned all these elimination events simultaneously, knowing he would only have a small window in which to accomplish each of them once the authorities realized they were connected. That preparation would pay off now.

If he had waited until he'd killed Fahey to look for his next victim and organize her demise, the chances of success would drastically diminish. But because he'd done all the prep work for each woman well in advance, all he had to do now was follow the steps in his detailed outline. The dominoes had already been lined up. Just giving one little push would topple them. It was exhilarating.

He was tempted to follow the cops to see where they would go next, but resisted the urge. If he did his job properly, it wouldn't matter where they went because their search would never lead back to him.

Besides, the next event would be occurring soon and he had to review all the elements to make sure everything was in place. There were a few variables that could complicate things and he needed to be certain nothing had changed since he last checked on the situation's status.

He'd been accused of overconfidence many times in his life. But he'd never been accused of not doing his homework. This would be no exception. By the end of the night, another woman was going to bleed.

CHAPTER ELEVEN

Hannah didn't pick up the first time.

Jessie, sitting in the passenger seat as Ryan drove them back to the Santa Monica police station, was tempted to leave a message. But she knew her sister rarely checked them so she called a second time. Just as she feared the call would go to voicemail again, her sister answered.

"What?" Hannah demanded without so much as a hello.

"What a warm greeting that was," Jessie said, unable to keep the frustration out of her voice. "How are you doing?"

"I know why you're calling, Jessie," Hannah said, still giving off a strong "leave me alone" vibe. "Yes, I know that it's two fifty-four p.m. Yes, I know my appointment with Dr. Lemmon is at three. And yes, my rideshare is almost there. I didn't forget."

"No one suggested you did," Jessie replied, though those were exactly the questions she had intended to ask. "I just wanted to check in with you. You may find this hard to believe but after being in hiding with government protection for over a week, it's going to take a while before I just casually assume all is well with the people I care about."

Though her statement was certainly true, Jessie had it admit, if only to herself, that her sister's *physical* safety wasn't the sole reason for the call. Ryan's skeptical expression from the driver's seat of the car suggested that she wasn't entirely believable.

"Okay, well now that you know I'm fine, can I go?" Hannah wanted to know. "The car is about to pull up to the building."

"In a minute," Jessie promised before delicately addressing the real reason she was checking in. "This is your first in-person therapy session with Dr. Lemmon since everything happened. Do you expect it to be any different from the telesessions you've been having lately?"

Even as she heard the words come out of her mouth, she knew they wouldn't convince anyone, much less her inherently suspicious little sister.

"Thank you," Hannah said, surprising Jessie with her polite response until she realized that she was talking to her rideshare driver. After the car door slammed, her sister responded more forcefully, though her voice was hushed. "I know you're wondering if I'm going to tell Dr. Lemmon about how the Night Hunter really died. Don't worry—I have no intention of saying anything."

"I'm not worried," Jessie insisted, although she wasn't exactly sure how she felt. "But someone is dead because of a choice you made and I think it would serve you well to discuss that, even in nonspecific terms."

"I'll think about it," Hannah replied. "But I'm about to get in the elevator and there are other people, so we should probably drop it for now."

"All right, I just—" Jessie started to say before she realized her sister had hung up. She sighed and said, more to herself than to Ryan, "That went well."

"Did you expect anything different?" he asked.

"I guess not," she admitted.

"Well, I have a good way to take your mind off it," he said. "You might have missed it while you were on the phone but Jamil texted us both. He says he had time to do a deeper dive into both victims' social media and he has some updates. You want to call him back?"

She nodded and did exactly that. Unlike Hannah, he answered before the end of the first ring.

"How's it going, Jamil?" she asked.

"Okay," he said. "I'm still processing the news about Detective Reid's heart attack. But doing this research has kept me occupied. I have some new information for you."

"Shoot," Ryan told him.

"First of all, I found that Gillian Fahey and Siobhan Pierson *did* have a few friends in common, at least online. They even had a couple of exchanges on different platforms, though they were very surfacy, just a comment here or there on the other one's feed. I get the sense that neither of them realized who the other woman was. They both used handles unconnected to their real names."

"Okay," Jessie said, trying to hide her disappointment, "anything else?"

"Yes," Jamil said definitively, "one small thing and one big thing. Which do you want first?"

"Start small and work your way up," Ryan suggested as they turned onto Olympic Boulevard. The Santa Monica police station was in sight now.

"All right, it appears that both women considered themselves amateur 'influencers,' and they weren't wrong. Praise or criticism of a business or service from either of them usually got lots of comments. In several cases, they talked about the same places. I'm still compiling a full list of establishments that both of them criticized. I thought that if someone's business might have been hurt by what they said, that might serve as motive."

"Good thinking," Jessie congratulated. "If that's the small thing, I can't wait to hear the big one."

She could almost hear Jamil blushing through the phone.

"Thank you," he said softly before finding his professional voice again. "The other thing is that I managed to access Gillian Fahey's direct messages. She has some from Ian Pierson."

Jessie turned to Ryan, her mouth open wide. Jamil had been underselling the big thing. As she regrouped, the researcher continued.

"There aren't a ton of them and they're several months old, but they're definitely worth checking out. I'll send them to you."

"Great," Ryan replied. "Can you summarize the gist though?"

"They're pretty nonspecific. I'd say intentionally so, as if they were written so that if someone—say a spouse—found them, they wouldn't be overtly incriminating. Even so, the fact that they exist at all seems noteworthy to me."

"No question," Ryan agreed.

So did Jessie. The itch that she couldn't scratch earlier when talking to Pierson returned with even greater intensity. Only now she knew why.

"Do the messages include their real names?" she asked.

"No," Jamil said. "Just handles. Why?"

"Just testing a theory," she answered cryptically. "Regardless, that's great work."

"Thank you. I'll send you the messages as soon as we hang up," Jamil said giddily, clearly proud that his discovery had met with so much enthusiasm.

"Thanks much. We'll talk again soon," Jessie said before hanging up and turning to Ryan. "You know that unsettled feeling I mentioned when we talked to Ian Pierson?"

"Yeah," Ryan replied.

"I know why now. It was a sense that he wasn't being straight when he dodged our questions about knowing the Faheys. He definitely knew her, and pretty well."

"How can you be sure?" Ryan asked. "Maybe they were just online friends."

"No," Jessie said firmly. "He called her Gilly, just like Simon Fahey did. That's personal."

Ryan seemed convinced, so much so that even though they were less than a block from the police station, he quickly pulled into the left lane and made a U-turn.

"I assume we're heading back to see Ian Pierson?" Jessie asked.

"You assume right."

CHAPTER TWELVE

Hannah was nervous.

That feeling—like so many emotions that others dealt with regularly—was so rare for her that it took a moment to identify it. But once she did, she knew why.

Sitting across from Dr. Janice Lemmon, as the legendary psychiatrist's eyes bored into her, would unsettle even the most emotionally anesthetized person, which was exactly how Hannah viewed herself.

Long before her adoptive parents were murdered in front of her; before she was kidnapped by a serial killer who wanted to sculpt her into becoming one too; before she gunned down the unarmed, elderly man who had been hunting her new family, Hannah Dorsey discovered that conventional emotions like apprehension, pleasure, and guilt were strangers to her.

Even more intense ones, like joy, fear, and anger, were hard to come by unless she put herself in extreme situations. In the last year, she'd sought them out by doing everything from confronting drug dealers to breaking into the home of a convicted pedophile to using herself as bait to catch a gang of sexual slavers.

And finally, less than two weeks ago, she'd shot and killed the Night Hunter. Yes, the primary purpose of that act was to prevent him from doing her family more harm. But she couldn't deny that firing that gun and watching the life leach out of him gave her a thrill. And that scared her.

"You seem like you're miles away," Dr. Lemmon said, pulling her out of her navel-gazing. "What are you thinking about right now? Hannah?"

Hannah looked back at the woman. Behind her thick glasses, Dr. Janice Lemmon fixed her with a warm but penetrating gaze. It would be easy to dismiss her at first glance. Her outdated perm was comprised of tight little blonde ringlets that bounced when they touched her shoulders. She was a small woman, barely over five feet tall.

But she was visibly wiry; probably a result of the Pilates that Jessie said she did three times a week. For a woman in her mid-sixties, she looked great. And those sharp, owl-like eyes missed nothing. Hannah knew that in addition to being a psychiatrist and behavioral therapist, Lemmon was also a highly regarded criminal consultant who used to work full time for the LAPD. She was not to be underestimated.

Hannah wanted to tell Lemmon the truth, to unburden herself of the weight of the secret. But she wasn't sure if she could say what really happened without consequences. Was the doctor bound by patient confidentiality? Or was she obligated to tell the authorities about something like this?

The police already knew that Hannah killed the Night Hunter. But they believed it was done in self-defense. And though he deserved to die, she could make the argument that it was. After all, she was protecting her family from a serial killer who had murdered over eighty people, and those were just the victims that law enforcement knew about. He was an evergreen threat.

But Jessie and Ryan seemed to think that by shooting the man when he was unarmed and handcuffed, she'd crossed some line. It felt arbitrary to her. Just two minutes before she'd shot him, the Night Hunter was holding an old woman hostage and taunting Jessie about which of her loved ones he would kill first. Just because he had been outsmarted and subdued, they were supposed to use kid gloves on him? That didn't seem right.

And yet, she hadn't told Lemmon the truth. Did that mean that some part of her believed that she had done something wrong? Clearly, if she was holding back, something about what she'd done was bothering her.

"Hannah?" Lemmon repeated. "What is it?"

Hannah realized that she still hadn't answered the doctor.

"Nothing," she lied. "Sorry. I just got distracted. You were asking me something about how school was going? What exactly was the question again?"

Lemmon frowned. It was obvious that she wasn't buying the "distracted" excuse.

"Tell me what you were thinking about just now," she repeated.

Hannah really wanted to. But how could she? How could she admit what was troubling her to Dr. Lemmon if she couldn't admit it to herself? The answer was simple: she couldn't.

*

This time, they didn't wait for Kelly Hoffs to lead them to Ian Pierson.

Ryan made a perfunctory attempt to greet the assistant when she opened the front door. But after the assistant let them in, Jessie stormed right past her into the foyer.

"Is he still in the game room?" she demanded.

"As far as I know," Kelly said, taken back. "What is this about?"

"We have a few more questions for your boss," Jessie informed her, already heading down the long hallway.

When she got to the game room door, she didn't knock before shoving it open. Pierson was lying in the same spot where they'd left him a half hour earlier. Only now he looked like he'd passed out.

"Pierson," she barked.

Startled, the man shot up, lost his balance, and tumbled off the couch to the floor. As she walked over, he looked up groggily.

"What's going on?" he muttered.

By now, Ryan and Kelly had caught up and were entering the game room as well.

"These detectives wanted to speak with you again," Kelly said, making a futile but admirable attempt to infuse the situation with some dignity.

"We'll take it from here, Kelly," Jessie said forcefully as she walked over to the man.

"Should I be calling Mr. Pierson's attorney to have him come over?" she asked Ryan.

"That will depend on the answers he gives," Ryan told her. "If we read him his rights, then yeah, but for now we just want to chat."

Pierson managed to pull himself upright and climb back on the couch.

"I thought I answered all your questions already," he said, squinting at Jessie, seemingly to make sure she was who he thought she was.

"We have others," she replied, before lowering her voice. "And unless you want your sweet assistant over there to know about some of the lies you told us earlier and lose that admiring, sympathetic look in her eyes, I suggest you send her on her way."

Suddenly, Pierson looked far less groggy.

"It's okay, Kelly," he said loudly. "You can go. I'll let you know if I need you."

Kelly nodded courteously and left the room, closing the door behind her. When she was gone, Jessie sat down, this time on the same couch as Pierson. She wanted him to feel the pressure of her presence. Ryan took a seat on the other couch.

"You weren't honest with us before, Mr. Pierson," Jessie said with a finality that let him know there was no point in denying it. He still made a lame attempt.

"I barely remember what I told you before," he murmured. "What are you saying I lied about?"

"When I showed you Gillian Fahey's photo before, you gave the impression that you weren't sure you knew her. But you did know her quite well, didn't you?"

"I..." he started before trailing off.

He looked torn between wanting to deny everything and wanting to come clean. Jessie knew he just needed a small shove. She allowed her features to soften and made sure that the next words she spoke didn't sound accusatory.

"Tell us about how you met Gilly, Ian."

That seemed to cause an emotional dam to break inside him. He choked back a sob, and then allowed the second one free rein. Jessie looked at Ryan, who clearly thought she was on the right track. He said nothing, not wanting to interfere with the connection she'd managed to establish. Pierson coughed a few times, and then seemed to regroup.

"One morning a few months ago, I was speaking at an event at her firm in Playa Vista," he said heavily. "At the reception afterwards, we started talking and realized we lived in the same area. I've even jogged past her house sometimes on the way to the pier. We really hit it off. After the reception, we kept talking; went to a coffee shop. Next thing I know, I look up and an hour has passed. Everything felt so natural."

He stopped, as if arguing with himself about whether he should continue. Jessie stayed silent. Now that he'd started, she knew he couldn't stop himself.

"We exchanged numbers," he continued. "I wasn't going to call but I couldn't stop thinking about her. So I gave in and contacted her, suggested another coffee get-together, officially to discuss the tech landscape in town. She agreed. I offered to pick her up so she didn't have to drive. I arrived in my limo. I wanted to impress her. It seemed to work."

"What happened then?" Jessie pressed. Pierson was talking but seemed hesitant to cut to the chase.

"We had another good conversation and afterwards I offered a ride back to her office. She accepted. But once we were in the limo, the vibe changed. I touched her. She touched me back. And it escalated from there."

"Be more specific," Jessie instructed.

Pierson looked at her with a pained expression, as if he couldn't believe she was going to make him say it out loud.

"We had sex in the limousine," he said softly. "After that, it became a semi-regular thing. For the next couple of weeks, we had multiple rendezvous; maybe five or six. But then we stopped."

"Why?" Ryan asked.

"For one thing, it was wrong," he answered. "As exciting as it was, I was consumed with guilt. I loved my wife and had just let this thing get out of control. Gilly—Gillian felt much the same way. I think it was even worse for her because she had kids. And beyond that, her husband and I both have high-profile positions. A sex scandal could ruin reputations and maybe even businesses. It just wasn't worth it."

"So you just ended it?" Jessie asked.

"Yes," he replied, "a couple of months ago. And we haven't communicated since then. Neither of us told our spouses. It almost felt like a dream, not quite real. In fact, after that, I hadn't heard the name Gillian Fahey until you said it to me earlier. Now I can't help but wonder if what we did somehow led to this. I already felt like Siobhan's death was somehow punishment for our indiscretion. And now Gilly—it can't be a coincidence. Can it?"

Jessie didn't know the answer to that yet. She looked at Ryan, wondering if he had any other questions. He leaned in and gave Pierson a hard look.

"Is there more you need to tell us, sir?" he asked. "Now would be the time to come clean about anything else you've been hiding. You don't want us to discover that you've been deceiving us twice."

"No," Pierson insisted, "I swear. That's it. I was just too shocked and ashamed to say anything before."

Ryan studied him for a long second before turning to Jessie. She could tell he wanted to confer privately before saying anything more.

"Give us a minute, Mr. Pierson," she said, standing up and leading Ryan to the far end of the game room. Once there, she asked in a hushed tone, "So what do you think?"

"I don't know what to make of it," he admitted. "If we can confirm it, his explanation makes sense. Jamil did say that he and Gillian Fahey hadn't DM'd in months. And we know he had an alibi for his own wife's murder, though his alibi for last night is sketchier."

"True," Jessie agreed. "But why would he kill Gillian Fahey? We don't have any indication that she was going to reveal their affair. It's not like she could tell Siobhan Pierson about it. The woman was already dead. As erratic as his behavior has been, and despite his lies, we don't have any evidence to suggest he's responsible for either murder. And it seems hard to believe that both weren't committed by the same person."

There didn't seem to be much else to say. They couldn't eliminate Ian Pierson as a suspect, but neither of them realistically thought he was their man. They returned to Pierson, who had poured himself a glass of something clear that Jessie doubted was water.

"Mr. Pierson," Ryan said sharply, gaining the man's full attention. "We're going to follow up on your statement. For now you're not under arrest. But you should expect either us or someone else to check back in with you. And I'm instructing you not to leave L.A. County without authorization. No trips to Bakersfield for board meetings until further notice, got it?"

Pierson nodded. Personally, Jessie doubted they had to worry that he'd leave the county. He didn't seem inclined to leave his couch.

They left him alone with his clear liquid and his TV remote to return to the Santa Monica police station, where they'd have to start from scratch. If Pierson was innocent, the killer was still out there. And Jessie got the strong feeling that whoever had committed these murders wasn't done yet.

CHAPTER THIRTEEN

Whitney Carlisle felt guilty.

She loved her husband, but there was something about a glass of white wine and having the whole house to herself that made her inappropriately—and therefore guiltily— happy.

She reminded herself not to feel *too* bad. After all, Gordo wasn't home because he was attending a bachelor party. She found it odd that it was being held on a Monday evening. But the wedding was a last-minute affair next weekend and the boys' night out had been thrown together on the fly. All she knew—all she wanted to know—was that after the night's festivities, the guys would be staying at a hotel in Orange County. Gordo was taking tomorrow off. She considered that a wise move.

She had considered calling a few girlfriends to come over but decided she'd prefer an evening of self-care. That meant sushi from the Japanese market by the pier, a bottle of Viognier, and a yet-to-be-determined trashy erotic thriller.

She looked out the window. It was late afternoon, almost 5:15 p.m. The sun was already starting to set. By the time she settled in for the evening, it would be dark out. She searched her streaming services for a movie that had the exact mix of scary and trashy that she was after and had narrowed it down to three choices when Yaz, her little schnauzer, started barking.

Reluctantly, she got up to see what had piqued his interest. She walked over to the living room sliding door that led to the half-finished deck and followed Yaz's gaze until she found what had him so agitated. There was a strange man in the backyard. A chill ran up her spine.

He was large, easily six foot two and 220 pounds. He had on jeans, work boots, and a hooded sweatshirt that made it impossible to see his face. He was walking straight toward her, though he didn't appear to have noticed her yet.

She darted behind the curtain out of sight. The man was all the way to the deck stairs now. She pulled out her cell phone and started to dial 911 when the man yanked the hood off his sweatshirt, revealing his face.

Whitney breathed an audible sigh of relief. She knew the man. It was Frank Marr, their contractor. He'd been working on some home renovations for them, including the deck, for the last few months. Even though she'd seen him almost every day, he had suddenly looked menacing and unfamiliar with his face covered by a hood. She put her phone back in her pocket and opened the sliding door.

"Hi, Frank," she said, stepping outside and walking over to the deck railing. "Everything okay?"

"Yeah," he answered, seemingly startled to find her there. "I'm just a little frustrated. I was headed home to Thousand Oaks when I realized I forgot my tool belt under the deck. I knew I wouldn't get any sleep if I didn't come and get it."

He bent down out of sight. After a few seconds, he reappeared with the belt, which he strapped around his waist.

"You could have called and we'd have kept it inside for you," Whitney told him.

"That's nice, but I didn't want to put you out."

"Okay," she said. "But next time, please give me a heads-up if you're stopping by. Yaz started barking at some 'unidentified' guy in a hoodie in the backyard and I freaked out a little. I almost called 911."

"Oh man," he replied sheepishly. "Sorry about that. It just got a bit chilly with the sun going down. Speaking of that, have you taken advantage of the deck yet for sunsets? It looks like this one's going to be a beauty."

He turned around. Whitney realized he was right. Their backyard faced west toward the Pacific Ocean and with the elevated deck, they now had an unfiltered view of the sun setting behind Point Dume. Streaks of orange, pink, and purple painted the sky just above the horizon, with the darkness of night closing in quickly just above them.

Both of them stood there silently for close to a minute as the last vestiges of sunlight dipped out of sight, leaving only dim remnants behind. Even Yaz had stopped barking in what she told herself was awe. Frank turned back around with a smile.

"Worse places to live," he said earnestly.

"No argument here," she agreed.

"Well, I'll see you tomorrow, Mrs. Carlisle. Things are moving along nicely. The office is done, as are the changes to the bedroom wing and the front door. We're on the last phase now with this deck. We should complete it by the end of the week. I expect my guys to show up around nine and I'll stop by before lunchtime to check on their progress. That sound okay to you?"

“It sounds good,” she told him. “You have a good evening, Frank.”

“You too,” he said and headed off toward the side door of the yard. Once he was out of sight, Whitney stepped back inside and locked the sliding door. She was about to pull the curtains across but then stopped when she got a glimpse of herself in the door’s reflection.

She liked what its shimmering, slightly gauzy effect did to her. Whitney knew that she was an attractive woman, with her yoga-firm body, short, dyed blonde hair, deep tan, and aquamarine eyes. But at twenty-seven, and after three years of marriage, she thought she could see the beginnings of the aging process at work. In the sliding door reflection, however, that was muted, leaving only the best parts.

“Enough narcissism,” she said out loud, turning away from the door and heading back to the kitchen to get the sushi and wine. Her phone buzzed. It was a text from her sister, Janey, which read: *While the boys are playing, you want company?*

Whitney had completely forgotten that Janey’s husband, Stewart, was also at the bachelor party. For half a second, she considered saying no. After all, this was supposed to a solo evening. But Janey was always good for a fun night. Besides, she liked trashy thrillers too.

So she texted back: *Sounds good. A nice bottle of white will guarantee you admission.*

Janey texted a thumbs-up emoji followed by: *See you soon.*

“Yaz,” Whitney called out, “we’re having company so you better be on your best behavior. No barking when she shows up.”

It occurred to her that she hadn’t heard Yaz bark at all recently, not since the sun set. In fact, she hadn’t even seen him.

“Yaz, where are you?” she shouted. “Yazoo, come to mommy!”

There was no response. She wandered through the kitchen, then the dining room, and back out to the living room but he was nowhere to be found. She tried the bedroom wing, opening each door and calling out for the schnauzer, to no avail. Frustrated, she returned to the living room and leaned against a couch.

Where is that little troublemaker hiding?

Whitney could feel anxiety rising in her chest but refused to acknowledge it. She’d already overreacted to the hoodie thing. She wasn’t going to do it again just because Yaz was messing with her.

*

He watched with malicious glee as she searched the house.

From his position in the coat closet near the front door, he could observe all her increasingly fretful movements as she moved from one room to the next. Of course, she wouldn't find her little Yaz. He was in the closet on the top shelf, with a broken neck.

Part of him wondered if he should leave a few breadcrumbs for those detectives he saw earlier outside the Pierson mansion. After all, so far it had been almost too easy.

While Whitney Carlisle and her contractor watched the sun set, he had slipped behind her on the deck and gone inside. She'd been oblivious to the dog's frenzied barks of warning, assuming they were still directed at the contractor and not the man who had silently entered her home.

After quickly dispensing with Yaz, he took the knife from the block on the kitchen counter and moved to the closet just as the woman and her contractor were saying their goodbyes. Then he watched through the slightly open closet door as she locked the sliding one and first admired her reflection in the glass, and then reprimanded herself for the admiration. After that came the dog search. And now there was the confusion and growing apprehension. It was magnificent. He imagined how fast her heart was already pumping and how far her blood would spurt.

She turned back to the sliding door and he knew he had to make his move. If she thought the animal was outside and went out to look for him, there were too many variables. What if she walked down the block? What if he had to pull her inside and she screamed? Or escaped? He had to act now.

He quietly opened the closet door and moved toward her in the shoes he wore specifically for this occasion. They made no noise and left no prints. He tiptoed quickly and was less than ten feet from her when he saw her back stiffen and realized his mistake.

He was visible behind her in the reflection of the sliding door. Before he could make his move, the woman darted to the left, back toward the bedroom wing. Despite his frustration, he was impressed. She hadn't turned to look at him or even screamed. Instead, she saw that she was in danger and did something to protect herself.

It wouldn't do any good, of course. He knew where she was going because of his previous visit and he'd written down a detailed sketch of the entire house as soon as he'd left it. That's how he knew that the room she was running to at the end of the hall on the left was a trap. Other than the one door, there was no way out unless she jumped out the window, which overlooked a cliff at least 150 feet high.

She locked the door from the inside just as he arrived. He stepped back and kicked, splintering it. The second kick finished the job as the door slammed open. He stepped inside the darkened room and turned on the light. She was nowhere in sight. The window was still closed so she had to still be in here. He was just about to kneel down to look under the bed when he noticed the room was different than he remembered.

It used to be much larger. And then, as growing dismay took hold of him, he comprehended the difference. A wall had been installed, turning one large bedroom into two smaller ones. More importantly, a door connecting the rooms had been added. Carlisle could have gone into the second bedroom and back out into the hallway.

He rushed back out. Sure enough he caught sight of her just as she tore from the hall back to the living room. He raced after her, expecting her to be at the front door by now. But she wasn't.

Just as he emerged, he felt a sharp pain as something solid slammed into his gut. He fell to the floor and rolled over to see Carlisle advancing on him with a thick, standing lamp she had yanked out of the socket.

Luckily for him, she led with her feet and not the lamp. Gasping for breath, he struck out at her leg with his foot and heard a sickening, beautiful crunch. She dropped to the ground, howling in pain. He allowed himself a moment to recover before getting to his knees and shuffling over to her. Then he removed his mask.

Through squinty, pained eyes she looked up at him. Those eyes widened and he knew she recognized him. That was almost his favorite part. She started to raise her hands in defense but she was just a hair too slow. By the time they were up, he'd already sliced the desired spot on her neck.

As he'd hoped, blood shot out to the left with incredible force. He had to dart to the side to avoid being splattered by it. Her hands were at her throat now, which made it easy to inflict the second wound, directed at her upper thigh. That one didn't bleed as dramatically because of the yoga pants she wore. But the carpet underneath the leg quickly turned dark.

He stood and looked down at Whitney Carlisle as the life drained out of her. She stared up at him with baffled, glassy eyes. But a few seconds later they lost their focus. She was gone. After dropping the knife beside her body, he was too.

CHAPTER FOURTEEN

They didn't stay at the Santa Monica police station for long.

When Ryan hit his limit in the overheated conference room, they decided to take the case files and their laptops and head over to the Third Street Promenade to work there for part of the afternoon. That's where they'd been ever since, sitting at a shaded table of an outdoor French bakery, where they spread out the case file paperwork and sustained themselves on a steady supply of croissants and cappuccinos.

They did their best to stay focused but it was occasionally a challenge. The Promenade was a walking-only, closed-off stretch of Third Street in downtown Santa Monica, just blocks from both the police station and the beach. There were high-end stores on either side of the street. In the middle of it, there were occasional kiosks—newsstands, sunglasses vendors, and folks selling tourist-friendly T-shirts. Multiple street performers—from break dancers to beat boxers to mimes—competed for window shoppers' attention. Despite the entertainment and the warm caffeine delivery system, Jessie was getting cold.

"Ryan," she said reluctantly, knowing he wouldn't like what she had to say, "it's too chilly to stay out here. And we're hitting a wall here. It's been all dead end leads since we left Pierson's place. I think we either have to go back to the station or head home. Besides, I need to check in with Hannah."

"You mean check *on* her, right?" he replied snarkily.

Jessie stuck out her tongue even as she called her little sister. Surprisingly, she picked up right away.

"You're going to be late getting home because of this case, right?" Hannah accused before Jessie could speak a word.

"Hello, little sis," she replied saccharinely, "nice to hear your voice. How are you?"

"Okay," Hannah said with slightly less surliness. "I *was* going to make some dinner but I don't know how many servings to prep."

"First of all, thanks for doing that," Jessie said, trying to get back on the right foot. "And to answer your question, as of now it looks like there's not much more we can do tonight, so we'll be coming home. But we're in Santa Monica so it'll probably be at least an hour. Time your meal prep accordingly. How was your session with Dr. Lemmon, by the way?"

She heard a brief hesitation before Hannah responded, just enough to make her worry.

"Fine—we talked about how I'm doing in school, my plans to go to that cooking camp in Wildpines over the summer, and the possibility of culinary school in the fall."

"Nothing else?" Jessie asked.

"Not what you're hinting at," Hannah replied.

"Okay," Jessie sighed, deciding not to push it any further for now. "We'll see you soon."

When she hung up, she helped Ryan gather the last of the files and put them in his satchel.

"She didn't tell Lemmon, huh?" he asked.

"Nope. I feel like if she just opened up about this, she could finally start to deal with it. I know it's eating at her."

"Maybe next time," he offered.

"Maybe," she conceded, though with little hope. "Hey, do you think it would be a good idea if I went to her next session?"

Ryan was opening his mouth to reply when his phone rang. They both looked at the caller. It was Decker.

"I've got a bad feeling about this," Ryan said before hitting the speaker button. "Hi, Captain, Jessie's here with me. You're on speaker."

"It sounds noisy where you are," Decker replied.

"We're at the Promenade," Jessie told him.

"Call me back as soon as you can talk privately," he instructed. "There's been another murder."

*

Hannah was just starting to mix the rub for the lamb chops when Jessie called back.

"Reaching out again so soon?" she asked.

She suspected from the pause before her sister answered that it was bad news. When she heard the deflated tone in her voice, she knew she was right.

"Hey," Jessie said, "right after I hung up with you we got word that there's been another murder. We don't know details yet but I'm certain that we'll have to go to the crime scene. I don't know when we'll be home."

"I guess it's dinner for one then," Hannah replied, trying to mask her disappointment.

"Actually, better make that for two."

"What are you talking about?" she demanded, suspicious.

"We don't know how long we're going to be out. It could be all night. So I asked Kat to spend the evening with you and stay over if need be."

"Jessie, I'm going to be eighteen in a couple of months," she pointed out. "I don't need a babysitter."

"She's not a babysitter, Hannah. It's just that you—we've all been through a lot lately and it would set my mind at ease if Kat was there."

"Why?" Hannah wanted to know. "Do you think I'm going slice my wrists? Or shoot some senior citizen as he walks down the street outside the house?"

"I can't do this right now," Jessie told her. "We have to call Captain Decker back and find out the details on the person who was just murdered. If you think you're old enough to stay home by yourself, prove it. Show the emotional maturity to handle having Kat stay with you tonight and then we'll talk about what happens in the future. Can you do that?"

Hannah wanted to come back at her hard for her patronizing tone but knew it would only make things worse. Once her sister—the brilliant, beloved profiler Jessie Hunt—made a decision, there was no talking her out of it.

"Sure, I'll do that. I just hope that I'm proficient enough with the oven that I don't accidentally blow the house up before she gets here."

She hung up without another word. It was only after the aggrieved feeling she was nursing began to fade that Hannah started to wonder if she could have handled the call better. But by then it was too late. Calling back to apologize was a sign of weakness. And Hannah didn't like to show weakness.

CHAPTER FIFTEEN

Three minutes by car.

That's how far away from them a woman was being murdered while they noshed on croissants. Jessie tried not to think about that as Decker updated them on the short drive over. Since the killing was so recent, there wasn't much to tell.

"The woman's name is Whitney Carlisle. She was found by her sister, who was going to spend the evening with her. She's still there so you can get more details from her. Same M.O.—two deep cuts with a sharp blade from the victim's home. She bled out on the living room floor."

"Is she married?" Ryan asked.

"Yep, just like the other two," Decker said. "The husband is a studio executive. He was apparently in Orange County. He's on his way back now."

"Captain," Jessie asked, "why didn't we get the call instead of you?"

"I wondered that too," he said. "It turns out I was still listed as primary on the case. I would have thought that SMPD would have switched it to Hernandez but I guess wires got crossed."

"Or Detective Gore just didn't give enough of a damn to do it," Ryan suggested.

"I don't know what that's all about, but I've had them switch it now," Decker replied.

"All right, we're pulling up to the scene now," Ryan said. "We'll keep you posted."

They stopped near the front of the house. Unlike the homes of the other two victims, it wasn't massive. Instead it was a nice, one-story, modern-looking home, with a cubist design comprised of four alternating brown and white sections. What made it notable was its location, only a block from the ocean. Jessie imagined that the view from the back was pretty impressive.

The place's charm was currently undermined by multiple vehicles with flashing lights in front of it. There were three black-and-whites, an ambulance, and a medical examiner's van. Police tape already surrounded the property. Neighbors had crowded around at the tape line, hoping to catch a glimpse of was going on inside.

They were about to get out of the car when Jessie had had idea. She typed out a quick text to Jamil that read: *Any luck on Ian Pierson's GPS location data yet, especially for the last few hours?*

As expected, his response came almost immediately, since Jamil Winslow seemed to never sleep. It said: *Still getting approval even though he OK'd it. Higher-ups want to follow every rule, considering who he is. Should have results by morning.*

That would have to be good enough for now. Besides, Jessie was just doing her due diligence. She didn't really think Pierson was their killer but she couldn't dismiss him just yet.

"Ready?" Ryan asked, as he opened his door.

"As I'll ever be," she told him.

They walked up the path to the front door, showing their IDs to the officer at the police tape. Once they got to the door, they were met by an older officer whose name tag read *Lovering*.

"Detective Hernandez and Ms. Hunt?" he asked. Apparently Decker had communicated their imminent arrival.

"That's right," Ryan said. "Who's in charge here?"

"You are, sir," Lovering replied. "My understanding is that HSS is taking lead on this and SMPD is in a support capacity. I'm Robert Lovering, the senior officer on scene, so I've been handling things up until now. The victim's sister is out back in the yard with a crisis counseling officer. She's pretty shaken up. I thought I could walk you through the scene until she's able to talk some more."

"Please," Ryan said, indicating for the officer to take the lead.

When they stepped inside, Jessie found that the interior style matched the outside. All the furniture was defined by clean lines and angles that reinforced the cubist theme. Officer Lovering led them through the foyer into the living room where Whitney Carlisle's body still rested.

She was lying on her back. Her blue eyes were open but vacant. Her left leg was bent awkwardly beneath her, contorted at an unnatural angle. Blood from the deep cuts at her neck and leg had pooled all around her. To her right on the carpet was a heavy lamp which had been unplugged from the wall.

"We also just found a dog in the closet over there," Officer Lovering said, pointing back to the foyer. "He was on the top shelf. His neck had been snapped."

As if she needed it, Jessie felt an extra twinge at that news. She knelt down beside Whitney, trying to imagine what had happened in her last moments. She closed her eyes and took several slow, deep breaths. The metallic scent of Whitney's blood filled her nostrils. When she opened her eyes again, a picture began to form in her mind.

"The killer likely hid in there," she said, standing up again and pointing at the closet. "I wouldn't be surprised if they watched while she searched for her dog, getting a kick out of her calling out the pet's name. At some point they came out to attack her but it didn't go as planned. She must have seen them come out."

"How do you know that?" Officer Lovering asked.

"Because of *that*," Ryan volunteered, pointing to the lamp. "She had time to grab it."

"You don't think they used it on her?" Lovering countered.

"Why would they?" Jessie asked. "They already had the knife. No—she saw them coming."

"But wouldn't they have been careful enough to wait until she was looking the other way?" Officer Lovering asked.

Jessie couldn't deny that he had a good point. She looked around, trying to put herself in Whitney Carlisle's shoes. Then she saw it.

"You're almost certainly right," she agreed. "With the other victims, surprise was essential. They never even had time to raise their hands, much less grab a lamp. But Whitney had an advantage."

"What?" Lovering wanted to know.

"That," she said, pointing at the sliding glass door. "From where we are now, I can see the foyer closet in the reflection of that door. If she was standing in about the same place, she would have seen it open and her assailant come out. The closet's far enough away that she would have had time to move."

"But enough time to pull that heavy lamp out of the wall socket?" Ryan wondered. "That seems unlikely."

Jessie deflated. He was right. It didn't make sense for her to grab a lamp. It made much more sense to run. She looked to the left, where an open door led down a long hallway.

"You find anything unusual that way?" she asked Lovering, pointing at the door.

The officer's face lit up at the question.

"Actually, yes," he said excitedly. "We didn't think much of it because all the activity seemed to be out here. But the door to the last bedroom on the left is broken."

"What do you mean, broken?" Ryan asked.

"Part of the frame and a whole section of the door is splintered, like it was forced open, maybe kicked in."

*

"Show us," Jessie said forcefully.

He took them to the door, which did indeed look like it had been forced open violently. In addition to the splintering, the top hinge was loose. They stepped inside.

"Was the light on in this room when you arrived?" Ryan asked.

"Yes. We haven't touched anything," Lovering assured him.

Jessie walked over to the window and looked out. The bedroom appeared to be situated at the edge of a cliff. In the dark she couldn't even see how far down the drop was. Turning around, she saw that the room had a second door.

"Does that lead to an adjoining bedroom?" she asked.

"Yes, ma'am," Lovering said.

All at once, an unsettling sensation overcame her, a feeling that something wasn't quite as it should be. It flickered briefly before fading away.

"What are you thinking?" Ryan asked her. He knew her expressions and she must have been displaying one that suggested she was on to something. Unfortunately, the sensation had gone as quickly as it came, like a wisp of smoke she couldn't grasp. As frustrating as that was, something else emerged in its place: a mental image that didn't fade. She focused on that.

"I'm thinking that Whitney ran down the hall to this bedroom and locked the door. I think the killer broke in. But while he did, she snuck out through the other bedroom. He must have realized it and chased after her back into the living room."

"But she didn't seem to get very far," Officer Lovering noted. "I would have guessed that she'd make it at least to the front door."

"That's a good guess, Officer," Jessie said, hurrying back down the hall to the living room. When he and Ryan caught up, she continued. "But I don't think she ran for the door. I think she was sick of running. I think she stood her ground here."

"You think that's when she grabbed the lamp," Ryan said, playing out the scenario with her. "Maybe she got in a whack, knocked him to the ground even."

"That would explain the leg," Jessie agreed. "Maybe she came at him a second time when he was on the ground and he kicked her, incapacitating her."

"She'd have been in incredible pain, unable to move," Ryan said. "That's when he used the knife, while she was lying on the ground, too focused on her leg to prevent what he did next."

All three of them stood there silently in communal horror, thinking about Whitney Carlisle's last terrified, excruciating moments. They were interrupted by another officer, who hurried over to Lovering.

"Sir," he said. "We have the security camera footage now. It's up on the laptop in the kitchen."

They all rushed over where another officer was waiting to play it.

"Can you set it to go straight to when the motion sensor was triggered?" Ryan asked.

The officer nodded and pulled up all the notifications indicating motion on the cameras. The last one prior to the first officers arriving on the scene was at 5:52 p.m., when a woman rang the doorbell.

"That's Carlisle's sister, Jane Smyth," Lovering said. "She said she came over to hang out because both their husbands were at a bachelor party in Orange County. That's about all we got out of her before she broke down."

They watched as Smyth repeatedly rang the bell and knocked on the door. In between, she used her phone multiple times to call and text.

"Didn't she have a key?" Ryan asked.

"That's something I intended to ask her before she fell apart," Lovering said.

After a full five minutes, she left camera range only to reappear at the back deck sliding door a minute later. She rapped on it several times before seeming to see something. Jessie could guess what it was. Smyth appeared to double over. The footage was silent but it was clear that she was screaming.

"We can move on," Ryan said.

The previous motion activation was at 5:28 at the front door.

"There's not much to it," the officer at the laptop said, "just a shadow barely in the frame."

Jessie's fingertips tingled at the sight.

"Play it again, please," she requested.

The officer was almost right. It did look like a shadow passing at the edge of the camera's range but it wasn't. Now her whole body was tingling.

"That's the killer," she said.

"How do you know?" Lovering demanded.

"Play it again," she instructed. "This time pause it at the 5:28:21 mark."

The officer did. When the image was frozen, everyone could see it. Someone wearing all black, including a watch cap covering the face, skirted the very corner of the frame.

"Play it at quarter speed," Jessie asked.

When the video resumed, the shadow person moved off to the right. The last thing visible before they disappeared was a left hand, which looked to have a latex glove on it.

"The killer knew exactly where the cameras were and how to avoid detection," Jessie said. "They wore dark clothing, masked their face, stayed out of frame, like they knew the place."

No one had a response to that.

"Go back further," Ryan finally said. "We need to see how they got in."

The video clip prior to that was at 5:17. It showed a man in a hoodie in the backyard walking toward the deck. The he removed the hoodie. His face was still hard to discern but she knew someone who could clean it up.

"We need to send that to Jamil," she told Ryan. "Maybe he can work his facial recognition magic."

Moments later, Whitney Carlisle stepped outside and seemed to speak to him. The man grabbed something from under the deck, but in the near darkness, Jessie couldn't clearly identify what it was. They talked a little more before they both stared, unspeaking, at something in the distance. They stayed that way for close to a minute.

"What's that all about?" the laptop officer wanted to know.

"I think they were watching the sun set," Jessie said quietly.

They spoke again briefly before the man wandered out of sight and Whitney returned inside. The timestamp read 5:19. Jessie got a shiver as she realized she was probably looking at the last time they knew for sure the woman was alive.

"So that's our window," Ryan said. "She was killed sometime between five nineteen and five twenty-eight. That's more than we had before at least."

"But we don't know how the killer got in," Lovering said.

"There might be other points of entry that aren't covered by cameras," Ryan replied. "If the killer knew where the cameras were, they probably knew where they *weren't* as well."

"Plus, there are blind spots," Jessie replied. "You can't actually see the sliding deck door from this angle. Someone could have shimmied along the back of the deck. If she didn't lock the door when she went inside, it'd be easy to get in and we wouldn't be able to see it."

Ryan tapped the laptop officer on the shoulder and handed him a business card.

"Can you send all this footage to Jamil Winslow? Tell him we're especially interested in ID'ing the man at five seventeen p.m."

The officer nodded and took the card. The group around the screen started to break up when a commotion from another room got everyone's attention. Ryan and Lovering moved to the kitchen entryway and Jessie followed close behind.

A woman was at the sliding deck door, trying to push her way past an officer who was awkwardly attempting to block her path. Jessie recognized her from the security footage earlier. There were mascara lines running down her cheeks and her eyes were red and puffy but there was no question: It was Jane Smyth, Whitney's sister.

Jessie called out to the officer holding her back.

"Let her in."

CHAPTER SIXTEEN

Smyth moved toward Jessie like she was a homing beacon.

As she ran over to them, Ryan whispered quickly to Officer Lovering, "Have your men cover the body."

Jessie silently berated herself for not thinking of that detail. She resolved to get Smyth back outside as quickly as possible. As the woman got closer, she noticed that her eyes were the same shade of blue as her sister's. She exhaled deeply, trying to project a calm she hoped she could pass on to her.

"Are you the one who's going to finally give me some answers?" she demanded.

"I hope so," Jessie said evenly. "I'm so sorry for what happened to your sister. My name is Jessie Hunt. And this is Detective Ryan Hernandez. We work for a special unit that focuses on cases like Whitney's. Why don't the three of us go back outside and we'll try to get you some answers."

That seemed to diminish the woman's ferocity slightly. She nodded and led them back in the same direction from which she'd just come. Jessie noticed that Ryan walked to Smyth's left, blocking any view of her sister's body.

Once they were outside, they all moved over to the edge of the deck, near where the railing met the stairs leading to the yard. It was almost exactly the same spot where Whitney Carlisle stood just over an hour earlier. Jessie looked out at the darkened Santa Monica Bay, dotted with lights that allowed her to see the outline of the coast from Malibu all the way south to the Palos Verdes Peninsula. This was the view that Whitney had been marveling at earlier, and which she'd never see again. Jessie turned to Jane. The time for stalling was over.

"Mrs. Smyth—" she began.

"Janey, please," Smyth interrupted.

"Okay, Janey, we don't know a lot yet, but I'll tell you what we *do* know. It might be difficult to hear though. Are you prepared for that?"

"No," Janey replied. "But tell me anyway."

"None of this is official yet, but this is what we believe: your sister was murdered with a knife from her kitchen. The killer sliced an artery on her neck and another on her leg. She would have died very quickly.

Prior to that, she appears to have tried to escape and subsequently, to fight back. During the altercation, she suffered a leg injury that made it impossible for her to get away. Those are the details about the actual incident. Are you comfortable with me continuing?"

She noticed that Janey had turned quite pale the more she talked.

"Go on," she said weakly.

"We believe that she was killed sometime between five nineteen and five twenty-eight—"

"Wait," Janey said suddenly. "I talked to her during that time. Well, not talked, but texted—she said it was cool for me to come over."

Jessie and Ryan exchanged an energized look they hoped didn't look too eager.

"Can you please show us your phone?" Ryan asked.

She unlocked it and scrolled to the text exchange. Whitney's last message, time-stamped 5:21, read: *Sounds good. A nice bottle of white will guarantee you admission.*

"Everything seems normal at that point," he noted, speaking Jessie's thoughts aloud. She looked back at Janey.

"Maybe you can help us," she said. "I know you said to the officer earlier that you came over to hang out. Can you describe the circumstances in more detail?"

"Yeah," she agreed. "Whitney's husband, Gordo—er, Gordon, and my husband, Stewart, were in Orange County for the bachelor party of a mutual friend. Whitney was going to have a solo night but at the last minute I thought it might be fun to hang out, just the two of us. You saw that she said yes. That's why I was so surprised when she didn't answer when I got here a little while later. I rang. I knocked. I called and texted."

"Didn't you have a key?" Ryan asked. "I figured that as sisters—"

"I used to," Janey cut him short. "But they were having some renovations done to the house. They did a bunch of stuff: bedrooms, an office, this deck, and they also replaced the front door. I just hadn't been over since they made the change. I bet she would have given me the new key tonight if…" She trailed off.

"What did Whitney do for a living?" Jessie asked, hoping to prevent the woman from spiraling again.

"She's—was a marketing executive at a studio." Smyth's voice quavered as she answered. Jessie sensed that she was struggling to hold it together.

"The same one as Gordo?" Ryan asked.

"No. They used to work at the same one, Third Millennium Wolf Pictures. That's where they met. But Gordo was offered a better position at Sovereign Studios. He said he could hook her up there too but she didn't want to commute all the way to Hollywood from out here." She paused for a breath before adding, "I hope they get here soon."

"They?" Jessie asked.

"When I found Whitney and the cops came, I called Stew to tell him what happened. I couldn't bear to tell Gordo myself so I asked him to do it for me. He said okay and that he would drive them both back. He didn't want Gordo trying to drive in that condition. But that was a while ago."

"I'm sure they'll be here soon," Ryan assured her. "Orange County is quite a drive and it's still rush hour. Tell me—how was Whitney and Gordo's marriage?"

He asked it so naturally that Janey didn't seem to register the interrogatory nature of the question.

"Good," she said. "I obviously saw them up close. They doted on each other. It was borderline gross. We would double date a lot and they'd feed each other bites of their meals at dinner. Whitney told me they had started to talk about having kids."

That was what broke her. Janey expelled something between a hiccup and a sob. She bent over like she had in the security video. Loud guttural moans came from somewhere deep inside her. Jessie moved to comfort her but before she could, a female officer appeared out of nowhere and wrapped her in her arms.

"I'm Nancy Caffey, the crisis counseling officer," she whispered to them. "Unless you absolutely need her now, I think it's time we get Janey to the hospital. She's been a trouper but she's in shock."

"That's fine," Ryan said as Officer Caffey escorted Janey down the deck steps and around the side of the house. Jessie watched them go, trying to keep it together herself. She couldn't imagine how she'd react if that was Hannah lying on the floor in that living room.

"Do we want to wait for the husband to arrive?" she asked abruptly once Janey was gone, hoping to shift her own focus away from thoughts like that.

"I don't think so," Ryan said. "We can always ask him to come in later. Right now I want to go through that footage again in more detail back at the station. I feel like we might be missing something."

"Sounds good," Jessie agreed. "Hopefully Jamil will get a hit on that guy in the hoodie. Plus we need to do a deep dive into Whitney

Carlisle's life. Maybe she has a connection to the other victims that can break this thing open. I would have loved to have asked Janey about that, but it'll obviously have to wait. In the meantime I have a call to make."

"To who?" Ryan asked.

"I'm going to ask Kat to spend the night with Hannah at our place. It sounds like we're in for an all-nighter."

CHAPTER SEVENTEEN

Jessie missed the sunrise.

When she looked up from the laptop she'd been staring at, the morning light was already pouring in through the Santa Monica police station windows. She put her head back in her hands. She'd been at it all night and for what? Not a single lead she and Ryan had pursued had panned out.

As far as she could tell, other than what they already knew, there was no useful connection among the three victims besides being wealthy and living in the same general area. They were different ages and traveled in different social circles. One had kids but the other two didn't. It was true that one had an affair with another's husband, but it was brief, it was months ago, and neither spouse seemed to have found out.

Her phone rang and she looked at it with bleary eyes. The call was from Jamil. She was about to answer it when Ryan, seated across from her, caught her eye. She turned around to see that Gordon Carlisle was walking toward them, escorted by a uniformed officer. She sent Jamil's call to voicemail and tried to look alert.

"Thanks for coming into the station again, sir, especially so early," Ryan said. "We have just a few more questions for you."

The truth was that they'd barely gotten to ask Carlisle any questions last night before he broke down completely. Part of that might have been that he was already deeply drunk from the bachelor party when Janey had called with the news. All they'd gotten out of him were some basics about where he'd been—enough to eliminate him as a suspect but little more. Their focus this morning would be on something much more specific.

"Of course," Carlisle said as he sat down, his voice hoarse. "The truth is, I didn't get any sleep last night anyway so I figured I might as well do something productive now that the sun is up."

He had two days' worth of stubble, uncombed black hair, and swollen eyelids. He was also wearing the same clothes as last night. Even with all that, Carlisle cut a dashing figure. He was well over six feet tall, with the rangy, relaxed look of a guy who surfed four or five days a week. Jessie imagined that when he and Whitney went out, they were a head-turning couple.

"We want to focus your attention on something we didn't get to discuss last night," Ryan told him, sliding over his laptop and pulling up the still image of the man in the hoodie from the previous night. He'd cropped the photo so that Carlisle couldn't tell that the man had been with Whitney at the time the image was recorded. They'd agreed before he came in that the fewer emotional distractions there were, the better.

"Do you recognize this man?" he asked.

Carlisle leaned in, squinting.

"Yeah," he said without equivocation, "that's Frank, our contractor."

"Frank?" Ryan repeated.

"Frank Marr—he and his guys have been doing all the work on our place: they redid my office, converted one bedroom into two, and replaced the front door. They're finishing up the deck this week." It took him a second to process that they weren't just curious. "Why?"

"We're checking on everyone that was seen in your security camera footage," Jessie said, not wanting Carlisle to jump to the obvious conclusion before they had anything on the man. "Would it have been normal for him to be at your place yesterday, late afternoon?"

"I'm not sure," Carlisle said guardedly. "Most days they were long gone by the time I got home. Whitney was the one who dealt with him day-to-day. Did he do this?"

He was sitting up straight now and his red eyes were attentive.

"Like I said, Mr. Carlisle," she repeated reassuringly, "we're just trying to identify everyone in the footage from yesterday. We didn't recognize him and were hoping you could. I wanted to ask you something else." She moved on quickly, hoping to get his mind off the man whose image he was currently staring daggers at.

"Do the names Siobhan Pierson or Gillian Fahey sound familiar to you?"

Carlisle sat back in his chair, thinking.

"Wasn't Pierson the name of that society lady who was killed a few weeks ago? I thought I saw that on the news."

"It is," Jessie confirmed, holding out a photo. "But did you or perhaps Whitney know her?"

"I didn't," he said, shaking his head, "and I don't think Whitney did either. She would have said something."

"And Gillian Fahey?" Jessie prompted, swiping to a photo of her. "Did you or your wife know her?"

Carlisle shook his head.

"I don't recognize her and the name isn't familiar. If Whitney ever mentioned her, I don't recall it. Why?"

Jessie wasn't sure how much they should reveal but Ryan shrugged at her. He didn't seem to be concerned.

"Both these women were killed in the same manner as your wife," he said quietly. "We're just trying to determine if there's a connection among them."

"Oh," Carlisle replied blankly, not seeming to totally get that his wife was the victim of a potential serial killer. "You have her phone, right? Did you check her contacts list?"

"We did," Jessie said. "Neither name was in there. That's why we wanted to talk to you, just to make sure."

Jessie's phone rang. It was Jamil again. Two calls in succession meant he had news.

"I have to take this," she said. "Detective Hernandez, can you finish up with Mr. Carlisle?"

She didn't wait for his answer, instead getting up and leaving the mini-conference room. Only when she was far enough not to be heard did she pick up.

"What's up, Jamil?" she asked as she passed through the station's lobby and stepped outside. She'd been inside for ten hours straight and the chilly air cut right through her.

"Did you listen to my message?" he asked urgently.

"No. We were doing an interview. Give me the good parts."

"I ran facial recognition on the guy you sent me and got a hit. His name is Frank Marr from Thousand Oaks."

"Thanks, Jamil. Great work," she replied, pretending not to already have that information. She didn't want him to think that all his hard work was for nothing. "What else did you find on him?"

"Not much—nothing but a couple of parking tickets in recent years. He was in a civil dispute with a client about a decade ago. He's a contractor and someone wasn't happy with the work he did. But they settled the case. That's really all I could find, at least on him."

"Okay," Jessie said. "We'll definitely look into him. Anything else? Oh wait, hold on. Ryan just walked over."

Ryan joined her outside, handing her the coat she'd forgotten to take with her. She muted the call and put on the coat

"Thanks for this," she said. "By the way, Jamil just confirmed the Frank Marr ID. I didn't tell him we already had it. He sounded so proud."

"Got it," Ryan said, smiling at her subterfuge.

"We're back, Jamil," she said, taking the call off mute. "I told Ryan about your ID of Marr. But I got the sense you had more to share."

"Right. We got approval to track Ian Pierson's location data. For the window of time you mentioned last night from five pm. to seven p.m., I initially thought he'd left his residence, but I was wrong. When I checked closer, I realized that it only looked that way because his house is so big. I pulled the most recent architectural plans on file with the city—"

"Of course you did," Ryan couldn't help but interject.

"*And*," Jamil went on, apparently not amused by the interruption, "it seems that he, or at least his phone, went from a large room on the western end of the estate to a small alcove just off what appears to be the kitchen. Then he went back to the larger room. Other than that, he never moved more than thirty feet at any given time."

"I think I can solve that mystery," Ryan said. "I'm pretty sure he went from the game room to the bar we saw just off the kitchen for more booze and then went back to numb himself some more."

"What?" Jamil asked, confused. He hadn't been read into Pierson's current mental state.

"Never mind," Jessie said. "Great work, as usual, Jamil. I know you've been looking for more social media connections now that you're able to plug Whitney Carlisle into your data set. Please let us know if you find anything worthwhile. Frankly, we've come up empty so far."

"You got it," Jamil promised.

Once they'd hung up, Jessie started to head back in but Ryan stopped her.

"You lucked out, by the way," he said.

"How's that?"

"About ten seconds after you left us, Gordon Carlisle had a delayed freak-out when he processed that his wife might have been murdered by a serial killer. I had to send him home."

"Sorry you had to deal with that on your own," Jessie told him.

"That's okay," he said, sounding as tired as she felt. "One more thing: I wouldn't say this officially to the folks inside just yet, but I think we can safely cross Pierson off our suspect list, especially now that we have Frank Marr. He's looking pretty good for this."

“What makes you so sure?” Jessie asked, surprised at how definitive he sounded.

“First of all, we can place him at the scene around the time of the murder. Plus he knew the house well from working on it. It makes sense that he’d know how to avoid cameras. And remember he picked up that thing under the deck. It looked like a tool belt. What if he ‘accidentally forgot’ it there so he would have to come back later to pick it up?”

He made some good points but something seemed off to her about the theory. She was getting the same unsettling sensation that had overcome her back in the bedroom with the splintered door at the Carlisle house, an instinct that told her there was something she wasn’t quite seeing clearly because she just wasn’t looking at it right.

“I think you’re wrong,” she said flatly.

CHAPTER EIGHTEEN

Ryan's jaw dropped open.

"What?" he managed to say.

She hadn't intended for it to sound so harsh. It was just that she was so lost in her own thoughts that when they coalesced, she spoke them aloud without thinking how they'd come across.

"I'm sorry. I didn't mean it like that. It's just that I'm not sure that Frank Marr is the home run you think he is."

To his credit, Ryan seemed to get over her abrupt tone quickly.

"Okay, why not?" he asked.

She had lots of reasons and did her best to keep them organized in her head.

"For one thing," she replied, "he was dressed differently than the shadow image we saw leaving the house in the front door security footage. Marr was in jeans and a hoodie. The killer wore all black."

"You don't think he could have changed in the house?" Ryan challenged.

"Possibly," Jessie conceded, "but we didn't see Marr carrying a bag that might hold other clothes. If he had them on underneath what he was wearing, we didn't see the hoodie or jeans in the shadow person's hands and we didn't find those clothes at the house. Maybe he borrowed Gordon Carlisle's clothes but you saw both men. Frank Marr has three inches and forty pounds on him. I doubt he could fit into anything of Carlisle's. Even if he could, we know that Whitney Carlisle was alive at five twenty-one and the killer left at five twenty-eight. That doesn't allow a lot of time to sneak in, kill the dog, chase her down, kill her, change clothes, and leave. You think he could do all that in seven minutes?"

"I'll admit it's tight," Ryan said. "But remember, he was working in the house for weeks. He knew the place well. If this was planned in advance, he could have stashed an outfit somewhere ahead of time."

As Ryan's words echoed in her ears, the wisp of smoky thought that had evaded her grasp twice now—at the house and just a minute ago—returned. Only now it didn't dissipate. It grew stronger in her mind until it was more like a rope she could almost physically tug on.

"You're right," she said, confidence rising in her chest. "He *did* know the place well. Something's been bugging me ever since I was in that bedroom at the end of the hall and I finally figured out what it is."

"What?"

"The killer chased Whitney down that hall. When the door was locked, he smashed it open. Then he went inside, allowing her to escape through the door to the adjoining bedroom."

"So?" Ryan said.

"If Frank was the killer, he might have broken down that door and peeked in but he wouldn't have stayed there long if he didn't see her right away. He would have known that she could escape through the other bedroom because he was the one who converted one bedroom into two. He would have waited in the hall for her to dash out. But she got all the way back to the living room and pulled a lamp out of the wall before he caught up to her."

"So you think the killer *didn't* know the house well?" Ryan asked.

"No. I definitely think they've been in that house, even in that bedroom, but not since the renovations. They didn't realize that the bedroom had been split into two rooms. They knew Whitney couldn't escape through the window because it overlooked a cliff so they assumed she was trapped. That's why they spent so much time in that room—enough for her to get back to the living room and yank out that lamp. Whoever did this was taken by surprise, maybe for the first time since all these killings started."

"You could be right," Ryan said sincerely. "Or Whitney Carlisle could just be a lot faster runner than her attacker."

"Listen, I'm not dismissing Marr as a suspect, not by a long shot. He should be interviewed. But do you really think this mastermind killer who meticulously slices arteries would be so sloppy as to show up right before the murder and show his face on a security camera for everyone to see?"

"That sounds like the exact argument a brilliant killer might make if he was arrested," Ryan countered. "Why would I be so stupid to let myself be seen on camera if I was the killer?"

Jessie sighed. They were at an impasse.

"I think we should have other HSS detectives talk to Marr," she suggested. "Meanwhile you and I should focus our attention on people who might have been in all three victims' houses, but not recently. I think we should look at caterers, massage therapists, yoga instructors—that kind of thing. If we can find someone who visited all three of them in the last few months, we'll have something to go on."

"But that could be anyone, not just vendors," Ryan pointed out. "It could be friends, relatives, guests who attended parties at all three homes."

"Then I guess we better get to work," Jessie said, smiling. Then she had an idea that made her smile even bigger. "I'll call Decker and ask him to have Nettles and Valentine talk to Frank Marr."

"You don't think Karen Bray should do it?" Ryan asked, surprised.

"No. She's probably wiped out because of all the stuff at the hospital with Reid yesterday. I think she could use a break. Besides, Valentine offered to help yesterday. Now that she and Nettles are done with their training session, I don't see why we shouldn't take her up on it. I say we don't tell them where either of us stand on Marr and let them pursue him free of any of our biases."

She neglected to mention that she was especially curious to see what conclusion Susannah Valentine might draw from an interview with Frank Marr. Would she leap at the chance to pin him to the crime, like Ryan was doing? Or would she see the flaws in the case against him?

"What aren't you telling me?" Ryan asked, pulling her out of her thoughts. She must have betrayed a look that suggested she wasn't being totally forthright.

"I was just wondering how Reid is doing," she fibbed, though now that she said it, she genuinely did wonder. "We should check up on him later."

"Okay," Ryan said slowly, apparently still not completely convinced, "and in the interim?"

"In the interim, we tell Jamil about my alternative theory and see if he can help us with it. Like you said, if I'm right, the culprit could be any one of dozens of people who might have had access to all three homes. All we know is that this person would be a keen observer who could memorize the layouts of the houses, what security systems were used, where cameras would be placed. They'd likely have a personable demeanor so that none of the victims would realize that the person's friendly curiosity was really just a front to case the place for when they came back to kill them."

"So," Ryan concluded sarcastically, "all we need to do is find out everyone who was in these women's homes for say, the last six months?"

"That sounds like a good start," Jessie said, refusing to let his skepticism infect her. "I hope you ate your Wheaties."

CHAPTER NINETEEN

109 people.

That's how many they started with. Jamil had helped them compile a list of every party guest, meeting attendee, service provider, or vendor who had been in the women's homes over the last half year. Jessie thought it could have been much worse.

Only one of the women, Siobhan Pierson, had held any formal events at her home during that time. Luckily, it was a philanthropic fundraiser board meeting rather than a party. There were just eight attendees. In addition to that group, they pulled together every contractor, handyman, landscaper, lawn maintenance worker, massage therapist, yoga instructor, acupuncturist, plumber, electrician, cable guy, and personal shopper who'd been at the homes. Anyone who did a job these people didn't want to handle themselves was checked. Then they started to cross-reference them.

"Maybe it's a security system technician," Ryan had proposed. "They would know the placement and capabilities of the installed cameras."

It was a good suggestion. Unfortunately, none of the victims used the same company and none of the techs overlapped, so they dived back into the sea of names. By 9:30 a.m., with Jamil on speakerphone the whole time, they had managed to cull the big list of 109 people down to fourteen who had been at two of the three homes.

But no matter how much they looked, they couldn't find a single individual that they could place at all three houses. Jessie was coming to the conclusion that they might never when she heard Ryan's name being called. She looked up to see Jim Nettles and Susannah Valentine walking into the Santa Monica police station bullpen. Ryan waved them over.

Jessie couldn't help but notice that Valentine looked amazingly fresh, especially compared to how she felt after the all-nighter. Her black hair was pulled back in a bouncy ponytail. Her hazel eyes sparkled. She wore slacks, a blazer, and a button-down shirt that was loose around the neck, highlighting her golden skin. Jessie tried not to hate her.

"Hey, guys," Ryan said when they came into the tiny conference room, "I didn't know you were going to stop by."

"What's going on?" Jamil asked over the speakerphone.

"Oh, sorry, Jamil," Ryan said. "Jim and Susannah just walked in. To what do we owe the honor?"

"We just finished talking to Frank Marr," Nettles said. "He was on a job site in Pacific Palisades so we met him there. Since we were so close, we figured it was quicker to just come by here to update you than to call. But I'm already starting to regret it. This room is a sauna."

"Don't get me started. It's like they're trying to sweat us out of here," Ryan griped. "I'm hoping you can make me forget about it. What did you find out?"

"I'm afraid it was a bust," Valentine said before Nettles could continue. "I know Marr looked promising because he was caught on camera and he knew the home layout. But when we dug in, it fell apart. He showed us a receipt from the In-N-Out Burger he said he went to right after leaving the Carlisle place. The timestamp is five thirty-one. We checked the restaurant's camera and he's right there at the pickup window at the matching time. It seemed unlikely that he could get from the house to the front of the drive-through line in three minutes—from five twenty-eight to five thirty-one—so we timed it ourselves. Sure enough, at a normal speed, it took us six minutes just to get from one place to the other, excluding wait time. There's no way he could have made it in half that. Not even I could do that weaving in and out of traffic at top speed in my Mini Cooper, though I'd like to try."

Jessie did her best not to mutter "humblebrag" under her breath.

"He also consented for us to check his phone location data," Nettles added. "Unless that shows something weird, it looks like a dead end."

"What was his demeanor like?" Jessie asked, focusing her question on Valentine.

"He seemed properly broken up when we told him about Whitney Carlisle's death," she answered. "If he was faking, it was very convincing. He said he had planned to stop by the house after lunch to see how today's work was going."

"Didn't his workers call him when they couldn't get hold of her this morning?" Ryan wanted to know.

"I asked him that," Valentine said, again leaving Nettles with his mouth open but nothing to say. "He told me that since his guys are working on the deck this week, they didn't need house access. They'd have no reason to reach out to her."

Jessie glanced over at Ryan, who looked crestfallen. Any satisfaction she'd gotten from being right about Marr's culpability was immediately wiped away at the sight of his forlorn face. It didn't help that Susannah Valentine, despite her inclination to cut her partner off, had passed her little test with flying colors. This morning was getting sourer by the second.

"I need some air," she said, and without waiting for anyone's response, headed outside.

*

Jessie luxuriated in the biting cold.

After Ryan's bad news about Frank Marr and the total failure to find a connection among the three victims, she had gone outside and sat alone on a bench outside the police station, embracing the sting of the whipping wind from the Pacific Ocean, only four blocks west. It was bracing but it seemed to help clear her head.

Realizing she hadn't checked in at home she texted Kat to see how the night had gone. The response came quickly: *Good so far. I'm working my accounting case. Hannah's still sleeping.*

For a second, Jessie freaked out. It was almost ten. The girl was super late for school. Then she remembered: there was no school today. It was a teacher in-service day and the kids had it off. She replied quickly: *Okay. Plan to stop by around lunch to check in and freshen up. Thanks again for doing this.* Kat responded with a thumbs-up emoji.

Jessie's mind returned to the endless list of vendors and service providers used by the victims, none of whom had overlapped at all the victims' homes. She just couldn't accept that three women who all lived within four miles of each had never shared any of the same providers. That seemed weirder to her than if they had a dozen overlapping vendors.

Suddenly, her mouth began to water. Looking around, she saw the reason. A Mexican food truck had set up shop across the street. The smell of sizzling meat made her swallow involuntarily. The side of the truck had pictures of the different meal options. Above them was a big notice in red letters that read: *CASH ONLY—no credit or phone payments.*

She stood up abruptly as a thought popped into her head, then dashed back into the station, looking for Ryan. He wasn't in the conference room. She suspected he'd taken a break of his own but she couldn't wait. She grabbed the phone and dialed Gordon Carlisle's number.

When he answered he sounded groggy.

"Hello?"

"Hi, Mr. Carlisle, It's Jessie Hunt. I'm sorry to bother you a third time but I really need your help with something."

There was a long pause before he replied.

"Hold on a minute," he said slowly. "I took some pills to help me sleep and I'm a little fuzzy. I just need to drink some water."

While she waited, Jessie tried to think of the best way to ask her question to a foggy-headed, grief-stricken husband. Before she'd figured it out, he was back on the line. She decided to just be clear and direct.

"Can you think of any in-home service Whitney might have used off-book? Stuff she didn't put in her calendar or some work that didn't require a receipt? Cash-only services?"

She could almost hear his brain searching for a suitable answer. When he responded, she knew immediately from his tone that it would be disappointing.

"I'm sorry," he said. "I can't think of anything."

She did her best to keep the frustration out of her voice when she responded.

"Thanks anyway, Mr. Carlisle. I'll let you get back to sleep. Please let me know if anything else occurs to you."

"I will," Carlisle said heavily, sounding like he might fall back asleep even before hanging up the phone.

Jessie sat silently in the conference room, listening to the station's hum of voices and typing outside the door. At this moment her brain felt as foggy as she imagined Carlisle's was. She closed her eyes, felt the heaviness of her eyelids, and considered giving in to it.

But she was ripped from her near catnap by the sound of the phone ringing. Her eyes snapped open and she looked at the display. It was Gordon Carlisle calling back. She couldn't answer it fast enough.

CHAPTER TWENTY

"She had a trainer."

"What's that?" Jessie asked.

"Whitney had a personal trainer," Carlisle repeated. "She usually met him at the gym. But when she was super busy, she'd have him come to the house. It wasn't a regular thing so she didn't have it in her calendar. And I remember that unlike when she trained with him at the gym, with all its corporate rules, she paid for the home sessions in cash. That's the only service I can remember her using that involved cash and no regular schedule."

"Do you remember his name?" Jessie asked, keeping her voice even so as not to betray her renewed optimism."

"Yeah. It's Vince Hutchence. He operates out of Pacific Performance Club on Colorado Avenue. Does that help?"

"I really hope so," Jessie said. "Thanks so much."

She had barely hung up before she was tearing through Gillian Fahey's file. First she checked her phone calendar for any reference to either Vince Hutchence or Pacific Performance Club. There were no mentions of him but it looked like Gillian used to be a PPC member until about a year ago, going regularly three times a week. She subsequently joined a different club but there was still hope. Since she went to PCC in the past, it stood to reason that she'd interacted with Hutchence.

She switched over to Gillian's hard copy appointment book. It was far less detailed than the one on her phone, more comprised of daily to-do lists than official appointments, all written in hard-to-read handwriting. She flipped through pages looking for the trainer's name but couldn't find it anywhere. She was about to give up when she saw a pair of letters, only just legible, out to the side of the list on a day about ten months ago: VH.

Silently chastising herself for not considering that the woman might have used initials to save time, she reviewed the lists again. Now that she knew what she was looking for, it came much easier. She found another seven references to "VH," all barely decipherable, the last one just three weeks ago. She was confident that they referenced the trainer.

If she was right, that was two women who used him. She just needed one more.

She began to search through Siobhan Pierson's schedule book for any reference to PCC or any variation on the name "Vince Hutchence." But there was nothing, not even a general mention of a trainer. Though she knew they were far less likely to have what she needed, she searched Pierson's digital files for the same thing. That proved equally fruitless. It didn't appear that the woman ever worked with the trainer or that she ever even went to PCC. Jessie could feel the optimism leaching out of her.

In desperation, she decided that if calling one grieving husband had worked, she might as well try another. She was just dialing Ian Pierson's cell phone when Ryan walked in.

"Where have you been?" she asked as she waited for Pierson to pick up.

"I went to the break room for a catnap," he said, looking at all the documents spread out in front of her with raised eyebrows "but I must have accidentally turned off my phone alarm because when I woke up, it had been forty-five minutes. It looks like I missed something while I was gone. Am I right?"

Pierson's phone went to voicemail so she hung up and tried his assistant, Kelly.

"I think I've found a possible connection among all three women. I've got two. Now we just have to confirm the third."

"What is it?" Ryan asked, all the sleep immediately draining from his eyes.

Before she could answer, Kelly picked up.

"Hi, Kelly, it's Jessie Hunt. I'm here with Detective Hernandez," she said, putting the call on speaker. "I'm trying to reach Mr. Pierson with an additional question but he's not picking up. Can you help?"

"I can try," Kelly said, "but he might not be in a very chatty mood. When I checked on him earlier, he was already in rough shape. I had to help him to the bathroom. Is there something I can assist you with?"

"Actually yes," Jessie said, realizing that Siobhan's assistant might be a better resource on this than her husband. "Do you recall Mrs. Pierson ever using a personal trainer named Vince Hutchence?"

"Sure," Kelly said so matter-of-factly that Jessie was momentarily speechless.

She couldn't believe it. They finally had another lead worth following. When she continued, she did her best to keep her excitement in check.

"Did she pay him in cash?"

"Yes—well, I made the actual payments on her behalf," Kelly answered. "He specifically requested cash; said it made things easier on his taxes, which sounded sketchy to me. But Mrs. Pierson was okay with it so I did what I was told."

"Did he ever train her at the house?"

"Yeah," Kelly said, "a few times—maybe three. But she dropped him after that."

"Do you know why?" Jessie asked slowly.

"Not really," Kelly said. "She mentioned something about him being a little too demanding but she didn't go into it. All I know is that she stopped seeing him and got a new trainer, a woman who came to the house twice a week."

Jessie was curious about exactly what "a little too demanding" meant. Did he push her to work too hard? Or did he maybe come on to her? The latter wouldn't be a shock but it would be bold. Making an unsolicited pass at a woman as powerful as Siobhan Pierson was a risky move. If she reacted badly and he felt threatened, was that a potential motive for murder?

"When was the last time he worked with her?"

"Oh, God, it was a while ago," Kelly replied. "It's late January now and I know it was just before her last birthday because she was hoping to look good for this tasting menu dinner a friend had gifted her. She wanted to be able to gorge all evening without feeling guilty. So, based on that, I'd say it was about four months ago."

"Thanks very much, Kelly," she said. "I guess you can let your boss sleep it off a little longer."

When she hung up, she looked over at Ryan, who was staring at her expectantly.

"Care to share?" he asked.

"All three women used the same trainer in their homes. At least two of them paid in cash. I'm guessing Gillian did too. And it seems like the visits weren't a regularly scheduled thing so they weren't in their phone calendars. That's why they didn't show up when we did our searches. Not even Jamil's advanced stuff would have picked them up."

"It sounds like we've got a legitimate lead here," Ryan said. "How do you want to go at it?"

"I say we surprise him and see how he reacts. I've got his website up now. I'm going to call his cell to make an appointment."

She was already dialing the number. It went straight to voicemail. His message was direct and to the point: *This is Vince Hutchence, peak performance trainer. Leave your name and number and I'll get back to as soon as I can to help you on your fitness journey. Have a healthy day!*

"Hi, Vince, My name's Jessie," she said before leaving her number. "I've heard that you're the guy who can get me looking good in my naughty nurse costume for my birthday party. It's coming up soon so please get back to me ASAP. Thanks!"

As she hung up, she saw Ryan's smirk and faked a pout.

"What, not convincingly shallow enough?"

"That's not it," he said. "I'm just wondering when *I* get to see that naughty nurse outfit."

"Play your cards right and maybe you'll get a surprise this weekend," she teased, before switching gears. "In the meantime, I don't want to wait for this guy to call me back. If he's our killer, every second is precious. We don't know when he might strike next. I think we can justifiably request a GPS search on that phone's location, don't you?"

"I think it will be a hell of a lot easier than it was getting the one on Ian Pierson," he replied, before smiling mischievously. "But can we go back to your promise about this weekend for a second?"

"Later, lover boy," she said. "Right now, we've got a peak performance trainer to visit."

CHAPTER TWENTY ONE

They didn't have to go far.

According to Jamil, Vince Hutchence's phone had been at the same location for the last half hour, an address in Santa Monica only six minutes from the station. They pulled up across from the house, which belonged to a divorcee named Eileen Schock.

They knew it was the right place because Hutchence's car, which Jamil had said was a red Jeep Wrangler, sat out front. Schock lived on a tree-lined street comprised mostly of impressive but tasteful two-story homes, almost all of which looked like they'd been built by the same three or four architects.

"It's almost eleven," Jessie said. "I guess we should just wait for him to come outside. It'll give us a chance to check him out."

"It looks like Jamil already did it for us," Ryan said, pulling up a message on his phone and reading from it. "He says that the guy has all the appropriate personal trainer accreditations. He's twenty-nine and has been doing this for three years. Most of the client comments and reviews are positive and they're all from women. Apparently he works exclusively with the fairer sex."

"Why am I not surprised?" Jessie said, rolling her eyes. "I was originally willing to bet the workout session would be ending soon, but maybe not, if there's some kind of 'overtime' involved."

"When did you become so cynical?" Ryan asked, pretending he didn't have the exact same suspicions as her. "I remember when I first met you and you ascribed the best of motives to people. Now you assume the worst. It's a crying shame."

"I don't know who you're talking about, Detective Hernandez," Jessie replied cheekily. "Maybe your other fiancée? Because I lost my ability to give most people the benefit of the doubt a long time ago."

"As long as it was before you met me," he said, wiping away an imaginary bead of sweat from his overly furrowed brow.

They may have been playing with each other, but Jessie didn't need any help remembering the exact moment that she realized the depths of depravity people were capable of. She was six years old, tied to a chair in a remote, snowy Ozarks cabin, when she watched her serial killer father slaughter her mother with a knife before turning it on her, cutting a long line across her collarbone that left an ugly scar. Then he'd left her to die.

She was there three days, slipping in and out of consciousness, before a pair of hunters happened upon the cabin and rescued her. Ever since, anyone she met started with a negative humanity rating. It took quite a few points just to get back to zero, much less enter positive territory.

She looked at Ryan, who had the highest point total going. He was wearing a frown. It took her a moment to realize that she'd never confirmed that her cynicism pre-dated him.

"Of course it was before you, Ryan," she said hurriedly. "I'd just as soon leave it there."

"Good, because for a second there, you had me wondering. I didn't know if maybe the last few weeks shook your confidence in me."

"What are you talking about?" she asked.

"You know, Alan Trembley," he said, referring to the detective who was murdered in a hostel bedroom while Ryan waited, unknowing, in a car on the street below.

"Ryan," she said, taking his hand in hers. "You have to stop beating yourself up over that. I know you feel responsible. And I'm not going to sugarcoat what happened that day. It wasn't your finest moment. But let's be real. You were still rehabbing after the coma. You wouldn't have been able to make it up the stairs of that hostel even if you'd gone inside with Trembley. The Night Hunter would have gotten the jump on him either way."

"But I might have been able to stop him in the lobby," Ryan insisted, "before he killed other people."

"Maybe," Jessie conceded, "or maybe in your diminished state, he would have gotten the jump on you and jammed an X-Acto knife in your throat too. You did what you could under the circumstances. I know you think you froze up when he came out of that hostel. And maybe you did. But what if you had tried to take a shot at him from across a crowded street? You said yourself that he used a family as a shield to escape. What if you accidentally shot one of them? Then you'd be flagellating yourself for coming back from rehab too soon and killing a civilian. It's time to make peace with what happened and move on. Trembley wouldn't want you to hold onto the guilt. He knew what I know in my heart: that there's no one on the force more brave or loyal than you. He'd want you to forgive yourself. He'd want you to be happy, because he loved you—maybe not the way I love you, but he did."

Ryan nodded, wiping away a tear from his eye.

"I just don't want to be a disappointment to you," he whispered.

"Would I have said yes that morning in Wildpines if I thought you were a disappointment?" she asked, her eyes watery too, before answering her own question. "Of course not."

He couldn't know that her doubts about pressing forward with a wedding weren't about the past but the future. Again, she wondered how wise it was to plan nuptials with everything so unsettled with Hannah, with their lives so in flux. But now wasn't the time to bring that up. She wasn't sure there ever would be an ideal occasion for that conversation. Luckily she didn't have to worry about it at that moment.

"Check it out," she said, pointing at the house, "it looks like Eileen's training session is over."

The front door was open and a man stepped out, waving to a woman in the doorway they could barely see. Jamil had sent them Hutchence's driver's license and the man walking to the Jeep was clearly him. But neither his license photo, nor the one on his website, did him justice.

The guy swaggering down the walkway looked like he might have been a former male model or a former football player. Jessie hadn't had time do research on him but she wouldn't have been surprised if he was once both.

Easily six foot five and 240 pounds, Hutchence's sun-bleached hair was as long as her own. He wore bike shorts and a tank top that revealed his broad, tanned shoulders and chiseled muscles. His brown eyes were huge, which gave him the look of an especially strapping puppy dog.

"This should be interesting," Jessie said, getting out of the passenger seat.

Ryan smirked in agreement as they headed over to meet the guy at his Jeep. As they approached, Hutchence noticed them and slowed from his peppy walk to a more leisurely, hesitant stroll. He stopped playfully swinging his workout bag in the air.

"Vince Hutchence?" Ryan asked.

"Yeah," the giant answered, his surfer dude vibe immediately apparent in his tone, "who's asking?"

"I'm Ryan Hernandez and this is Jessie Hunt. We're with the LAPD and we have a few questions—"

He hadn't even completed the sentence before Hutchence dropped his bag, turned, and started sprinting back in the direction he'd come from. He looked to be headed for the open side gate of the house next to Eileen Schock's.

Jessie and Ryan exchanged a quick, unspoken glance that both immediately understood. Ryan wasn't yet in condition to go sprinting after anyone. There was frustration in his eyes, but also an acknowledgment that he just wasn't up to it. That meant Jessie was on chase duty. As she started after the trainer, she heard her partner and fiancé shout out after her.

"I'll call for backup and try to loop around."

She hoped that worked but couldn't count on him having success. As she dashed toward the gate that Hutchence had disappeared beyond, she undid her gun holster and removed her weapon. She hoped she wouldn't need it but if the guy took her by surprise and she wasn't prepared, she doubted it would go well for her.

When she reached the gate, she scanned the backyard. It was huge, with a large kidney-shaped pool in the middle. A big play structure, complete with monkey bars and a curling slide, sat further back in the yard, and just beyond that, a trampoline. Suddenly, she saw movement. Hutchence had already run around the pool and past the structure and trampoline. He was preparing to scale the tall, wooden back fence, which looked to be at least ten feet high.

She skirted by the edge of the pool just as he leaped up to grab the top of the fence. But he lost his grip and dropped back to the ground. He looked back. Seeing Jessie with the gun in her hand seemed to give him a renewed burst of energy. This time when he leapt up, he got hold of the top of the fence easily and hoisted himself up and over. In the place where he'd been moments earlier, now there was nothing.

She stood there in momentary shock. Then she saw a ray of sunlight that was poking through two fence planks briefly disappear. It happened to another one to the left, and then another. He was running that way. Somehow the small discovery of which direction he was headed in gave her an unexpected surge of hope. This wasn't over yet.

She started running again and as she approached the fence, a crazy idea popped into her head. There was no way, even at her considerable height, that she could scale that fence unassisted. Hutchence had barely done it with the advantage of seven extra inches and triple the arm strength. But maybe she could get an assist.

Without taking time to think about it, she reholstered her gun and scurried up the play structure stairs to the wooden bridge leading to the slide. Then she started running. When she got to the slide, she took one step near the top and leapt through the air.

For one endless moment, she was flying. Then she locked her knees as her shoes landed solidly on the surface of the trampoline. She felt the material give and then shoot her back up into the air in the direction of the fence.

It came up on her fast and she barely had time to process two things. First, she was definitely high enough that she could grab the top of the fence. Second, she was going to slam into it hard.

She was right on both counts. Her right hip smashed into the wall, right where her gun and holster rested, sending shooting pain through her pelvis. She was so high up that she almost toppled over the thing entirely. Then gravity did its work and she slid back downward, barely managing to hook her armpits over the top of the fence to stop her momentum. The wood dug into the tender skin there, but compared to her screaming hip, it was nothing.

Gasping for breath, she looked left and saw Hutchence dashing west down the back alley, in the direction of the next cross street. He was moving fast. There was no way she could catch him at this rate.

Still, she heaved herself up and over the fence, then dropped the rest of the way. When she landed, she stumbled and fell back onto the gravel road, feeling the little bits of rock dig into her backside. Ignoring it, she gritted her teeth, got to her feet, and started after the massive being that was almost to the end of the alleyway.

Hutchence looked back in her direction, and seeing that she was easily fifty yards back, he gave a satisfied smile as he reached the next street. Jessie watched as he turned around, just in time to see the open passenger door of Ryan's car slam into him. She watched him soar a good ten feet before landing in a heap in the street.

Even from as far away as Jessie was, she could hear him groan. Ryan got out of the car and looked down the alley toward her. They might have been fifty yards apart, but the proud grin on his face was impossible to miss.

CHAPTER TWENTY TWO

She had to admit she was impressed.

As Jessie stared at Vince Hutchence through the one-way mirror of the SMPD interrogation room, she marveled that the guy was even sitting upright.

After cuffing the dazed trainer and tossing him in the back of the car, she and Ryan thought they might have to make a pit stop at the hospital. Jessie was even looking forward to it, on the off chance she could stop in to see Callum Reid.

But the mountain of a man recovered enough that it was clear no stopover was needed. In fact, it had taken three good-sized officers to drag him into the room where he sat now, handcuffed to a table that was bolted to the floor, looking far less like a puppy dog than before. His expression was surly and his eyes were flinty.

"You ready?" Ryan asked from beside her.

"What I'm ready for is a good bath," she said. "My hip is killing me."

She didn't mention that she was also so tired that she thought she might keel over then and there.

"Maybe we should have stopped at the hospital to get *you* checked out, Evel Knievel. I don't know what you were thinking."

"I clearly wasn't," she admitted. "I'll be fine once the ibuprofen kicks in. Let's see if we've got our guy, shall we?"

They walked into the room and, as she had while waiting in the observation room, Jessie stood in quiet wonder at the modern touches the Santa Monica police station had that Central Station did not. The technology in both was state of the art. Most of the stuff they used downtown was approaching a decade old. Here, the interrogation room was soundproofed, with hidden microphones intended to make suspects forget they were being recorded. The multiple cameras were built into the walls for the same reason. At Central Station they were lucky if all their recording equipment worked.

"Hello, Mr. Hutchence," Ryan said. Jessie knew he was addressing the guy formally to remind him in one more subtle way that he wasn't in charge. No one would be fawning over his good looks and physique here. "So I read you your rights back in the vehicle. I know you weren't at the top of your game then, what with your run-in with the car door. Are you willing to talk to us now?"

Though Ryan had Mirandized Hutchence in the car, they hadn't tried to question him then. He was angry and volatile and they didn't want him invoking his right to an attorney, so they'd held off until he was a little calmer.

"I don't even know why I'm in here," he said belligerently. Jessie considered the fact that he was speaking at all to be a good sign. She decided to take advantage of it.

"Do you know Gillian Fahey or Siobhan Pierson?" she asked as if she was merely curious about the weather. His face softened slightly at the names.

"Yes. They were both clients of mine. It was awful what happened to them."

"Not just them, Vince," she said, using a gentle tone and his first name to make their interaction more informal, as opposed to the one with Ryan. It was classic good cop, bad cop, or in this case, good profiler, bad cop. "Someone else was killed too—Whitney Carlisle."

"What?" he said with a look of disbelief on his face.

"I believe she was a client of yours as well, correct?" she noted, not hinting that under her comparatively affable visage, she was just as skeptical of Hutchence as Ryan.

"Uh-huh," he said, slack-jawed, before adding, "I had no idea."

Ryan jumped back in.

"Are you really trying to tell us that you didn't know she was killed last night?"

Hutchence first looked dumbfounded, then appalled.

"How would I know?" he demanded, before seeming to finally put the pieces together. "Wait, you think *I* did this—killed three of my own clients?"

"It's not a crazy assumption. You did run when we identified ourselves," Jessie pointed out.

"Not because of that though," he insisted.

"Why then?" Jessie asked.

Suddenly the guy looked much less willing to talk. There was unmistakable guilt in his eyes.

"I'm not sure I should say..." he said before trailing off.

"Vince," Jessie replied, sitting down in one of the chairs across from him and leaning in, "if you have an explanation that doesn't involve you killing three women, you'd be well advised to provide it. Whatever it is, it's preferable to being charged as a triple murderer."

She was skeptical that he could explain himself out of this one and waited for him to either confess outright or fumble through a lie. The first was obviously preferable but if he tried the latter and failed, that could be useful at trial. He sighed heavily before answering.

"It's just that I'm little behind in paying my taxes."

Jessie hadn't been expecting that answer, though she did her best to hide it.

"How far behind?" she asked, waiting for him to get to the point.

"About six years."

"That doesn't explain why you ran," Ryan reminded him.

"The IRS has been sending me letters for a while now. I thought that maybe they were taking it to the next level, like sending the cops to arrest me."

Jessie didn't know how to react to such an absurd claim. She tried to keep the bewilderment out of her voice when she replied.

"You're saying you believed the IRS would send an LAPD detective to arrest a personal trainer for not paying back taxes?"

He shrugged.

"It seemed possible. Some of those letters they sent are really intense."

Jessie looked over at Ryan and could tell he was thinking the same thing as her: either Vince Hutchence was one of the dimmest bulbs they'd ever encountered or he was brilliant at acting the part. Getting an answer to that question was crucial. If he was as stupid as he seemed, there was no way he could have pulled off such complicated murders. If he was faking his cluelessness, then he was still their best suspect.

"Let's talk about Siobhan Pierson," she said, pivoting to a rawer subject. "She was no longer a client of yours, right?"

"Yeah, we had different fitness metrics for her so we decided to part ways."

"I don't know what that means," she pressed.

"I'm guess I'm trying to be polite. I just thought she could work a little harder."

"Is that what she was talking about when she told her assistant that you were 'a little too demanding'?" Ryan challenged.

"That's probably it," Hutchence answered unconvincingly.

Jessie knew in her bones that he was lying. She decided it was time for her to play a little hardball too—no more "good" profiler.

"Don't insult us, Vince," she growled. "If you keep lying, we're going to toss you into county lockup for the night—general population. You know what that means? You'll be surrounded by a lot of guys bigger and meaner than you. And I can't guarantee how friendly they'll be to a pretty boy in bike shorts and a tank top with long, flowing blond locks and puppy dog eyes. They might want to dirty you up a little. So tell us the truth: what did she mean by 'demanding'?"

"Okay, okay," he said, holding up his hands and inadvertently making the cuffs attached to the table rattle. "She probably meant that I came on to her. Sometimes I provide 'extra services' to my clients if they express interest. That's part of why I get paid in cash—because even a top trainer isn't going to charge a thousand bucks for an hour-long private HIIT workout. It would look suspicious on a receipt. But with Siobhan, I couldn't tell if she was into extras or just wanted a legit training session. After a while I got restless. She's so rich that if she wanted a more private workout, I could charge her way more than other clients. So at the end of the session I went for it. It turned out to be a mistake—she wasn't interested *and* she was pissed. I apologized and left right away. I didn't want her to post a bad review so I didn't even charge her for the last session. That's the last time I saw her. It was months ago."

That answer made sense but Jessie couldn't help but wonder if he'd decided to make extra certain that Siobhan didn't badmouth him by silencing her for good. Of course, if he wanted to do that, why wait until four months after their last appointment?

"Did you provide your 'extra services' to Gillian Fahey and Whitney Carlisle too?" she asked.

"With Gillian, yes—eventually. The sessions started off legit but at some point she asked for extra. That only happened a couple of times though. She told me she felt guilty and wanted to stop. After that, it would have been weird to keep training her."

Jessie noticed a pattern with Gillian. She seemed to enjoy short-term liaisons, which were followed soon thereafter by shame and a need to shut them down. That's what had happened with Ian Pierson and if Hutchence was to be believed, she'd done the same thing with him. She wondered if there were others.

"And what about Whitney?" she asked.

"No. She never gave any sign that she had interest in anything other than working out. She wanted to sweat, to be pushed to the limit. But that was it. Once the hour was up, I left. She seemed really into her husband." The way he said it made it sound like that was a weird concept to him.

"Where were you last night?" Ryan asked, abruptly switching gears.

"Um, it depends on the time. Can I have my phone to check my schedule?"

"You need your phone to remember where you were yesterday?" Ryan challenged.

"I need my phone to remember where I was an hour ago," he conceded sheepishly.

An officer brought it in and gave it to Ryan, who handed it over. Hutchence pulled up the calendar.

"What time?" he asked.

"Between five p.m. and seven p.m.," Ryan told him.

"Okay," he said, scrolling until he got there. Once he did, he smiled. "Oh yeah, I had an extended session with a client whose husband is out of town. I was there from five until six-thirty. That was my last appointment for the day. I went home and showered, then chilled out playing some video games."

"What about Sunday night?" Jessie asked, "Between midnight and three a.m.?"

"Oh, that was a rough one," Hutchence said, chuckling despite his current circumstance: handcuffed to a table in an interrogation room.

"Go on," Ryan said impatiently.

"I also do some work as an adult dancer," he said with a mix of pride and sheepishness. "I was working a bachelorette party at a house in Thousand Oaks. I arrived at midnight, worked the crowd for an hour. Then I went to a bedroom with the bride for a solo show that lasted another hour. I left a little after two, I think. I can't say for sure but I think I went straight home. I had a client training session at eight the next morning so I doubt I'd have stayed up."

"What about January sixteenth, between eight p.m. and midnight?" Jessie asked, referring to the date and approximate time of Siobhan Pierson's murder, though she was starting to question the point of pursuing this. If what he said was true, he'd have an alibi witness for last night and potentially a dozen or more for Sunday night.

"That was also an 'extra services' training session," he said when he got to the date.

"You seem to spend more time on the extra services than the actual training," Ryan noted drily. "We're going to need all those clients' names to confirm your whereabouts."

"Okay," Hutchence said, "but could you talk to them, like secretly? I don't want to lose any clients and I think some of their husbands might be mad if they found out."

"Ya think?" Ryan asked, finding it difficult to hide his disdain.

Jessie wasn't in the mood to condescend. She was too busy coming to terms with a harsh reality: Hutchence was a bust as a suspect. Even if his alibi witnesses didn't all vouch for him on the record, one thing was clear. The guy was just too damn stupid to pull off these murders.

It was back to the drawing board.

CHAPTER TWENTY THREE

Jessie was almost home.

As she made the last few turns, she reviewed their leads again in her head. And just as before, she concluded that they were all dead ends. That was what Ryan had said to her forty-five minutes earlier when he sent her home.

"You're all beat up," he'd said. "Take my car. Go back to the house. Get cleaned up. Check on Hannah. Maybe grab a quick nap and a bite to eat. I'll take a shower here at the station and dive back into the leads we let slide to pursue Hutchence. We'll meet up afterward."

Pulling into the garage, she felt an unexpected mix of relief and exhaustion. She could finally ease up on the throttle a little, but the thought of that made her suddenly, incredibly tired. She walked into a surprisingly quiet house.

"Anyone here?" she called out.

"In the kitchen," Kat shouted back.

Jessie rounded the corner to find her friend at the breakfast table with an early afternoon coffee and dozens of papers spread out so that not an inch of wood was visible.

"What are you up to?" Jessie asked.

"Just working on what might the most boring case I've ever taken on," she replied, waving at the documents laid out before her. "Remind me never to accept another one involving malfeasance at an accounting firm, no matter how big the retainer. This is not Philip Marlowe stuff. I think my eyes almost started bleeding for a moment there."

"I'm sorry to hear that," Jessie said without much sympathy. "Maybe you can console yourself by rolling around in your bed with the piles of cash you're getting."

"I'm willing to give it a shot," Kat replied straight-faced.

"Before you do that, can you tell me where my sister is?"

"She left about a half hour ago for that coffeehouse she likes. I believe she mentioned something about FaceTiming with someone named Chris?"

For the briefest of seconds, Jessie was tempted to call Hannah to check on her. But knowing it would only alienate her, she fought the urge and instead focused in on Kat's unspoken question.

"Ah yes," Jessie said. "He's the cute boy she met when we were up in Wildpines. To be honest, I think he's half the reason she wants to go to culinary camp there this summer."

"Would that be the end of the world?" Kat asked.

"Actually, that would be just about the most reassuringly normal behavior that kid has engaged in for a while. I'm all for it. Speaking of behavior, how was hers last night?"

Kat gave a half-hearted smile.

"After she got over the seething resentment that I was here at all? Not too bad. We ate popcorn and watched a marathon of *Nailed It!*"

"Well, thanks for doing it on short notice."

"No problem," Kat assured her. "I can do this kind of work from here just as well as the office so it wasn't a sacrifice. How's your case going? You look a little…pooped."

Jessie couldn't help but laugh.

"That's very diplomatic of you. The truth is that it's not going great."

She explained the circumstances of the murders and their all-night search for a connection among the victims, before wrapping up with the Vince Hutchence imbroglio.

"So after using a trampoline to scale a fence, which left me feeling like I need a hip replacement, it all ended up being for nothing. He's got alibis for all three murders and he's too dumb to hold a knife, much less use it as a weapon. Ryan's following up on other 'leads,' but we're basically treading water here."

"I'm sorry, Jessie," Kat said sincerely, "that really sucks."

"It really does," Jessie agreed. "But I've decided that I'm going to put all that out of my head for the next half hour. I need a shower, a thick layer of deodorant, and something to eat. Then I'll start up again, maybe not smelling fresh as a daisy, but not as bad as a dead fish either."

"You do have a way with imagery," Kat said, scrunching up her nose.

*

When Jessie got out of the bathroom after her shower, Kat was sitting on her bed with a gleam in her eye.

"Okay, you don't look creepy at all," Jessie said, rewrapping the towel around her.

"Sorry, it's just that I had an idea while you were showering and I couldn't wait to run it by you," she said excitedly.

"Can I at least get dressed first?" Jessie asked. "Maybe put on a bra and panties?"

"You dress, I'll talk."

"This better be good, Kat. I was actually relaxed there for half a second."

"I think you may find this is worth the awkwardness," Kat said. "I was thinking about what you said earlier and something occurred to me."

"I'm all ears," Jessie said as she searched for something clean to wear.

"So you talked about how you were trying to find some kind of vendor or service provider who'd been to all three victims' homes," Kat said, standing up and grabbing a presentable looking shirt on a hanger. "But I noticed that most of the people you considered would be repeat visitors."

"What do you mean?" Jessie asked, taking the shirt approvingly.

"I mean, you mostly looked at people like this Hutchence guy: in-home trainers, yoga instructors, gardeners, personal manicurists, that kind of thing. But if this person is as sharp as you think they are, they might only need one visit to each house to get the lay of the land. It could have been someone adept at understanding home layouts, like a contractor who came by once to give an estimate on home remodeling or a delivery person who brought a piece of furniture inside. Maybe the killer has a photographic memory for where everything—including security cameras—is. My point is: I think you may be limiting your pool of suspects."

Jessie slumped down on the bed.

"What's wrong?" Kat asked. "You don't think it's possible?"

"No," Jessie sighed. "Now that you mention it, I think it's entirely possible. That's the problem. You just increased our potential suspect list exponentially and I don't know how we can possibly narrow it down in time. We've had murders on two consecutive nights. Who's to say the killer won't go for three in a row?"

Speaking the words out loud made her realize that the time for casual conversation was over. She had calls to make and sustenance to force into her body if she was going to prevent another death tonight.

CHAPTER TWENTY FOUR

Multi-tasking was hard under the best of circumstances, but was especially bad without having had any sleep for over thirty hours. As she rushed through her errands around the house, Jessie felt both harried and like she was moving in molasses. She was currently making herself a quick sandwich while carrying on a conversation with Callum Reid in the hospital.

"I'm sorry I haven't been able to drop by yet," she said. "This case has been so crazy that I haven't had any down time until now."

"That's okay," he told her reassuringly. He sounded surprisingly chipper for a guy who just had a heart attack. "The docs tell me that I should be discharged tomorrow."

"That's great," she replied as she hurriedly loaded up the turkey sandwich with lettuce and tomato slices. "What's the long-term prognosis?"

"They say it depends on my lifestyle. If I continue to work in a high-pressure job that requires periodic all-nighters, this could happen again. But we both know that's not in my future. I actually plan to call Captain Decker right after I hang up with you. I originally wanted to tell him about my retirement plans in person. But I don't think it's fair to him to hold off any longer when my mind is made up."

"I'm happy for you," Jessie said, adding a cheese slice to the pile of food. "I know you were worried about leaving him in the lurch. But with HSS getting all the new funding and personnel, it's never been in a better position. You can say goodbye with a clear conscience."

"Thanks, Hunt," he said. "Hell, I may want to conference you in for backup in case he gives me a hard time."

"Hey, if I can stay awake and you need me, I'll do it."

"I'm just kidding," he said. "This is a one-person job. Besides, I want you to keep all your focus on working your case and staying upright."

They said their goodbyes and Jessie returned her attention to the sandwich. As she added the second piece of bread and pressed everything down, she tried to stop her weary mind from fixating on the multitude of worries scraping at the edge of her skull.

She was concerned about Hannah's mental health. She was anxious about Ryan's physical health and whether he was pushing too hard to get back to where he used to be before the stabbing and coma. She wasn't sure about the wisdom of planning a wedding in light of everything going on.

And to top it all off, she couldn't think of an efficient way to narrow down the suspect list that Kat had just helpfully but mercilessly expanded. Frustrated, she grabbed the knife and sliced the sandwich down the middle. But her grip slipped slightly and she cut a gash into the outside of her left thumb.

"Damn it!" she shouted.

"What's wrong?" Kat asked from the living room, where she'd relocated all of her paperwork.

"I just cut myself," Jessie answered, grabbing a paper towel and pressing it against the spot. Kat came in immediately.

"Let me see," she said, and after Jessie removed the bloody paper towel, she added, "That's more than just a nick. Where do you keep your first aid kit?"

"In the hall closet on the second shelf," Jessie told her.

"I'll go get it while you run your hand under some water."

Jessie moved over to the sink and let the cold water pour over the wound. It didn't look like it would require stitches but it was quite ugly. As she watched the blood seep out, run down her thumb to her wrist, and then trickle into the drain below, she had an unexpected random thought: there might be a way to narrow down that list of suspects in the case.

She remembered what Ryan had said at the morgue while looking at Gillian Fahey's body—that the cuts to the carotid and femoral arteries had been clean and meticulous. But it wasn't just her. That was true of all three victims.

There was a precision and exactitude to them that suggested the perpetrator was someone with a steady, professional hand. She wondered if they ought to focus their search on service providers, or even friends, who did that kind of work. Maybe they needed to skip the yoga instructors in favor of acupuncturists, tattoo artists, and surgeons.

Kat walked in with the first aid kit and got to work. As she cleaned, then wrapped the thumb, Jessie silently played out the possibilities in her head.

"All done," Kat said, pulling her back into the moment. "Almost good as new."

"Thanks so much, Kat. As long as you're in favor-granting mode, can I ask you for one more?"

"What's that?"

"Can you stick around a little longer to keep an eye on Hannah when she gets back? I had a possible brainstorm and I need to get back to work on the case."

Kat looked like she'd been expecting the request.

"I'll do it as long as she makes me one of those fancy dinners this evening. Last night she was too aggrieved to make anything."

"Deal," Jessie said as she grabbed her sandwich and headed for the garage. "And if she balks, I'll make you something myself."

"That's okay," Kat said, turning up her nose at the idea of a Jessie-cooked meal. "Aren't you at least going to tell what this epiphany is?"

"Maybe later, and only if it proves fruitful. I don't want to jinx it."

*

He didn't want to make the same mistake as last time.

Walking briskly down the charming neighborhood street in the early afternoon, he resolved that he wouldn't. As well as the actual elimination events had gone—clean and without much fuss, this last effort had gotten complicated. In retrospect he should have known better.

The previous time he had been at Whitney Carlisle's house there was no backyard deck. He ought to have anticipated that the couple might have had work done inside the house as well. But he hadn't noticed anything when sneaking inside or hiding in the closet, so it never occurred to him that the very bedroom Whitney ran into to escape might have been changed from one bedroom into two. It almost cost him.

Truthfully, if the woman had just kept running for the front door instead of trying to take him out with that lamp, he probably wouldn't have caught her in time. He wasn't going to chase her into the street and try to drag her back inside by her hair. After all, his goal wasn't to terrorize these women. That defeated the purpose of the kill. Each one was designed to prove his skill. He couldn't make elegant cuts if the victim was flailing wildly about.

He needed to do better this time, be more cautious and less cocky. That was especially true after discovering that the woman he'd photographed leaving the Pierson mansion wasn't a detective at all. She was the celebrated criminal profiler Jessie Hunt.

It only took a quick Google search of her exploits to appreciate that he'd need to be at the top of his game to outwit her. It was one thing to have an air of unshakable confidence at work, but for this kind of job, a little humility was required. Besides, these were people's lives he was taking and he needed to do it properly, not in slipshod fashion but with some respect.

That's why he was down the street from the next subject's house right now—to make sure things ran smoother this time. He walked slowly down the block as he studied the place again, looking for any sign that things had changed since he'd been inside the home two months ago. Everything looked the same.

Just to be sure, he pulled on his hoodie—the one he'd picked up from Goodwill earlier in the day—then continued down the sidewalk until he was in front of her place. He noted happily that her husband's car was in the driveway. That comported with what he'd already confirmed: Dr. Colin Lennox wouldn't be on duty at the hospital until 5 p.m., leaving his lovely wife, Sheena, alone for the night.

As he passed by the house, he checked to make sure the security cameras were still in the same place and that there was still that loose board in the fence on the right side. He was reassured to find that both were exactly as they had been the last time he walked by yesterday evening.

He got an unexpected jolt of giddiness when he glanced though the window and actually saw Sheena there in the sitting room. She appeared to be playing the piano with her back to him. Her brown hair was pulled up in a bun and her professional blouse and skirt suggested she might not be finished showing houses to clients yet today. A Realtor's work was never done.

He kept walking another half block so it wouldn't look suspicious when he crossed the street and returned back in the direction from which he'd come. As he stepped off the curb onto the street, he stumbled slightly. He recovered quickly but the jerky movement made him inhale in sharp pain.

The blow that Whitney Carlisle delivered to his ribs with that lamp last night had really done a number on him. He didn't think any of them were broken but they were definitely bruised. It stung whenever he inhaled deeply.

He tried to put the discomfort out of his head as he walked back to the end of the block. He might be hurting right now, but in just a few hours, he would be the one inflicting the damage.

CHAPTER TWENTY FIVE

Jessie was barely off her own street when she had both Ryan and Jamil on the phone.

"Where are you?" Ryan asked before she could share her theory.

"I just left the house," she said. "I'm headed back to you."

"I thought you were going to try to nap a little."

"I was," she replied, getting irked. "But something came up, and if you let me, I'll explain what."

"Sorry," he said, sounding a little hurt. "What is it?"

"I appreciate the concern but you'll understand in a second," she replied quickly, trying to smooth things over. "Are you still there, Jamil?"

"I am," he said after a pause. "I just didn't want to get in the middle of that little spat."

"Wise man," Jessie said jokingly, though she felt bad for the poor kid. "Here's what I've got. Ryan, do you remember how, when we were at the medical examiner's to look at Gillian Fahey's body, you talked about how deliberate and clean the arterial cuts appeared?"

"I remember."

"Okay," she said, "but we never really took it to the next level. I think we should be looking at people who make these kinds of precise slices for a living—I'm talking about butchers and surgeons, that kind of thing. I think we should even expand it to people who just require steady hands for a living, like acupuncturists and makeup and tattoo artists. I'm sure there are other professions I'm forgetting."

"That makes a lot of sense," Ryan agreed. "Any job where people need to use their hands in skilled, detailed ways. We could include carpenters and mechanics."

"Or jewelry designers," Jamil volunteered, getting into the act, "and artists like painters or sculptors."

"Exactly," Jessie said. "And Kat pointed out something else to me. We shouldn't assume the killer is a regular visitor to the victims' homes. Some people can go to a place once and memorize everything about it, and if the killer was at the victims' homes with the specific intent to return, they'd be even more attentive. This will probably expand the search to an unpleasant degree, but I think that we need to include anyone who was at each house even one time. Is that doable, Jamil?"

"Sure," he said confidently. "I've already uploaded all their calendars. It's just a matter of expanding the search parameters. I'm sure it will yield results. But there are two problems."

"Of course there are," Ryan groaned.

"The first," Jamil said testily, "is that we won't necessarily know if some of these services were in-home or at another location. I'm assuming a butcher didn't cut meat for these women in their houses, but an acupuncturist? Who knows? You guys will have to make the calls to find out. The second issue is the same one we had with Vince Hutchence. If these transactions were conducted in cash and they were one-time only, it's very possible the victims didn't log them in their calendars. All three of these women were pretty organized, but there's a limit."

"Noted," Jessie said. "Just do the best you can and we'll take it from there, Jamil. Ryan, I'm hoping to meet you at the station in about a half hour. I should be there by two p.m. Fingers crossed we have something to work with by then."

*

Jessie was halfway to Santa Monica when she got the call.

She recognized the number immediately. It was the main line for the Twin Towers Correctional Facility. She answered right away, steeling herself for some horrible news. Had Hannah not really been at the coffeehouse but rather out doing something that had gotten her arrested?

"Hello?" she said urgently.

There was a long pause. Then an automated female voice said, "Collect call from Twin Towers Correctional Facility—Women's Forensic In-Patient Unit. Will you accept a collect call from—?" The voice stopped abruptly and was replaced by another, far more familiar one that loudly and quickly declared, "Hey, lady. It's your favorite sociopath, Andy. Say yes!"

Jessie had forgotten all about Andrea Robinson. But now she knew what the call would be about: Andy's request to support her relocation to a different prison in exchange for information supposedly more valuable than her Night Hunter intelligence. The beep indicating she should reply sounded. With just a moment to answer, she made the only choice she could.

"No decision yet," she said hurriedly. "I'll let you kn—"

A beep cut her off before she could finish. She didn't know how much of that Andy had heard but she wasn't going to wait to find out, so she hung up.

Even if she *had* already decided whether or not to accept the proposal, there was no way she was going to have a conversation with Andrea Robinson in her current state. Andy was tricky enough to deal with when Jessie was at the top of her game. But right now she was exhausted, stressed about the case, and had a throbbing hip. Talking to the woman now would be like throwing herself to the wolves.

She was still thinking about it when Jamil called. She was surprised to hear from him so soon. This was likely very good or very bad news.

"Ms. Hunt, I've already got Detective Hernandez conferenced in," he said. Before she could reply, he continued. "I'm still searching but I wanted to let you know about the potential hit I just got. I think it's promising."

"Go ahead," Ryan said without the teasing tone from before.

"I found a plastic surgeon named Dr. Roland Gahan that all three women used," he said excitedly.

A tide of enthusiasm washed over Jessie. A plastic surgeon made perfect sense.

"Wow!" she exclaimed. "That could be a home run—works with his hands *and* knows all about human anatomy."

"Exactly," Jamil agreed. "But as much as he would be a good match, at first I thought I'd hit a stumbling block: what surgeon does procedures in people's homes, right? But when I checked his website I made a discovery—he offers free initial in-home consultations. If a potential patient is apprehensive about being seen at his office or if their schedule is just too full, he'll go to them."

"It fits together nicely," Jessie marveled. "That's exactly the kind of appointment that a person might leave off their calendar or at least note cryptically. And since the consultation is free, there'd be no bank or credit card record."

"All true," Jamil said. "But there had to be a record of payment for the actual procedures, which is how I know that all three women made payments to something called "R.O.S.E."

"What's that?" Ryan asked.

"That's what showed up on their billing statements. It's not technically correct but it's supposed to be an acronym for Roland Surgical Enterprises."

"I guess that works better than using his last name and having it be R.G.S.E.," Ryan said. "That one doesn't exactly roll off the tongue."

"No, but either would afford them some privacy," Jessie noted. "So Jamil, these billing records definitively show that all three women underwent procedures with Gahan?"

"I can't say for certain what they were paying for, but these bills are for thousands of dollars and they match the going rate in town for a few specific plastic surgery procedures."

"How long ago were they?" she asked.

"Siobhan Pierson has several bills. The most recent is last spring. Gillian Fahey was well over a year ago. Whitney Carlisle saw him in September. Her bill was also the least expensive."

"So none of these women conclusively saw him more recently than four months ago, and some much farther back than that?" Ryan mused. "That's a long time to harbor a grudge."

"If Dr. Gahan did do this," Jamil said, "I think I know a reason why he might have waited so long to act."

"Why?" Jessie asked. It was always nice when someone else could suggest a motive.

"I've been looking him up while we were talking. It seems like he's fallen on hard times of late. A highly touted plastic surgeon from New York relocated to Santa Monica about six months ago. It looks like he started siphoning off Gahan's patients. It didn't help that about two months ago, one of Gahan's patients sued him over dissatisfaction with a procedure. They settled but word got out. Between the new doctor in town and the lawsuit, he started losing patients fast. I'm seeing lots of nasty online comments. It almost looks like there was an organized campaign against him."

"Were any of the negative comments from the victims?" Jessie asked.

"I'm searching now using all their known handles," Jamil said. There were several seconds of silence before he responded. "I'll keep searching but I'm not finding anything so far."

"Of course that doesn't change much," Ryan pointed out. "They could have smeared him through old-fashioned literal, in-person word of mouth. It's harder to track that. And if they *were* bad-mouthing him, it could easily have gotten back to him."

"I think it's time we talk to the good doctor in person," Jessie concluded. "I want to look in his eyes when we ask him about this stuff. Can you send us his address, Jamil?"

"Doing it now," he said.

Jessie stopped at the next light and glanced at the map on her phone.

"I can be there in ten minutes," she said, energized by the potential of the new lead.

"I'll meet you there," Ryan told her. "And please, don't go in without me."

"I wouldn't go anywhere without you, lover," she said gleefully, as much to make Jamil uncomfortable as to tease her secret fiancé.

"I'm officially hanging up now," the young researcher said.

Jessie continued chuckling long after the line went dead.

CHAPTER TWENTY SIX

Jessie got there first.

After she arrived at Gahan's office building in Ryan's car, she got out and stared at the building that might harbor a triple murderer. Her muscles tensed involuntarily at the thought of what she might be facing in suite 505.

That was the top floor of the steel and glass tower that dominated the block. Every other structure near the corner of Arizona Boulevard and 14th Street was residential. But none of the surrounding homes or condo complexes was higher than two stories. Just then, Ryan's rideshare pulled up right behind her and he hopped out. He looked up at the building as he walked over.

"If Gahan is struggling financially," he said, "I'm surprised that he can still afford to keep his practice here. This is a prime location."

Jessie tended to agree. Maintaining a practice in an area like this would require a steady stream of income, something that the doctor was allegedly having trouble with.

"Let's see how he manages that," she said, leading the way inside. They took the elevator to the top floor. Once they stepped out, she looked at the directory on the wall.

"There are only six suites on this entire floor," she noted. "They must all be huge. Can you imagine the rent for one of them?"

Gahan's office was situated at the southeast corner of the building. That meant the views inside would include downtown Santa Monica and the entire bay. She could almost taste how desperate Roland Gahan must be to keep his practice here and maintain the illusion that all was well.

Ryan opened the office door and they stepped inside. Jessie instantly sensed that something was off. The waiting room was empty and there was no one at the reception window. In fact, peering past it, she noticed that, other than the room they were in, it looked like all the lights were off everywhere else.

"Awful quiet in here," Ryan whispered, unsnapping the holster of his gun.

Jessie nodded.

"Almost like the office is closed and someone forgot to lock up," she added.

"I don't like it," he muttered.

"Let's find out what's up," Jessie said. Ryan nodded.

"LAPD—anyone here?" he called out.

When no one replied, she too unsnapped her holster. Ryan tried again.

"This is the Los Angeles Police Department. Is there anyone currently in this office?"

Again, there was no response. He moved quietly over to the door connecting the waiting room to the rest of the office and turned the knob. It wasn't locked. He opened it and looked back at Jessie.

"Exigent circumstances," he mouthed silently before stepping across the threshold. Jessie followed right behind him. Sometimes they fudged whether a situation was really exigent, but in this instance it felt completely legitimate.

The rest of the office was as massive as she'd anticipated, with tinted windows that gave an unobstructed view of a chunk of the California coastline. No lights were on and the only illumination came from outside. They searched the exam and procedure rooms, as well as the lab, but came up empty. The nurses' station and break room were also unoccupied, as were all the bathrooms.

They moved silently to the very corner of the suite, where the door to the only room they hadn't checked was closed. Bold letters on the door's name plate read: *Dr. Roland Gahan.* From somewhere inside, Jessie heard an indistinct, barely audible sound that she couldn't identify. Ryan noticed it too. As he took out his gun, he motioned for her to open the door.

She grabbed hold of the knob and silently turned it before gently pushing the door open. Inside, a man in a suit sat behind a desk with his back to them. His body was shaking slightly and though it was muffled, it sounded like he might be crying.

"Dr. Gahan?" Ryan asked. "I'm Detective Ryan Hernandez with the Los Angeles Police Department. Can you please turn around slowly?"

The man didn't appear to startle at the words. Instead, he slowly swiveled his chair around to them. Jessie saw that he was indeed sobbing softly. But that's not what bothered her. Roland Gahan was holding the muzzle of a revolver in his mouth.

The sight of it made her own mouth suddenly go dry. She could feel her heart pounding against her chest wall. She tried to control it as she quickly evaluated the situation.

Gahan, a heavyset, moon-faced man in his fifties with glasses and the remnants of blondish-gray hair, looked like he'd been sitting there for a while. His eyes were puffy, suggesting he'd started crying some time ago. There were also now-drying strands of saliva on his dress shirt, which indicated he might have had that gun in his mouth for a while, drooling intermittently as he debated whether or not to pull the trigger.

In that instant, she decided she needed to take the initiative. The man in front of her was twitchy and his index finger was curled around the trigger way too tight. If he killed himself, it might take hours or even days to find out for certain if he was their murderer and they didn't have days, maybe not even hours. Besides, it didn't seem advisable to have the big detective with the gun try to talk him down.

"Hi, Roland," she said softly, keeping as still as possible. His eyes darted from Ryan over to her. "My name is Jessie. I'm not a cop. I'm a consultant for the department and I'd like to help you if I can. Is that okay?"

He said nothing but his eyes seemed to lose a bit of their panicky energy. She took that as a yes. Kneeling down to make herself less imposing, she continued to speak in gentle measured tones.

"Can you tell me what has you so upset? Maybe I can help you find a way to work through it."

Gahan studied her for several seconds without responding. Finally he pulled the gun out of his mouth. Unfortunately, he promptly pressed the muzzle against his temple. As he did, his considerable double-chin quivered.

"My life is basically over," he croaked. His voice was raw and scratchy.

"Why do you say that?" she asked.

He snorted at the question.

"Oh, I don't know," he snarled. "Maybe it has something to do with ninety percent of my patients leaving in the last ninety days for some guy with a nice tan and a silky voice. Maybe it's because I'm being vilified on social media for something I didn't actually do wrong. Maybe it's because I can't pay my bills and I'm being kicked out of this office at the end of the month. Or maybe it's because once the cash supply ran dry, my wife of twenty-eight years left me. I got the papers earlier this afternoon, right around the time my one remaining nurse and the office manager quit. They did it together, which had an extra special sting. So you can see why I'm not feeling all that chipper right now."

He was out of breath and the speech seemed to sap some of his passion. Jessie took advantage.

"You said you were vilified for something you didn't do wrong. What was that?" she asked, hoping that self-righteous pride might take hold and make him want to defend himself. She watched the gears turn in his head as he recalled the injustice he'd supposedly suffered.

"A patient accused me of going too far with her neck lift. She said it was obvious that she'd had work done and sued me. But *she* was the one who insisted on such a dramatic procedure. I specifically told her if she was hoping for subtlety, we should do the work gradually over several visits, otherwise it would look too different from before. But she was adamant. And when I finally did exactly what she asked, she didn't like it and alleged malpractice. I had documentation of our conversation but my lawyer said it didn't matter. The jury would see how ridiculous she looked and blame me. He said I was much better off settling and keeping it quiet. So I did."

"But it didn't stay quiet, did it?" Jessie said sympathetically. "The word spread, maybe not organically but with the assistance of the guy with the nice tan and the silky voice, and you couldn't shut off the spigot. Patients left in droves, am I right?"

His eyes were wide. He was clearly stunned that someone not only understood what had happened, but seemed to empathize with him. Out of the corner of her eye, she noticed Ryan slowly lower his gun so that it wasn't pointed directly at Gahan. It was a small move intended to help lower the temperature.

"You are exactly right," the surgeon said.

"Let me ask you, Dr. Gahan," she said, shifting gears. "Do you have any children?"

He appeared surprised by the question but answered anyway.

"I have a twenty-six-year-old daughter and a twenty-two-year-old son."

"Have you thought about what this will do to them?" she asked delicately. "Do they know everything you told me—about the unjustified lawsuit or the campaign to steal your patients and ruin your good name?"

"No," he said, embarrassed. "I didn't want to burden them with it."

"I understand," Jessie said, leaning in toward him slightly. "But imagine the burden this will put on them. If you do this, they'll assume the allegations against you were true. They'll think you ended your life because you were ashamed of your actions rather than because you'd been maligned unfairly. If you don't tell them the truth, who will?"

She watched as he silently considered the question. Feeling like she was making progress, she continued.

"More importantly, don't you want to show them that you can pull yourself out of this moment; that you can get up when you're knocked down? You're their father. What lesson do you want them to learn from this?"

He was quiet, which she took as a hopeful sign. She decided to keep going.

"I say you sue this patient for sullying your character, and if you can, go after this other surgeon too. To me, this sounds like an orchestrated attempt to destroy your business and your good name. Don't let them do it, Dr. Gahan. Fight back. Reclaim your reputation!"

For an interminably long time, he said nothing. Then, without any warning or ceremony, he dropped the gun on the ground.

CHAPTER TWENTY SEVEN

Roland Gahan didn't realize he was in an interrogation room.

He wasn't cuffed and Jessie had asked an officer to lay down a tablecloth over the metal tabletop so that it didn't seem so sterile and intimidating. He was sitting in a chair with a blanket over his shoulders, sipping coffee. Jessie and Ryan watched him for a few minutes through the one-way mirror as they determined their plan of attack.

"We better get in there," Jessie said when they were done. "We don't want him to get any twitchier than he already is."

"Let's go for it," Ryan agreed, opening the observation room door for her.

They had barely entered the interrogation room when Gahan hit them with a question.

"Why am I still here?" he asked, more pleading than demanding.

Jessie walked over and sat in the chair closest to him. Ryan took the other chair. When she spoke, she kept her voice low, almost conspiratorial.

"Before we let you leave, we need to make sure you're safe. Dr. Gahan, I called a department psychiatrist to come and talk to you. She's on her way."

"But I'm fine now," he insisted.

"I believe you," she said, leaning in as she had back in his office. "But only thirty minutes ago, you had a gun in your mouth. It would be irresponsible for us to just send you on your way without at least having a professional give you a clean bill of health."

He sighed, obviously frustrated.

"Don't worry," Jessie continued. "She'll be here soon and I doubt it will take her too long to clear you. In the meantime, why don't we take advantage of your presence? There were a few technical questions we were hoping you could help us clear up. Would that be okay?"

"I guess," Gahan said, shrugging.

He looked wiped out but Jessie couldn't tell if it was part of some larger act. She still wondered if his suicide threat was legitimate. It definitely seemed to be. But even if so, was it really about his career and personal life falling apart? Or might it have been his desperate last move when he thought he was about to be arrested for killing three women? Was he just trying to generate sympathy to throw them off his scent?

"Great, thanks," she replied, smiling kindly to hide her doubts. "Before we do that, Detective Hernandez is going to read you your rights. It's just a formality but an important one."

Ryan impressed her by proceeding to deliver the least intimating recitation of the Miranda warning Jessie had ever heard. He was doing his best not to raise any red flags for Gahan. As he did, Jessie watched the doctor closely for any sign of distress or evasion but couldn't discern anything overt. He seemed to be miles away, his thoughts focused elsewhere.

"Now that we've gotten that out of the way and with those rights in mind," Ryan concluded, "are you okay talking to us?"

"Uh-huh," Gahan muttered.

"Thanks so much," Jessie replied. "We're trying to find out about a few of your patients. That's actually why we came to your office earlier. Do you remember a woman named Whitney Carlisle?"

She had decided to start with Carlisle because she was the most recent victim and the one an innocent man would be least likely to know about. Her death hadn't yet made the news.

He looked at her fuzzily for a few seconds before something in his head seemed to click.

"I want to help," he answered, "but HIPAA requirements prohibit me from discussing information about a possible patient."

"We understand that, Dr. Gahan," Ryan said, "but as I'm sure you're aware, there's an exception to the law that allows you to disclose information to law enforcement when the patient has died and that death may have been a result of criminal conduct. And I'm afraid to say that Mrs. Carlisle died yesterday."

"Oh my god—how?"

"She was murdered," Jessie said, studying him closely. His shocked reaction appeared genuine but someone capable of such a crime might also be capable of unparalleled deception. "Do you remember her?"

He was quiet for a second, seemingly searching his memory.

"The name sounds familiar," he finally said. "But I'm not sure. I have hundreds of patients."

Jessie pulled out her phone and showed him a picture of her.

"Yes, I remember her now," he said, leaning in close to the phone. "She came in a few months ago. If I recall, it was a minor procedure to improve the look of a scar from a burn she suffered on her leg a few years ago."

As he talked about the case, Jessie noticed that his posture improved, as did his spirits.

"What about Gillian Fahey?" she asked. "Was she a patient of yours?"

"She was," he confirmed. "I heard about her death on the news—terrible."

"And Siobhan Pierson?" Ryan wanted to know.

"Oh yes. Siobhan was a long-time patient. She'd been coming to me for years before…what happened to her. Oh my, that's three of my patients who have been killed in just the last few weeks."

"We thought it was unusual as well, Dr. Gahan," Jessie told him. "That's why we came to speak with you. We thought that perhaps you might be able to discern some similarity among them that we aren't able to see."

He scrunched his eyes in concentration before looking at her apologetically.

"I'm afraid I can't think of anything. As I told you, I've seen hundreds, probably thousands of patients over the years. Most of them live on the west side of town. It stands to reason that there would be some connections among them, myself included."

"That's a good point about them all living in the same part of town, Doctor," Ryan said, circling closer to where they wanted to get. "It reminds me—I saw on your website that you regularly offer in-home initial consultations. Did you do that for these women?"

Jessie watched to see if he would balk at the question but he seemed so focused on remembering that he appeared to miss the underlying implication.

"I definitely remember going Siobhan's place. If you've been there, it's hard to forget. The place is the size of a museum. I also recall going to Gillian Fahey's home. When I saw footage of it on the news after her death, I recognized having been there before. As to the third one, what was her name again?"

"Whitney Carlisle," Ryan prompted.

"That's right. I don't have a specific memory of going to her house, but if she lived close by, it wouldn't surprise me. I try to be as accommodating as I can. Why?" he asked, and for the first time his eyes narrowed in suspicion. "Hold on—all three of these women were killed in their homes, weren't they?"

"They were," Ryan acknowledged.

Roland Gahan looked down at the floor for several seconds. When he met their eyes again, his expression was different, fearful.

"Am I a suspect?" he asked, dumbfounded.

Jessie took that one.

"Let's just say that we'd love to eliminate you as a person of interest. The more forthright you are with us, the more likely we are able to cross you off our list. We all share the same goal here. So I think the fastest way to clear you of any suspicion would be to find out if any of the women we've been discussing was among those who bad-mouthed you."

This was the moment Jessie had been waiting for: the chance to look in the suspect's eyes in search of the truth.

"Were they bad-mouthing you, Dr. Gahan?" she asked, then held her breath waiting for the answer.

They were in dangerous territory now. When they last checked with Jamil before entering the interrogation room, he still hadn't found any online comments from the victims about Gahan. But as Ryan had noted earlier, that didn't mean they *hadn't* cast aspersions that made their way back to him.

Still, the only way to gauge that was to observe how the doctor responded to the question. It was risky. Gahan could invoke his right to an attorney at any time. He could simply clam up. Or he could demand to leave the room, which would force them to either release or arrest him.

He did none of those things.

"Ms. Hunt, I wouldn't know if they were disparaging me," he said calmly, his eyes cold. "I stopped reading the online comments when I determined that they were taking a toll on my mental health. And it's not like someone would tell me about something like that in person. If you're suggesting that I killed these women because they might have said something mean about me, you're wrong. If I killed every woman who said something cruel about me in the last few months, half of Santa Monica would be littered with bodies."

"We're getting close," Ryan said, his tone challenging.

Jessie took a deep breath as she waited for the doctor's reaction.

"I'm not a murderer, Detective," he said evenly.

Despite anticipating this moment, Jessie was at a loss. Nothing in his demeanor gave away either clear guilt or innocence. She doubted pressing the issue would change that.

"Let's move on to where you were last night," Ryan said, aggressively switching subjects. He must have felt they'd hit a wall too.

"That's easy," Gahan said with a raucous snort. "I've spent every night for the last few months in the same place: at my house, pouring myself a Seven and Seven, drinking it, and repeating the process until I pass out."

"There seems to be a lot of that going around," Jessie said quietly, noting that drinking oneself into numbness seemed to be a recurring theme with rich, down-on-their-luck Santa Monica men these days.

"Yeah," he said, "well, when your business is for crap and your wife runs out on you because you're a loser, it tends to make you want to shut out the world a bit."

The man was clearly peeved, but even when they poked at him, his reaction didn't rise to a level that Jessie would call angry. She looked over at Ryan, unsure how they should proceed. He took the lead.

"Can anyone verify that you were at home last night, or the night before, or on January sixteenth?" he asked, though Jessie was sure he knew the answer already.

"I'd tell you to check my calendar but that doesn't typically include interactions with teenage cashiers at burger joint drive-thru windows, pizza delivery guys, or the staff at the neighborhood Thai food takeout place."

"Well, if you consent to let us look at your bank information and GPS data, it might go a long way to—" Jessie began before Gahan cut her off.

"Screw that! I'm through helping you people railroad me."

He seemed genuinely upset. Before she could reply, a loud knock at the door interrupted them. Ryan opened it and motioned for Jessie to join him, where an officer with a nervous grimace was waiting.

"The psychiatrist is here," he said.

Ryan looked at Jessie.

"You think we should go at him again or let the doc break things up a little?"

"I think he's on the verge of demanding to leave," she said, "in which case we'd have to arrest or release him. Maybe sending the psychiatrist in will buy us some time to make a decision."

"I agree, go get the doctor," Ryan said to the officer, before turning back to Gahan. "The psychiatrist is here. We're going to take a break and let you talk to her."

They stepped outside and closed the door. Ryan flashed Jessie a big smile.

"What are you so happy about?" she asked.

"I think we may have our guy," he replied.

"What makes you so confident?" she wanted to know. She felt far less so.

"What *doesn't* make me confident?" he countered. "We can check his bank and GPS data, but it sure sounds like he's not going to have any alibi witnesses, which could be by design. If he knew months ago that he was going on this spree, he had lots of time to prep this 'non-alibi' alibi, complete with claims of solo drunkenness."

"Go on," Jessie said. She couldn't argue with his logic there.

"It sounds like he's been to all three houses," Ryan pointed out. "Hell—he admitted to being in two of them. And as a surgeon, he obviously knew how to make the most effective, damaging cuts with those knives. We don't have a motive locked down, but revenge against women who might have helped destroy his career is a pretty good one."

"We have no proof of that yet," Jessie reminded him.

"And we might never, if the bad-mouthing was only verbal," Ryan replied. "Come on Jessie, you have to admit, this guy fits the profile."

She *did* have to admit it. Gahan had the skill set, the opportunity, a weak alibi, and a potential motive, yet she wasn't sure.

"It's not that I think you're wrong," she said, thinking aloud as she spoke, "he's clearly sketchy and I couldn't get a good bead on whether he was lying, which is a troubling sign on its own. But I have some nagging reservations."

"Like what?"

"Like, do we really think Gahan is capable of sneaking into these women's homes and doing what he did without leaving a trace? At his size, I'm not sure this guy could walk up a flight of stairs without getting winded. And if he really has been drinking that heavily lately, I'd expect him to be sloppier at the crime scenes."

"Is that really your main concern?" Ryan pressed. "Because if that's what his lawyer takes to the jury, I think we're in pretty good shape."

"It's not just that," she said, frustrated with her inability to pinpoint the source of her uncertainty.

"What is it then?"

Something about Ryan's challenging tone was instantly clarifying. Suddenly she understood where her reticence came from. It was due to Gahan's surprising willingness to answer questions, even after he knew why he was in that room.

This was a man who was about to commit suicide when they found him. If he was telling the truth, he'd already been drinking himself to death for months. He'd been willing to go his grave with a ruined professional reputation.

Yet, he had insisted that he hadn't committed these murders. Why put up a fight when he thought his life was over anyway? The very fact that he was willing to die but not willing to admit killing these women was the strongest argument in favor of his innocence.

Even so, that argument wasn't enough to justify letting the guy walk. Her misgivings wouldn't mean much if Gahan left the station and sliced up someone else. She needed something more.

"Jessie, what is your main concern?" Ryan, who had been waiting for her answer, asked again.

"I'm not sure," she finally said.

"So we arrest him?" Ryan said expectantly.

"Yeah," she said reluctantly. "I guess we have to."

Even as she said the words, she hoped she wasn't helping give permission for a whole police department to let its guard down. She hoped she wasn't giving a killer a better chance to strike again tonight.

CHAPTER TWENTY EIGHT

Jessie wished she'd been wrong, but she wasn't.

The second that word spread throughout the Santa Monica Police Station that a suspect had been arrested in the case, she felt the entire place sigh in simultaneous relief. Unable to justify why she didn't share it, she retreated to the conference room while Ryan went to call Decker and brief him on their status.

She sat down at the table and stared at the mountain of papers spread around and on top of her laptop. The sight of it made her whole body sink, as if she'd been caught in quicksand comprised exclusively of exhaustion and stress. She desperately wanted a moment, however brief, to rest her eyes, to rest her brain.

But that moment could be the difference between another woman living or dying. She had to keep pushing. Despite her body silently screaming at her not to, she sat up straight. There had to be an answer here. She just needed time to find it.

Though she couldn't officially justify it, she pulled out her phone and texted Ryan: *Tell Decker not to release a statement to the press for another hour. I want to follow up on some loose ends. Please.*

It took nearly a minute before he responded. She could almost hear the tone of reluctance in his voice as she read it: *One hour.*

That was all she could reasonably expect, even from her partner and fiancé. There was no credible reason for the delay and yet she'd just asked him to put himself on the line because she had a hunch, and barely one at that. She needed to make the most of it.

So she dived back into the list of vendors and service providers that they'd compiled with Jamil. If Dr. Gahan was going to be supplanted by another suspect, then it had to be someone so inarguably suspicious that even Decker couldn't balk.

She flipped through the names, which were all notated in a database Jamil had set up, with columns that included in-home service, multiple/single visits, cash/gift payment, and expertise with hands. Nothing jumped out at her. Other than Gahan, there was no one that could be definitively checked off in all the categories. Some people didn't even have enough information to fill in more than one box.

For example, one box, for Siobhan Pierson's birthday tasting menu dinner, only had "gift" checked off. It didn't even list the catering company she'd used. The only other listing that even mentioned a gift was for something Whitney Carlisle had calendared as "fancy dinner."

Jessie was tempted to move on. After all, it was unlikely that the caterer who did a socialite like Siobhan's tasting menu dinner was also responsible for Whitney's "fancy dinner," which was apparently such an unusual occasion that it had to be set off with quotations. But she didn't have any better ideas and her hour was down to fifty-four minutes, so she decided it was worth a shot.

She called Siobhan's assistant first, mostly out of cowardice. She didn't want to ask brand new widower Gordon Carlisle to detail old meals he'd had with his now-dead wife. Kelly Hoffs picked up on the first ring.

"Hello, Ms. Hunt," she said. "I'm afraid that if you need to speak to Mr. Pierson, he's out for the count today."

"Actually, I was hoping to talk to you, Kelly."

"Oh, okay. What can I do for you?" she asked.

"I remember you mentioning that Mrs. Pierson was working out hard with the trainer, Vince Hutchence, because she wanted to be able to pig out at a birthday tasting dinner she had coming up."

"That's right," Kelly said. "She'd been looking forward to it for months."

"Can you tell me the name of the catering company she used?" Jessie asked.

"Oh, it wasn't a catering company," Kelly said. "It was an in-home chef. That's why she was so excited. I guess it's all the rage now to have celebrated chefs cook for you in your own house. And this guy had worked in several Michelin-starred restaurants so it was kind of a big deal to have him in her house, using her kitchen and her equipment to make this fancy meal."

Hearing those words, Jessie felt a prickling sensation overwhelm her entire body. She tried not to let her eagerness seep through as she asked her next question.

"Do you recall the chef's name?"

"Sure. It's Curt Sumner," Kelly said.

"And where was Mr. Pierson that night?" Jessie asked as she scribbled the name down furiously.

"He was at the Pierson Farms headquarters," Kelly said wryly. "I remember because he moved heaven and earth to find a credible reason not to be at that dinner. In the end, he just told her he had 'urgent company business' to take care of. But he privately told me that he would have used any excuse, even driving to Bakersfield, not to be around Siobhan's friends all night."

"Do you know if this chef takes checks or credit cards?" Jessie asked, her tone impressively even.

"Since it was a gift from one of her friends, that topic never came up," Kelly said. "I left before he showed up anyway. But however people pay, I know it's expensive. That gift card was worth five grand."

"Thanks very much, Kelly," she said.

"Does that help?"

"I don't know yet," she answered. She didn't want to say anything that might tip her hand.

Jessie hung up, ordering herself to do the mental work before reaching out to Ryan. She reviewed what she knew for sure. A man experienced in the use of knives was in Siobhan Pierson's home, in her kitchen, in fact. At some point during the evening, he may have even used the very knife that killed her.

Spending an evening at the house, he would know its layout and have had casual access to multiple rooms. At least in this case, he was compensated through a method that had no real paper trail and wasn't even paid for by Pierson herself. It all fit, but unless she could confirm that Curt Sumner had prior access to the Carlisle and Fahey homes too, he still wasn't as strong a suspect as Dr. Gahan.

That meant the next step would be an unpleasant one: calling Gordon Carlisle. She dialed his number and waited anxiously as the phone rang. Just as she though the call would go to voicemail, he picked up.

"Hello?"

"Hi, Mr. Carlisle, it's Jessie Hunt. I'm sorry to bother you but I was hoping you had a minute. Do you remember me?"

"Of course, Ms. Hunt, you're working on Whitney's case. Do you have news for me?" he asked.

The man sounded unfathomably tired. As exhausted as she was, it was nothing compared to the combination of sleeplessness and grief that he was suffering through. She almost backed out but managed to steel herself. She was trying to help him, even if it might hurt first.

"I'm sorry. No, not yet. I was actually hoping that you could help me. This might sound out of left field but I'm trying to track down something that was in your wife's calendar from a few months ago, late November actually. She mentions a "fancy dinner" on the twenty-ninth. It looks like there was a gift card involved. Do you recall that?"

He was quiet for a moment. She wondered if he might have fallen asleep.

"Nothing rings a bell," he finally said. "Is that all you have on it?"

"It's possible it might have involved an in-home chef," she volunteered.

"Oh yeah," he replied, borderline excited. "I remember now. Someone I work with gave me a gift card for a dinner to be prepared in your home by a private chef. The reason I forgot was because I didn't go."

"It didn't happen?" Jessie asked.

"No, it did. But that same afternoon, a friend of mine landed courtside seats for a big Lakers game. Whitney knew I wanted to go so she said I should do it. We tried to postpone the dinner but the chef had a twenty-four-hour cancellation policy. So rather than waste the card, she had her sister come over instead."

He went quiet, though Jessie could sense he wanted to say more. When he finally did, his voice was trembling. "Looking back on it now, I wish I'd stayed home with her."

"I'm sorry," Jessie said quietly. "Is there any chance you remember the chef's name?"

"No. I think it might have been something like Kent but I'm not sure. I know he was a big deal, used to work in award-winning restaurants."

"Thank you," Jessie said. "One more question: you mentioned that this was in late November. Do you recall when you started having the work done on your house?"

"Sure. They started mid-December, took a break for the holidays, and then picked up again just after the New Year. What is this about, Ms. Hunt?"

"We're just following up on every lead," she told him, not wanting to offer false hope. "I saw the 'fancy dinner' reference and just wanted to get some clarity on it. But I promise to keep you informed if we find anything substantive."

She said goodbye, doing her best to ignore the fact that she'd ended her conversation with Carlisle with a lie. They *had* found something substantive—a suspect currently in custody for the murder of his wife. But considering she had increasing doubts about the man's guilt, she decided it was best not to go there just yet.

Instead she sat quietly with her developing theory for a minute. It sure sounded like Whitney Carlisle's chef might have been Curt Sumner. The name "Kent" wasn't far off. And if it *was* the same man, he would have been in the house before the bedroom at the end of the hall was converted into two. That would explain how he might have assumed Whitney was trapped in the room. Jessie knew she could confirm the chef's identity with a call to Whitney's sister, Janey Smyth, but didn't want to take that step until she had some indication that Sumner had been in the Fahey house as well.

So, with a churning stomach, she made her second call in five minutes to a mournful widower. Only this guy was now also a single father, something she tried not to think about while she waited for the call to connect. When it did, the phone was answered by a woman.

"Fahey residence, how may I help you?" an older-sounding female who wasn't the house manager, Ann Roth, asked warily.

"Yes, hi," Jessie said, surprised. "My name is Jessie Hunt. I'm a criminal profiler with the Los Angeles Police Department. Is Simon Fahey available?"

"Are you involved in Gillian's case?" the woman pressed.

"Yes, ma'am, with whom am I speaking please?"

"I'm Olivia Copeland, Gillian's mother."

"Oh, Mrs. Copeland, I'm terribly sorry for your loss."

"Thank you, dear," she said resignedly, as if she'd been accepting condolences for days, which she probably had. "I'll get Simon. Forgive my curtness before but I'm trying to be a mama bear and protect everyone from unnecessary intrusions."

"Of course," Jessie said.

When Fahey got on the line, he sounded slightly more composed than Gordon Carlisle had. Of course, Jessie noted cynically, he'd had a whole extra twenty-four hours to come to terms with the loss of his wife.

"Thank you for speaking with me, Mr. Fahey," she began. "I won't take up much of your time. I was just hoping you might recall if you or your wife had an in-home chef cook a special dinner for you at some point recently?"

"We did, but not recently. It was six months ago."

Jessie waited until the inappropriate thrill that consumed her entire being had settled down a little before following up.

"Did you receive a gift card for the dinner?' she asked.

"No," he said. "It was a gift, but it was from me to Gilly for our anniversary. I paid cash—a thousand bucks for the evening."

"But it wasn't in her calendar," Jessie noted.

"No, it wouldn't have been. I meant it as a surprise gift. Unfortunately, I never got to partake."

"Why not?" Jessie asked.

"It was scheduled, but I ended up having to go to D.C. to meet with a senator about a bill that was being voted on the next day. I tried to reschedule the meal but it was too late. We would have lost the entire payment. So Gilly's mom, Olivia, who you just spoke to, took my place. I remember I left an envelope of cash in a drawer for the chef. I felt like a drug dealer or something." He stopped talking and Jessie thought he was done, but before she could ask her next question, he wistfully added, "I was going to rebook the chef just for us but never got around to it."

He sounded just like Gordon Carlisle.

"I'm so sorry, Mr. Fahey," she said. She tried to think of a delicate way to ask her next question but couldn't so she just came right out with it. "Do you perhaps recall the name of the chef?"

He didn't seem offended.

"Not anymore, but I bet Olivia would. Let me put you on speaker," he said, and then called out to his mother-in-law. "Liv, do you remember the name of the chef who cooked at the house for you and Gilly the night I had to go to D.C. on our anniversary?"

Moments later Olivia was back.

"Absolutely, his name is Curt Sumner. He was so good that I recommended him to some of my friends. The meal was delicious. Why do you ask?"

"Oh, we're just trying to recreate Gillian's timeline as far back as possible," Jessie lied. "You've been very helpful—both of you. I'll be in touch when I have more."

Only once she'd hung up did Jessie allow the excitement she'd been containing to fully bubble up. They now had a credible alternative suspect to Dr. Roland Gahan. She still had to confirm that he'd been in the Carlisle house via a call to Whitney's sister, Janey. But if that panned out, she could finally go back to Ryan and tell him that they might have the wrong guy.

And if they did, they needed to move fast to find the right one. Looking outside, she saw that the sky was darkening. That meant the clock was ticking for another woman. The perpetrator had killed on each of the last two nights. And night was fast approaching.

CHAPTER TWENTY NINE

"Are you sure?" Ryan asked.

Jessie tried to be patient as she caught him up. Maybe the heat of the tiny conference room was starting to get to her too.

"I just got off the phone with Janey Smyth and she confirmed that Curt Sumner was the name of the in-home chef that came over to their place. That means the guy had access to all three victims' homes, including going to the Carlisle house *before* they had the bedroom converted into two smaller ones. Because he gets paid in cash, there was no paper trail to track him."

"That definitely explains why he didn't pop up in our initial searches," Ryan conceded.

"Right," Jessie said, barreling on. "And he obviously has expertise with knives. Also, remember that we agreed this killer was painstakingly detailed in committing these crimes. Just like surgeons, most successful chefs are meticulous and organized about their work. Finally, Sumner is much younger than Dr. Gahan—he's thirty-six. And at least according to the picture on his website, he's in better shape too. It's not hard to see him effectively sneaking into a house or chasing down a victim who was running away."

With each word she said, she saw Ryan becoming increasingly apprehensive. She understood why. He'd thought they had their man. But if he was wrong, the real killer was out there right now, possibly preparing for his next attack.

"Have you gotten a warrant to check his location data yet?" he asked.

She shook her head in mild aggravation.

"Considering that I only made all these connections a few minutes ago and I came to you right afterward, that would be a no," she said, finding it difficult to contain her growing frustration. "I figured that I should talk to the lead detective on the case before making any command decisions like that."

"Right," he said, pretending not to notice her tone. "Then we should loop Jamil in ASAP."

"And you should call Decker to make sure he doesn't go public claiming we have the killer in custody," she reminded him. "HSS doesn't need another black eye so soon after finally getting out of the dog house."

Ryan looked pained at the suggestion.

"Listen," Jessie said, softening her tone, "there's no downside to pulling back. We still have Gahan in custody. If he's the killer, we know he can't do any harm from a cell. In the meantime we can look into Sumner. If he turns out to be our guy, then HSS's reputation hasn't been tarnished by a big press conference identifying the wrong man as the murderer. That's why I asked you to hold off an hour."

Ryan looked at his watch.

"It didn't even take half that time for you to come up with this lead. I shouldn't have jumped the gun," he said, sounding defeated.

"Hey, don't do that," she scolded. "Everything pointed to Gahan. He may still be our killer. I just had a funny feeling that he might not be. You couldn't go to Captain Decker with my funny feelings."

"Maybe I should start," he muttered before seeming to move past his self-flagellation. When he spoke again, his voice was loud and forceful. "Okay, I'll call Decker while you reach out to Jamil about getting a court order for Sumner's phone. Then we should go pay him a visit."

Jessie nodded, heartened and a little turned on by the fire that had returned to her fiancé's eyes. It was time to get back to work.

*

Sumner's office, like so many places they'd visited on this case, was only minutes from the station, located on 4th Street near Wilshire. Jessie noted to herself that it was also only a ten-minute walk from the Fahey house.

They walked up the exterior steps to the office, which was one of several on the second level of a brick building with a chic handbag boutique down below. They had tried calling the numbers listed on the website but everything went to voicemail, which was full. So while they waited for Jamil to get back to them with other contact numbers for the guy, they decided to make the three-minute drive to the address listed on the website.

Ryan knocked on the door, which had no business name, only the suite number 202. They waited, neither of them optimistic that anyone would be here at this hour. It was close to 6 p.m. and the sun had completely set.

To their surprise, a light came on behind the door's frosted window. Ryan undid his holster, then rested his hand back against his leg. The door opened to reveal a petite, young blonde woman that Jessie doubted was older than twenty-five. She looked like she spent more time at the beach than in an office.

"I'm sorry," she said. "But we don't take in-person bookings. You need to fill out the form on the website. Someone will get back to you within forty-eight hours."

"We're not customers," Ryan told her, taking out his badge. "We're with the LAPD and we need to speak to Mr. Sumner."

The girl's pouty certitude melted away.

"Um, he's not here right now," she said shakily

Jessie decided that if they were going to get this girl's help, they needed her to be calm and focused rather than terrified, so she stepped in.

"What's your name?" she asked warmly.

"Cyndi Butler," the girl answered. She looked like she was on the verge of tears.

"Cyndi, I'm Jessie. Why don't we go inside and explain why we're here?"

"Okay," the girl replied, holding the door open for them.

When they stepped inside, Jessie was surprised at how tiny the space was. There was only room for one desk with a rolling chair and another folding chair beside it. A large cabinet rested against one wall. On the back wall were dozens of kitchen implements, all hanging from hooks. There were pots, pans, and assorted cooking utensils, some of which she didn't even recognize.

Ryan closed the door behind them and Jessie had Cyndi sit in the rolling chair while she took the folding one.

"We need your help, Cyndi," she said. "It's important that we find out where your boss is right now. Do you know?"

"No," she answered flatly, wincing in apprehension that she didn't have the right answer.

"Can you pull up his calendar?" Jessie suggested.

"Did he do something wrong?" Cyndi asked.

"It's nothing like that," Jessie said with an assurance that surprised even her. "We'll explain more later, but right now we really need to see that calendar. Can you access it?"

"I can," she told them, as she clicked on the desktop screen. "But I don't think it will help."

"Why not?" Jessie asked gently.

"Because Curt doesn't have a House Cook—that's what we call them—tonight, so there's nothing scheduled," she said, clicking onto the calendar page on the screen. "It does say he's tentatively planning to do a video tutorial tonight for a YouTube cooking channel he partners with."

"What does that mean?" Ryan asked, taking Jessie's cue and keeping his tone of voice less threatening than before.

"He provides the channel with weekly content, usually on Tuesdays. Sometimes it'll be a real-time professional cooking tutorial. Other weeks he does a Q&A session. He occasionally switches up the day but he always likes me to keep Tuesdays open."

"Does he usually do those from his place?" Jessie asked. "It doesn't look like this office is equipped for that kind of thing."

"Yeah," Cyndi said. She was still nervous but seemed to settle down with each passing moment. "He's set up his whole kitchen with lighting and mics. It's very professional. That's the main way he gets clients, other than through word of mouth."

Jessie wanted to dive into more detailed questions about what was in his calendar for the dates of the murders. She was even tempted to have the girl call Sumner to ask where he was. But she sensed that Cyndi needed a little more comforting before going there, so she asked a question she knew the assistant could handle but might still prove valuable.

"So Cyndi," she asked in her best "curious" voice, "what is a House Cook exactly? I hear they're very popular these days."

"They are," the young woman agreed, launching into a spiel that Jessie suspected she'd used many times before. "It's an opportunity for anyone to have a fine restaurant-quality meal prepared in the comfort of their own home by a top level chef. You don't have to provide anything other than the appliances and kitchenware. The chef brings all the food and can even select a wine that pairs well with the meal. You can just relax and hang out or, if you like, most chefs will walk you through the dinner as they prepare each course."

"That sounds really cool," Jessie said. She sensed that the girl was now calm enough to handle a more challenging question. "I know Curt used to work at some impressive restaurants. Why did he switch to in-home cooking? I mean the *real* reason, not the official version on the website."

Cyndi's expression soured slightly when she realized she wouldn't be able to go with the authorized explanation. But she shrugged and answered anyway.

"Curt was previously the executive chef at Porcine when it earned a Michelin star. Then he moved on to Glutton, which also got a Michelin star during his tenure. But about a year and a half ago, he got a negative review from the new food critic at the *Times*, not so much about the food quality but about his culinary arrogance. I'm not even sure what that means, but it had an impact. One day he had the perfect image and then just like that, it was ruined. Business dropped off and he was dumped so the restaurant could do a refresh. He told me he was devastated."

"Is that when he started the House Cook thing?" Ryan asked.

"Not right away. After Glutton fired him, he couldn't get work as an executive chef and he wasn't willing to answer to anyone else. He lived off his savings for a while. That's when some other chef friends told him he should try this. He was reluctant at first because it seemed like a step down. But when he did some research, he discovered that if he catered to wealthy clientele exclusively, he could rake it in. His cheapest package is five hundred dollars for two people on a weeknight. If you want more, like four people, or a weekend night, or for him to use ingredients from a farmers' market he visited that day instead of just a grocery store, we're talking over a grand. Some larger groups have paid five to ten times that. Now he's so in demand, he's lucky if he gets a night off, other than the YouTube Tuesdays, which is still work, I guess."

The girl had stopped shaking was speaking normally again. Jessie figured it was time to get into the really detailed questions.

"That is amazing," she said. "And you say he works almost every night, even on Mondays? Like, did he go to someone's house last night?"

Let me check," Cyndi said, looking at the screen. "Yep, he had a seven p.m. House Cook here in Santa Monica."

Jessie looked at the address. It was less than half a mile from the Carlisle home.

"Does he always stick to this part of town?" she wanted to know.

"Not always," Cyndi said. "He'll go just about anywhere for the right price, but I know he prefers to stay close if he can. And to be honest, he can. There's so much demand from folks around here that he doesn't really need to travel much. In fact, a lot of times the clients live so close that he can walk there from his place."

"Where does he live?" Ryan asked innocently.

"Up on 10th Street," Cyndi said. "It's only about six blocks east of here near El Cholo restaurant on Wilshire, so he'll walk in to work most of the time too."

Jessie knew the location. It occurred to her that both Sumner's home and office were within a half hour's walk of all three victims' homes, not just the Faheys'. From the look on his face, Jessie was certain that Ryan was thinking the same thing.

"What about Sunday?" he asked. "Did he have a House Cook then too?"

Cyndi looked back at the calendar.

"Yes," she said, "that was a big one—eight guests. It was nearby too, up on Montana Avenue near 5th Street."

Jessie didn't even have to look at a map to know that intersection was only blocks from the Fahey place. They were two for two.

"Let's check a date a little further back," Ryan suggested as if they were playing a little game. "How about the sixteenth?"

That was the night Siobhan Pierson had been killed.

"Sure," Cyndi said, checking. "Oh, that's interesting."

"What?" Ryan pressed.

"That was a Wednesday, which is usually a House Cook night, but he switched it up and did a video tutorial, a popular one too. Last time I checked, it had over half a million views."

"Any particular reason he switched nights?" Jessie wondered.

Cyndi scanned the screen for a few seconds before her eyes lit up.

"Yeah, I remember now. He did a House Cook in Palm Springs the night before. It was a big deal. With the travel and the dozen guests, he pulled in twelve grand for the night. I'm sure he was spent after that and considered making a video to be a breeze in comparison." She paused for a moment and Jessie knew something had changed. Cyndi added, "He gave me a five-hundred-dollar bonus for putting that Cook together."

"That was nice," Jessie said, sensing what was coming.

"Tell me again why you're looking for him," Cyndi said, her voice harder than before.

Loyalty was beginning to trump fear. Jessie looked over at Ryan, unsure how forthcoming they should be. Sumner was looking like a credible suspect, but if they told the girl the truth and they were wrong about him, there could be lawsuit implications. But if they were right and she warned him, he might escape or worse, someone else might die.

“The truth is that we think he might be in danger,” Ryan said in a hushed voice. “We need to reach out to him, but if the threat to him is nearby, maybe even listening in, he could be at real risk.”

“Oh my god!” Cyndi said, putting her hands to her mouth. “What kind of threat?”

“We’re not at liberty to say,” Ryan said cryptically but firmly.

“That’s why we need *you* to call him,” Jessie added. “And when you do, you have to sound totally normal, for his sake. His life could depend on it.”

CHAPTER THIRTY

Curt Sumner was out on what looked like a leisurely walk.

In reality it was a stakeout, as he waited for Sheena Lennox to follow the next step in her evening routine: walking the dog. She should be heading out in the next few minutes.

Her doctor husband, Colin, had already left for the hospital over an hour ago. Curt knew that because he lived just two streets over from them and just "happened" to be on another brief stroll right as Dr. Lennox backed out of the driveway.

After watching him drive away, Curt had returned home to brush his longish, black hair, which had gotten windswept outside. Then he checked the status of the video tutorial he intended to post tonight. He'd actually completed it a week ago, but he planned to have it automatically uploaded about an hour from now.

He'd carefully orchestrated the shoot, even altering the clocks on the oven and the wall to match the time he anticipated slicing up Sheena. That would make for a nice alibi.

Just before leaving the house, he'd changed into a different outfit from the one he'd worn for either of the earlier walks today. The pants, hooded sweatshirt, and shoes had never been worn. He'd bought them all with cash months ago at a sporting goods store in San Pedro, a good thirty miles southeast of here. After he completed the task tonight, he would bleach and bag them. Early tomorrow morning he would drop them in a nearby Taco Bell dumpster just minutes before the trash truck came by.

To go that one extra step, he'd left his cell phone in the kitchen and had his calls forwarded to a burner phone he kept with him, so it looked like he'd never left the house even when he was out. He loved it when all the pieces fell into place.

That's what these killings were about—precision, balance, striving for perfection. That's not how it began, of course. There were other motivations the first time he cut a woman with a knife. But now he was all about testing his limitations, going beyond his comfort zone while still doing work he could be proud of.

It's not like he had anything against Sheena Lennox. When he'd done the House Cook for the couple last summer, both she and Colin had been quite lovely. His talents were an anniversary gift from another couple who had used him, so they were happy to have him at all.

Curt found that the guests who were gifted his services were usually far more gracious than those who paid for them themselves. The latter always seemed to be judging whether a particular morsel of food was worth the price they'd paid. It was exhausting.

But the Lennoxes had been wonderful. Sheena played a few songs on the piano before he started cooking. Colin offered him a beer, which he declined. He was on the job after all. He didn't mention that he needed to stay alert so he could memorize all the details of their house for a future, uninvited visit.

Nor did he say that he lived only two blocks over. He had decided almost the second he learned how close their homes were that the Lennoxes would be ideal for an upcoming Elimination Event, his preferred name for these special evenings.

On the night he cooked for them, he made sure to give special attention to their golden retriever, Georgie Boy, scratching his tummy and giving him scraps from the meal. He hoped that when they were reunited momentarily, the dog would remember their previous positive interaction and not bark at the sight or scent of him. That hadn't worked out so well with the Carlisles' dog, Yaz, but maybe he'd have better luck this time.

He stayed half a block down, out of their security camera's line of sight. Only when he was sure Sheena and Georgie Boy were at least a block away would he follow the specific route that would allow him entry to the back door, which he'd learned was never locked until they went to bed.

He was reviewing the route in his head when his burner cell phone rang, forwarded from his regular one. It was Cyndi. She rarely called after hours. He was the one who might occasionally reach out while on a House Cook with a frantic request for her to pick up an ingredient he'd forgotten. He was tempted to let it go to voicemail, what with Sheena about to walk the dog any minute. But because she called so rarely, he decided to pick up. Besides, this might actually help burnish his alibi.

"Hey, Cyndi, what's up?"

"Hi, Curt," she said. "I just wanted to double-check the schedule with you. I got a reminder alert on my phone to reconfirm the time of your Cook tomorrow in the Palisades. Is it still at eight?"

She sounded a little odd. Curt wondered if she might be tipsy.

"That's right," he said. "Unless something changed that I'm not aware of."

"No, we're good. For a minute I thought you might be double-booked but I think I just forgot to close out an old Cook from last week. How's everything going?"

"Good," he said. "How are you?"

He was pretty sure she wasn't drunk but she definitely sounded more prim than usual, like back when she was on her best behavior in those first weeks after he hired her.

"I'm okay," she answered, "just closing up the office. Sorry to have bothered you. I hope I didn't interrupt the tutorial."

"No," he said without hesitation. "I was actually taking a little break to tweak the lighting before finishing up. I'm planning to eat my work afterward."

"Not many people can say that," Cyndi said before laughing awkwardly.

"No, I guess not," he replied. "Hey, Cyndi, is everything all right with you?"

"Yeah. Totally. Everything's cool. I think I'm just a little tired. Is everything cool with you?"

Just then, Sheena and Georgie Boy emerged from the front door of the house.

"It will be when I finish up this tutorial," he told her. "You mind if I get back to it?"

"No. Of course. Sorry. You should do that."

She sounded genuinely flustered now.

"I'll see you tomorrow, Cyndi," he said. "Get yourself a good night's sleep, okay?"

"Yeah. You too. Goodnight."

It took Curt a second to realize that she had hung up. He looked at the phone as if it might offer an explanation for her bizarre behavior. Glancing up, he saw that Sheena and Georgie Boy were already a half dozen houses up the street. In another minute they'd round the corner and head out of sight.

This was the last walk of the night. It typically lasted twenty to thirty minutes, which should give him more than enough time to get inside, grab the knife, and be ready to do the deed. He crossed the street and started in their direction, staying well back so as not to spook Sheena.

He was already an intimidating presence because of his height. If she glanced back and saw a tall guy in a hoodie only a half block behind her, she might panic and call 911, messing everything up. So he shuffled along slowly, planning to dart to the edge of their yard only when he could no longer see Georgie Boy's golden fur.

He was now in front of the Lennox home. For all intents and purposes, he looked like just another unidentifiable neighborhood guy out for an evening stroll. A few more steps and he'd be out of range of the camera, able to sneak along the fence line to the side gate.

Just then, Sheena paused to let Georgie Boy poop, so Curt stopped moving too. To stall, he bent down to untie and then retie his shoe. As he did, he winced audibly. His ribs were still sore from where Whitney Carlisle had whacked him with the lamp last night.

While he waited, his thoughts drifted back to that odd conversation with Cyndi. Why had she sounded so jumpy? It wasn't like her. That's one of the reasons he'd hired her in the first place—her chill, unruffled demeanor.

He wondered if that was her awkward way of hitting on him. She'd never given any indication that she was into him. And though she was cute, he wasn't interested in her for any number of reasons, foremost among them, that it would complicate nights like this.

But if she *was* into him, was this her way of finding out if he was really home so she could surprise him? The thought gave him a flicker of trepidation. Cyndi said she was just closing up at work. If she made an impromptu appearance at his house, it would ruin everything.

He told himself that he was overreacting, that she was just tired like she said. Looking up, he saw that Georgie Boy was done with his business. He and Sheena were just passing the house on the corner.

It was now or never. If he waited any longer, he wouldn't have time to properly prep for Sheena's return. And because of the couple's complicated schedule, if he didn't do the Elimination Event tonight, it might be weeks before he'd get another chance. Not to mention that he was really hoping to make up for the missteps with Whitney Carlisle last night. He was still reprimanding himself for not anticipating that bedroom issue.

He stood up, this time moving slowly. It didn't help. His ribs were throbbing. He started to doubt whether he'd even be able to scale the house's side fence in this condition.

Again he thought of Cyndi's peculiar vibe on the phone. Something was definitely up with her, even if he couldn't decide what it was. In that moment he decided: he was calling it off.

Between the ribs and his assistant's unsettling, potentially longing phone call, it was just too much. He couldn't chance the girl showing up on his doorstep and him not being there. Sheena Lennox would have to wait. He needed to get home. There was work to do and not much time to do it.

CHAPTER THIRTY ONE

They pulled up just down the street from Curt Sumner's house fourteen minutes after Cyndi hung up with him.

Even that was longer than Jessie would have liked, but they couldn't risk her calling Curt back once they left the office. So they took her back to the station, where she was left with an officer who would hold onto her phone until given an all clear. Once they dropped her off, they sped toward Sumner's home. On the way, they called Jamil to see if he'd gotten the court order to check Sumner's phone.

"It's pinging at his house," he answered before being asked.

"That was fast,' Ryan said, impressed.

"What can I say?" Jamil replied more brashly than usual. "I'm good at what I do. His vehicle GPS is also pinging from the house."

"Nice," Jessie said. "Since you're feeling so cocky, how about I give you a few more requests? Maybe they'll actually challenge you."

"Go for it," Jamil tossed back.

"Okay, first, I need you to check Sumner's criminal history."

"Already done,' Jamil told her. "I was about to tell you before you started questioning my skills. He got a DUI twelve years ago, but nothing before or since."

"Okay, smart guy," Jessie replied. "That was the easy one. I'm about to send you a full client list we got from Sumner's assistant. Can you look into whether any of them have been hurt or killed? Start with the most recent and work your way back."

"Will do," Jamil said confidently.

"And one more thing," she added. "Be careful."

"Why?"

"Because," she said, "I'm worried that with your skinny frame and your head getting so big, you might topple over."

She hung up without waiting for a response. Ryan's broad smile from the driver's seat was almost as satisfying as the dig itself.

But now, sitting in the car a half block from Sumner's house, all vestiges of jokiness were gone. They both activated the hidden wires they'd been given by an SMPD tech and tested that they were working with their support team.

As they got out of the car, Jessie tried not to think about how poorly Cyndi's call with Sumner had gone. She'd never heard those two people talk to each other before but she knew it couldn't normally be that stilted. And if she sensed it, Sumner surely did too. That might be all the forewarning he needed to hide evidence of his crimes. They walked over to one of the two squad cars that had arrived with them. The officer in the lead car lowered his window.

"Stay here out of sight until you see us enter the home," Ryan instructed. "That is, assuming he lets us in. Then you all can wait out front. Hunt and I are both wired up so don't go breaking down any doors unless we say something or you hear gunshots, okay?"

"Got it," the officer said.

Jessie and Ryan made the short walk to Sumner's home. It was more modest than those of the victims, but then again, that was true of ninety-five percent of the houses in L.A. His place was a cute, one-story cottage-style place. Getting on her tiptoes, Jessie could see over the fence to the edge of a small yard in the back. Even though the whole place was probably less than twelve hundred square feet, she estimated that it would probably go for over two million dollars if Sumner tried to sell it today.

"You ready?" Ryan asked, unsnapping his weapon's holster when they reached the front door.

"As I'll ever be," she replied with a smile of confidence she didn't really feel. She also released her holster guard.

Ryan was reaching out to ring the bell when the door opened, revealing a darkly handsome, very tall, very pale man with stormy gray eyes and black hair pulled back with a tie. He reminded Jessie of Trent Reznor twenty years ago. He was wearing jeans, a casual dress shirt, and an apron with traces of something red splattered on it.

"I have a motion detector," he said when he saw their surprised faces. "So I figured I'd save you the trouble of ringing the bell."

It occurred to Jessie that the man would also have a heads-up when the uniformed officers arrived at the door. Hopefully they'd heard what he said on the wire and would act accordingly.

"Do you always open your front door to strangers?" she asked, hoping to throw him off guard and get a sense of his real reactions before he realized what this was all about.

Sumner smiled comfortably.

"To be honest, no," he admitted. "But I just finished prepping dinner and was feeling sociable. Besides you two don't exactly look like you're selling bibles door to door. Have I made a terrible mistake?"

"I hope not, Mr. Sumner," Ryan said, "Although you might find us more objectionable than bible salesman. We're with the LAPD. I'm Detective Ryan Hernandez and this is Jessie Hunt. She's a consulting profiler for the department."

"I *knew* I recognized you from somewhere," Sumner said, pointing at Jessie excitedly. "You're the one who stopped that old guy a few weeks back, right? What did the news call him—the Senior Citizen Serial Killer or something like that?"

"That's what the news called him," Jessie confirmed, cringing at the memory of how much fun the media had turning a man who likely killed hundreds of people into a cheesy alliteration.

"But you guys had another name for him. Wasn't it the Night Killer?"

"The Night Hunter," Ryan corrected.

"Right," Sumner said before asking the obvious question. "So what brings you to my doorstep?"

"We're actually investigating a suspicious death involving a former client of yours, a woman named Siobhan Pierson," Ryan said, giving only the most bare bones information. "We've hit a bit of an investigative wall so we're reaching out to all manner of folks who interacted with her, trying to get some background, anything that can help us. At this point we're really grasping at straws."

Sumner nodded sympathetically. He appeared generally concerned but otherwise personally unflustered.

"Of course," he said, opening the door wider. "I was stunned when I heard about that on the news a while back. Anything I can do to help. Please come in."

They stepped inside and he closed and locked the door behind them.

"So how exactly can I help?" he asked.

"Maybe we should sit down somewhere for that," Ryan suggested.

"Sure," Sumner said. "Do you mind if we go to the kitchen? I was just wrapping something up in there."

"Lead the way," Ryan said.

Sumner walked down the narrow hall, which opened into an amazing kitchen that Jessie suspected took up a full third of the home's square footage. There was a giant island in the middle with seating for four and a six-burner stove next to a large butcher block. She paid particular attention to the knife block on top and noted that all the knives were accounted for.

Sumner also had two double ovens and a refrigerator the size of small shed. Connected to the ceiling above were several overhead lights and a couple of boom mics that hung down just out of view of the multiple cameras in the room. On top of all that, something smelled incredible.

"Whoa," she muttered despite herself.

"Thanks," Sumner said nonchalantly. "I'm a chef, mostly for private events. I call them 'House Cooks.' But another part of the chef gig these days involves doing on-camera tutorials for an online cooking channel I work with. I just finished one. In fact I posted it right before you arrived. I was just about to enjoy the fruits of my labor. Would you like some? I made enough to serve four. I was just going to freeze what I didn't eat myself."

Jessie looked at the counter by the sink, where a serving dish was filled to the brim with bubbling cheese and some kind of red sauce. In the sink were several bowls and pans, piled high. She could feel the residual heat from the overhead lights and the closest oven, even though they were all off now.

She found it all impressive but disconcerting. Was Curt Sumner the kind of person who could cook an entire meal for a viewing audience, then eat it, all before going out to slice a woman to death? Or was this his reward for a job already well done?

"I don't think we'll be here that long," Ryan said to the dinner offer. "But I don't want it to get cold so you go ahead. We can talk while you eat."

"Okay," Sumner said, scooping a healthy portion of what looked like something Italian into a bowl. "Please have a seat."

"What is that?" Jessie asked as they sat at the kitchen island barstools. She was sure Hannah would have known the answer upon sight. Thinking of her sister reminded her that she hadn't checked in for a while and probably wouldn't be able to for some time. She forced the needling guilt she felt out of her system. There was no time for it right now.

"Just eggplant Parmigiana," he said dismissively. "I'm in the middle of a 'hearty meals for winter' series. Sometimes I go more upscale but this dish is designed to be something easy that can feed a whole family. Nothing complicated about it, although I always like to add a few personal touches."

"Like what?" Jessie asked, both interested and hoping to keep the vibe casual for as long as possible.

"In this case, some brown sugar, along with sun-dried tomatoes for a hit of tanginess," he said, opening the fridge. "Would either of you like a drink?"

"Not for me," she told him.

She'd learned the hard way from Andrea Robinson never to accept food or beverages from someone connected to a case. The peanut oil that Andy had snuck into her Mojito on their ill-fated girls' night made her throat close up so fast that she nearly asphyxiated. Ryan shook his head as well.

While Sumner picked out something to drink for himself, Jessie looked around the kitchen. She was impressed with how he managed to keep everything so orderly. Not a cookbook on the bookshelf was out of place. Every appliance was perfectly equidistant from those on either side of it. Even the hand towels hung immaculately on their hooks.

She supposed she shouldn't have been surprised. Hannah was the same way when she cooked. Jessie shivered slightly at the thought of comparing her sister to a man who might have killed three women. But the fact remained: there was nothing out of place, at least not in the kitchen.

She did notice that in the adjoining living room, a pair of black pants and a black, hooded sweatshirt had been tossed carelessly on the back of the couch. It was at odds with everything else but maybe his attention to detail only extended to what he considered the most important room in his house.

Sumner, who had chosen a bottled IPA to go with his dinner, took the seat next to Jessie. She eyed the beer bottle warily, fully cognizant that it could easily be turned into a makeshift weapon.

With that realization fresh in mind, she decided that he was as comfortable as they could make him. If they were going to catch him in a deception, this was the ideal the moment. The time for pleasantries was over. She looked him directly in the eye as she asked her question.

"So Curt, what can you tell us about Gillian Fahey and Whitney Carlisle?"

CHAPTER THIRTY TWO

It wasn't that he didn't react. He did.

The problem was his reaction was completely normal, the response of a reasonably confused person.

"Who are *they*?" he asked, curious but in no way tense or startled.

"You don't know those names?" Ryan pressed, clearly getting what Jessie was trying to do.

"Should I?"

"Those are the women who were killed on the last two nights in precisely the same way as Siobhan Pierson," Ryan told him.

"That's terrible," Sumner said, putting down his beer empathetically. "I hadn't heard about this. Three women killed the same way? Shouldn't that be all over the news?"

"I'm sure it will be soon," Jessie replied. "Do they sound familiar to you, Mr. Sumner?"

He appeared to search his memory for a few seconds.

"I don't think so," he finally said, "but I'm getting the strong sense that you think they ought to."

"It's just they were also both clients of yours," she "informed" him, though she had her doubts about just how hazy his recollection really was. "You did events—House Cooks, I think you called them—for both of them in the last six months."

"Wow," he said, shaking his head in seeming disbelief. "That is a horrifying coincidence. And now I'm embarrassed that I don't remember their names. I know this is awful to say but I do private events five or six nights a week. They all start to run together after a while. The only reason I remember Siobhan Pierson was because she was a public figure and lived in this over-the-top, ornate mansion. So when I saw her on the news after she died, it all came flooding back. I'm ashamed to say these other women didn't stick out like that."

"That's understandable, Mr. Sumner," Ryan said. "But we're hoping that if we showed you pictures of them and their homes, then that might refresh your recollection. Would you be willing to do that?"

"Of course," Sumner offered. "Do you have them with you?"

"Unfortunately no," Ryan said. "They're all back at the police station over on Olympic. But hopefully that won't put you out too much. We just came from there and it only took about five minutes to get here."

"I know where it is," he said with good cheer. "My office is actually in downtown Santa Monica. That's fine. What time is good for you? Maybe I could stop by in the morning before I go to work."

"Actually," Jessie said, gently putting her hand on top of his—the one without the beer, "we were really hoping you might come over now."

Sumner frowned but didn't object outright. She continued before he tried.

"It's just that we've got these grieving families and every second counts," she said, delicately removing her hand from his. "It's like Detective Hernandez said earlier, we're at our wits' end here. We have virtually no good leads. That's why we're bugging a chef who cooked for them months ago in the hopes that seeing some photos might jog a memory that could be useful. We're really pulling at every loose strand at this point. Detective Hernandez and I got the lucky assignment. There's another detective currently interviewing these victims' plastic surgeon. I guarantee you that cop wasn't offered eggplant Parmigiana."

"I don't know—" Sumner started to say before Jessie cut him off.

"Speaking of dinner, why don't you package it up and take it with you?" she suggested. "You can eat while we review the photos. Hell, we'll give you a ride so you can take your beer too. Please, you'd be doing us a huge favor."

Sumner was quiet for several seconds. Jessie sensed that he was, against all odds, actually considering the idea. She decided to give him an extra push.

"Of course," she added, "if the idea of going to a police station is too intimidating for you, I get it. Not everybody is up for it. You'd be surprised at how many people can't handle looking at a few photos or answering a question or two from a cop. It's nothing to be ashamed of."

She started to get off the barstool as if to leave when he suddenly raised his beer bottle. For a long moment she thought he might smash it on the counter and attack her with it. Instead he put it to his lips and chugged what was left. Then he wiped his mouth and gave her a big smile.

"Let's go."

*

Sumner seemed mostly unfazed on the drive to the station. As they passed the homes in his neighborhood, he talked comfortably with Ryan about whether the Lakers or Clippers would finish the season with a better record.

The only time he seemed even momentarily distracted was when they passed an attractive woman returning home from a walk with her cute golden retriever. In the rearview mirror, she saw the chef's gaze linger on the woman a little longer than usual. Jessie wondered if he was imagining sleeping with her or killing her.

After that, the basketball talk resumed, which was fine with her. It kept Sumner relaxed and chatty and allowed her to settle on the best approach once they had him at the station. Unfortunately, the ride over lasted all of six minutes and by the time they pulled into the station lot, she hadn't come up with any brilliant ideas.

She looked at the man as he eased slowly out of the car and ambled leisurely into the station beside them. Carrying his dinner in a Tupperware container, but seemingly without a care in the world, his lack of concern had her starting to doubt herself.

Could someone this accommodating, this unflustered, be their guy? The answer, in her experience, was absolutely. The problem was, even if they had the right guy, if they couldn't prove it and he didn't implicate himself, there was nothing they could do.

They led him into the same interrogation room where they'd questioned Dr. Gahan, who was now on suicide watch in a holding cell downstairs. The tablecloth they'd used to mask the sterile metal surface underneath was still there.

"Don't you guys have an office or at least some desk we can use?" Sumner asked when he saw the barren room.

"We've actually been working out of here," Ryan said without missing a beat. "Our station is downtown. We've been helping the SMPD out on this case and this is what they had available. It doesn't really matter where we are though. We'll bring the laptop with the pictures in here. Just give us a minute to get organized."

"So I should wait here?" Sumner asked, looking around as if he couldn't believe how far from Michelin-starred restaurants he'd come.

"It's nothing fancy," Jessie admitted. "But have a seat. Enjoy your dinner. We can't offer you a beer but I can get you a soda or coffee if you like."

"Water's fine," he said, "and maybe a fork for my food."

"You got it," she told him, jokingly assuming a faux snooty tone. "Only our best plastic utensils for you, sir."

He chuckled politely as they stepped outside and closed the door. Ryan turned to her.

"I'll get the laptop while you get the other stuff," he offered. "Maybe on the way back, one of us will figure out how to break this guy, because he is the coolest customer I've come across in a long time."

"Don't hold your breath," she said. "I've been trying to figure that out since the second we left his place and I've got nothing so far."

"Well, I'd say we've got about five minutes before he starts to get suspicious and bails or worse, asks for a lawyer."

Jessie thought about that for a second and a crazy thought came into her head.

"Maybe that's not such a bad idea."

"What—let him walk?" Ryan asked incredulously.

"No, preempt him on the lawyer. One thing I've noticed about Curt Sumner is that he's pretty pleased with himself. He hides it underneath the gracious manner but the guy clearly has a massive ego. The very fact that he came here at all, that he's sitting in that room, willing to talk to us, suggests that he thinks he's playing a game that he can't lose. Set aside the potential triple murderer thing. He's still got the arrogance of a celebrated chef who was done wrong. He wants to prove just how clever he is. I say we let him."

"How?"

"Read him his rights when we get back in there," she said. "Make it seem like you're embarrassed to have to do it at all, but procedure requires it. Dare him to ask for a lawyer. I think he's too proud to do it."

"That's an awful big risk, Jessie," Ryan warned. "If he actually asks for an attorney, we're screwed."

"I have a feeling we may be screwed anyway. If Sumner is guilty, that means he's been planning each of these murders for months. Other than a temporary setback because of one bedroom that was converted into two at Whitney Carlisle's house, he hasn't made any mistakes that we know of. Right now, we don't have anything definitive to tie him to these crimes. I think we have to try something bold. Are you with me?"

Ryan smiled.

"Jessie Hunt," he said staring deeply into her eyes, "I don't know if this will work, but I can promise you one thing: I'm always with you."

CHAPTER THIRTY THREE

Ryan waited until the time was right.

First he and Jessie showed Curt Sumner the photos of the women and their homes.

"I remember that house now," he said, referencing the Faheys' mansion. "It was pretty impressive. But the woman doesn't jump out at me."

Ryan placed a photo of the Carlisle home in front of him.

"Does this look familiar?" he asked.

"I'm sorry," Sumner said, shaking his head regretfully, "but it really doesn't."

Ryan dropped another photo on the table, this time of Whitney on her couch, hugging Yaz the dog. He studied Sumner's face but the man didn't react to it at all. He looked up.

"I feel bad," he said. "But at a certain point, a lot of these folks just start to run together for me."

Ryan nodded as if that was perfectly normal.

"Thanks for looking at all of them," he said. "I do have a few more questions for you that might really help us, but in order to ask them, we have to go through the whole 'read you your rights' thing. I hate to throw that at you when you've been so cooperative. But it's technically required and since you don't seem to have any issue being forthcoming, I'm hoping it won't change anything. You mind?"

He thought he'd done a pretty good job of seeming uncomfortable with what he was asking while simultaneously making it seem like no big deal. But that wasn't really the point. He didn't honestly think he was tricking Curt Sumner. Like Jessie said, they were challenging him. Would he end this shared veneer of polite engagement? Would he get cold feet when facing actual stakes?

"It's a little weird," Sumner said, "but I guess I don't mind, though I can't promise I won't change my mind along the way."

"Totally reasonable," Ryan said, before launching into the Miranda warning. When he finished informing their guest that he could remain silent and had the right to an attorney, he wrapped up as casually as he could. "So after hearing all that, are you still cool talking to us?"

"For now, sure," Sumner said cautiously, though his body language—he was almost vibrating with anticipation—suggested he was eager for what was coming.

"Great, thanks," Ryan said. "So, to formally get it on the record, you said you remember Siobhan Pierson and her home as well as Gillian Fahey's home, but you can't specifically recall Fahey herself, or Whitney Carlisle?"

"That's right," he confirmed.

"Did you ever run into them after the House Cooks you did?"

"No. If I had, I suspect they would have said something to me, which would have helped me remember them better," he pointed out, borderline condescendingly. "But since I don't, I assume I never came across them."

"It's just that despite the population, this seems like a pretty small town," Jessie noted.

"That's true," Sumner agreed. "And I *have* definitely bumped into clients in the past but I usually don't recognize them. They'll see me and reintroduce themselves. I try to be polite about not recalling them but like I said, I have so many events that it's really hard."

"Understood," Ryan said, before making the best of an awkward transition. "Just to get it out of the way, where were you last night?"

Sumner smiled.

"Is this the alibi portion of the interview?' he asked.

"It is."

"Last night I had a House Cook," he replied without hesitation.

"What time was that?" Ryan wanted to know.

"Seven p.m."

"What about before then?" Jessie asked.

"I was home prepping for it."

"From when to when?" Ryan pressed.

As Sumner answered their rat-a-tat questions, his head bobbed back and forth like he was at a tennis match. But he didn't seem rattled. He looked like he was enjoying himself. Ryan had never seen a suspect, innocent or guilty, delight in an interrogation so much. He didn't know what to make of it.

"I left the office around four thirty," he answered. "Then I went home for my usual late afternoon walk. It's my one chance to decompress all day. After that I spent the next hour and a half prepping before heading over to the client's."

Ryan noted that the guy claimed he was "prepping" during the exact window of Whitney Carlisle's death.

"You drove?" Jessie asked.

"Walked actually," he corrected. "A lot of my clients live close enough for that. In this case, I just put the supplies in a wagon and wheeled everything over."

It went on like for that for a while. When they moved on to the night before last, when Gillian Fahey was murdered, Sumner's answers were equally succinct and unflappable; same thing for the night of Siobhan Pierson's death. At no point did the man look like he was sweating it.

Ryan glanced over at Jessie, who was giving him her patented "we need to talk" expression.

"Why don't we take a break for a few minutes?" he suggested. "Everyone can stretch their legs, use the restroom. Since we missed dinner, Ms. Hunt and I can grab a quick snack."

"Okay," Sumner said, standing up. "Do we have a lot more of this or are we nearly through?"

"I think we're almost done," Jessie said quickly, surprising Ryan. "We just need to dot some i's and cross some t's."

"Can't we just do that now?"

"We could," she said, guiding him to the door, "but to be honest, I really have to pee. I promise we'll be quick."

Once outside, Ryan motioned for a young, dark-haired officer named Wiedlin, who was standing guard outside the room, to come over, then turned back to Sumner.

"Guests aren't allowed to wander the station unaccompanied so Officer Wiedlin will escort you to the facilities," he said. "Let's meet back here in ten."

Sumner left with the officer while Ryan and Jessie retreated to their stifling conference room.

"Please tell me you're holding back some incredible insight," he said once they were alone, "because from where I was sitting, that interview was a disaster for us."

"That's *why* I wanted the break, Ryan," she said. "I agree that it was disaster. I just wanted to stop the bleeding."

"Well, we better think of something quick," he replied, "because our case against this guy is on life support."

*

Jessie had lied.

She didn't really need to use the restroom. But it turned out that Ryan did, which left her sitting alone at the conference room table with her head in her hands. A little voice in her head began to ask if maybe she hadn't gotten it wrong again; if perhaps the real killer was out there right now while she was wasting time in here. Shaking her head, she silently ordered the voice to shut up. Running out of time and ideas, she called Jamil.

"Any updates?" she asked hopefully.

"Nothing that will make you happy," he told her. "I checked Sumner's phone and vehicle data for the nights of all three murders. Both were exactly where they should have been during the time of each death."

"What about that client list?" Jessie asked, trying not to let the bad news overwhelm her.

"Still looking," he replied. "I've gone back about four months so far, but haven't found anything suspicious. One male client died about six weeks ago but it doesn't look connected. He was on vacation in the Bahamas at the time. It was declared a heart attack. Also, he was eighty-seven."

"Okay, keep looking," she instructed. "Anything else before I let you go?"

"I also screened the YouTube tutorial Sumner did tonight. It was uploaded at the time he said that it was, which supports his alibi. The clocks in the kitchen are visible and they match his story too."

"Okay, thanks, Jamil. I'll get back to you."

She hung up and let everything he'd said sink in. She consoled herself with one bit of positive news. If Sumner was making the YouTube video up until they knocked on his door, at least he hadn't had time to kill anyone between when he left work and their arrival at his house. So that left two options: either he really *was* planning to kill someone for the third straight night soon after preparing and enjoying a hearty Italian meal, or he had decided to take a night off from murdering women.

Jessie could feel the hands of the clock in her own head clicking loudly with each passing second. She was absolutely certain that Curt Sumner, and not Dr. Gahan, was their killer. It wasn't so much his answers as the way the presented him.

There was a coolness to him that seemed at odds with the circumstance he was in. No matter how innocent a man was, being brought in and questioned about the murders of multiple women he'd interacted with should have been a bracing, even scary experience. But

Sumner didn't exude even a hint of apprehension. It just felt wrong. It felt like the behavior of a guilty man who knew he was going to get away with it.

But she couldn't prove it. And if they had to let him go, the pressure on Captain Decker to publicly announce Gahan as the culprit would be overwhelming. An innocent man might go to prison or worse, while a guilty man walked free, all because she couldn't do her job.

Stop it! Focus. Work the problem. Find the solution. There has to be one.

She lifted her head, closed her eyes, took a deep breath, and fixed all her attention on Curt Sumner. He was so smooth, so practiced. She cast her mind back to when they first arrived at his place and did a mental scroll through their visit, trying to recall if there was any point when he hadn't been completely in control. For a full two minutes, she stayed like that—eyes closed, breathing deeply in and out, reliving all the moments leading up to this one.

Suddenly her eyes popped open.

There was no time at the house when Sumner was even slightly off his game. But there *was* a moment when he lost his discipline ever so briefly. It just wasn't in his house. It was in the car on the drive to the police station.

She reached for her phone. Ryan had to get back in here now.

CHAPTER THIRTY FOUR

"Slow down," Ryan demanded, swallowing a big piece of granola bar. "I'm gone a few minutes and the whole world explodes. What did you have Jamil check again?"

Jessie silently instructed herself to speak clearly and with deliberation. It wasn't that easy with so many thoughts pinballing around in her brain at once.

"Let me back up," she said more calmly than she thought possible. "A lot has happened while you were getting yourself a snack but leaving me hungry. When we drove Sumner back here from his house, I was watching him in the rearview mirror. He was happily chatting away with you about basketball teams. The only time he wasn't 'on' was when he got distracted by a woman returning home from walking her dog. He watched her for just a second longer than casual interest would justify."

Ryan walked over to her without a word, removed another granola bar from his pocket, and placed it on the desk beside her.

"Sorry," she said meekly.

"Forgiven," Ryan replied. "Okay, so he was hot for some neighbor?"

"That's what I thought at the time. Actually, that's one of two things I thought—that he wanted to sleep with her or to kill her. And that's when it hit me: maybe that wasn't just gallows humor. Maybe he really *did* want to kill her."

She paused briefly, waiting to see if he had any questions.

"Don't stop on my account," he said.

"Okay," she continued. "So I used Google street view to find the house again, and then gave the address to Jamil to work his magic. Want to know what he found?"

She couldn't help but allow herself this one moment of self-satisfaction. Ryan generously let her luxuriate in it before replying.

"Yes please."

"The couple who live there are Colin and Sheena Lennox. He's a doctor. She's a real estate agent. They are also former clients of Chef Curt Sumner. Before I even asked, Jamil was pulling up footage from their security cameras. He sent them to me. Take a look."

She watched Ryan as he studied the same clips she just had. In the first one, Sheena Lennox left her house with her dog and headed left along the sidewalk for a few paces before disappearing from the frame. The screen went black.

"Jamil said this next clip is from forty-five seconds later," she said.

It showed a man walking on the sidewalk in front of the same house. He was very tall and wore black pants and a black hooded sweatshirt that hid his face. He stopped directly in front of the house and bent down to tie his shoe. He moved gingerly, as if in pain. He stood up with similar caution. Then after staring in the direction Lennox had gone for several seconds, he turned and walked back in the same direction he came from. He moved tentatively, as if still in discomfort from bending down. He left the frame and the clip ended.

"You obviously think that guy was Sumner, right?" Ryan said.

"I'm sure of it," she insisted.

"Because he's tall?"

"That's just the cherry on top. Did you see the way he struggled when he bent down and stood up? How careful he was when walking away? It's almost as if he was dealing with a rib injury, the kind you might get if you'd been recently whacked with a big lamp."

"Jessie—" Ryan started to say, his tone suggesting more skepticism than she liked.

"Hold on," she told him. "I haven't gotten to the best part. When we were in Sumner's kitchen, I peeked into the living room and saw some clothes lying on the back of the couch. It was a pair of black pants and a black hoodie."

Ryan was quiet for a moment. When he started to talk, Jessie immediately knew she hadn't convinced him.

"You're right," he said. "It probably *is* him. Hell, I'm even willing to buy that he was there, scouting for a future attack. But that's not enough to arrest the guy. Remember, he lives a couple of blocks away. It's not unusual that he would pass by a neighbor's house, especially one he'd cooked for. We already know that he likes to do his House Cooks close to home. Nothing we saw on that video would convince a district attorney to charge him. It's all easily explained away."

Officer Wiedlin, who had shepherded Sumner to the bathroom, poked his head in.

"I took your guy back to the interrogation room five minutes ago. He's asking what's taking so long. What should I tell him?"

Jessie looked at Ryan, who shrugged resignedly.

"I think we have to cut him loose," he said.

Jessie desperately wanted to argue but no matter how much she wanted to, she couldn't come up with a reason to keep him here. She sighed heavily. Ryan took that as a sign.

"Tell him we'll be back in a minute to escort him out," he told the officer.

Wiedlin started to turn to leave. Something about the finality of the act made Jessie's chest ache.

"Hold on," she said, standing up. "Tell him we'll be back in five minutes. Say we're sorry for the delay—that we're following up on a suspect we like and we're just finishing up."

"Jessie," Ryan implored, "what's the point of delaying the inevitable?"

"You gave me an hour earlier today and I used less than half that to throw doubt on the Gahan case. All I'm asking for is five minutes."

Ryan grinned despite himself. He turned to Officer Wiedlin.

"Tell him what she just said," he instructed, "The whole thing—the suspect, the apology, the five minutes."

The officer nodded and left. When he was gone, Ryan turned back to Jessie.

"Okay, consulting profiler Hunt," he said. "What are you thinking?"

"Right," she said, sitting back down. "Let's start simple. We know he did it."

"We just have to prove it," Ryan replied.

Jessie smiled.

"Or at least make him think we can prove it," she said. "Maybe if we can get him on the defensive, he'll let something slip."

"He hasn't so far."

"Maybe not out loud," she conceded, "but I keep coming back to those clothes on the couch. I thought it was odd because everything else in his house was in its proper place. Maybe we poke him on that, comment on how not everything in the home was up to snuff, and see if he gets flustered."

"That's feels like a Hail Mary to me."

"You're right," she admitted, though she couldn't let it go. There was something about the clothes that felt important, like it might unlock everything else. "I just can't get past why a guy that anal would just toss that stuff on the couch. It doesn't fit the profile. It's like…"

She stopped mid-sentence as her brain opened up a door she hadn't known was there.

"Like what?" Ryan asked.

When she spoke, it was with confidence that she had finally discovered the clue that would lead her to the truth.

"It was like he had rushed home to change and didn't have time to put the clothes in the laundry."

She stared at her fiancé as one realization cascaded into the next. She didn't wait for him to respond.

"That's what it looked like because that's exactly what he did," she continued, grabbing her phone and calling Jamil. "He rushed home because he knew we were coming."

Ryan stood silently, waiting for her to explain how she was so sure. But that would have to wait.

"Hello," Jamil said after one ring.

"I need the time stamp on the second clip you sent us, the one where the guy in the hoodie ties his shoe."

"One sec," Jamil said without hesitation, his fingers audible as they flew across his keyboard. "It starts at 5:54:21 p.m. and ends at 5:55:09."

"What time did we have Cyndi call Curt Sumner?" Jessie asked Ryan.

"A few minutes before six," he said. "Remember, she was getting ready to close up the office when we got there."

Jessie nodded in agreement.

"I'm willing to bet that she called him right before this footage," she said. "I think he was about to sneak into Sheena Lennox's house. I think he had it all planned. He knew when she walked the dog. That was the perfect time to slip in. He was going to wait for her to come back and kill her. But something stopped him."

"The call?" Ryan asked. "You think Cyndi tipped him off somehow?"

"I think she didn't have to. That conversation was so awkward and she sounded so nervous that he had to know something was up. Look at the video again. He's staring off in the direction of Lennox and her dog, then he turns and leaves. I think that's the moment when he decided he had to abort. He couldn't risk it. If the cops were coming to his home, he had to get back fast."

"That's not the only reason he had to get back," Jamil chimed in excitedly. "Like I mentioned earlier, that tutorial video he uploaded has two clocks in it—one on the oven and another on the wall. They show the time he starts the lesson as five thirteen. He ends it at six-oh-one. If you guys showed up and he wasn't home, that would prove that he wasn't really home during that time, that he'd faked when he shot it.

And that would mean he might have faked the timing of other videos too."

"Like the night Siobhan Pierson was killed," Jessie said. "He had to get back to his house tonight in order to salvage his alibi for the night of Siobhan's murder. That's why he just tossed the clothes. He knew we were coming from his office and he had a good five-minute walk to get back home. He barely had time to change when he got there."

"Okay, but doesn't the video upload have a time stamp?" Ryan asked. "Wouldn't that show when he posted it?"

"Sure," Jamil answered. "But when it gets posted doesn't depend on when it was shot. It's easy to auto-upload a video at a predetermined time. Lots of people do it."

"That means that *everything* was probably faked," Jessie told them. "The tutorial was pre-shot. The food was pre-cooked. He could have just microwaved it. Meanwhile he turns on the oven and the overhead lights for a few minutes so they'll seem recently used. He changes into the more camera-friendly clothes he had on in the video. He even splatters some red sauce on his apron. But in all that rushing around, he forgot to move his other clothes into the bedroom, something this guy would never do under normal circumstances."

They were all quiet for a moment.

"This is great stuff," Ryan finally said. "But we've got a suspect in there who expects us back *now*. He could walk out of that interrogation room at any second. And because he didn't actually kill Sheena Lennox tonight, it doesn't matter that he faked his alibi because there was no crime to cover for. We don't have proof that he faked the video the night Siobhan Pierson was killed. Unless he confesses, he still walks."

Jessie thought about it for a second before replying.

"You're right," she admitted. "This guy is too good. We might never catch him in a mistake that we can tie to one of the murders. That's why we need to come at it a different way."

"A different way?" Ryan repeated, flabbergasted. "How do you propose to do that in the next three minutes?"

"I'm not going to," she said. "Jamil is."

"Excuse me?" the surprised researcher said over the phone. "How?"

"First I need you to get a warrant to search Sumner's house," she told him. "But that's just for insurance. This next part is more important."

"I'm listening."

"If we can't connect Sumner to these murders," she explained, "then our best bet is to find out *why* he's committing them. Are you still searching that client list?"

"Yes," he said. "I'm about halfway through; still nothing."

"Change of plans," she told him. "Stop working backward. If we want to learn the motive for these murders, we need to start at the beginning. Something clearly set him off. But he didn't begin killing women until months after cooking for them. Maybe whatever started all this began a while back too. Go back to the beginning, Jamil."

"Okay," he said. "I'm on it."

"We don't have any more time, Jessie," Ryan insisted to her. "We have to get back in there now."

"I know," she replied. "While Jamil's doing his thing, we'll be in with Curt Sumner."

"Doing what exactly?" Ryan wanted to know.

"Well, like you said, we don't have anything solid on the guy and we can't be sure that Jamil will come up with anything new. So we're going to do what you said."

"What did I say?" Ryan asked.

"You said the only way to stop him is to get him to confess. So that's exactly what we're going to do."

CHAPTER THIRTY FIVE

"Sorry for the delay," Ryan said to Sumner when they returned to the interrogation room. "We were following up on a time-sensitive lead involving a possible suspect."

"I hope it bore fruit," Sumner said. He was leaning back in his chair, comfortably sipping at his water bottle.

"We're still in wait and see mode," Ryan replied. "But we didn't want to keep you waiting any longer that we already have. So let's get back to the i-dotting and t-crossing, shall we?"

"Hold on," Jessie said. "Don't you want to remind him of his rights again?"

Ryan looked at Sumner questioningly.

"Would you like me to do that? It all still applies but I can do it if you like."

"I'm good," Sumner told him. "I can remember things for longer than twenty minutes."

"I'm sure you can," Jessie said, baiting him as she and Ryan had predetermined that she would. "But are you sure? I mean it can't hurt to have a lawyer to help out if there are questions you're not equipped to answer."

She thought she saw the slightest glimmer of irritation in his eyes, though she worried that she might have imagined it.

"I said I'm good," he repeated slowly and with emphasis. When he was done speaking she saw that any impatience had been replaced by self-assurance. His relaxed demeanor was back. He thought he had her right where he wanted her. She could read it all over his face—he wanted to outsmart Jessie Hunt, the famous profiler who had just caught the legendary serial killer, the Night Hunter. At least now she had something she could use against him.

"I was surprised by how messy your house was," she told him in an intentional non sequitur.

"What?" he asked, temporarily flummoxed. "You're kidding, right? Other than a few dirty dishes in the sink, it was immaculate."

"No, you're right," she replied, waving her hand dismissively. "The kitchen was fine. I was talking about the living room, all those sweats draped over the couch."

The briefest cloud of uncertainty crossed his face before quickly fading away.

"I went for a walk earlier," he explained. "It was cold so I dressed warm and I lost track of time. By the time I got home I was behind schedule on prepping the tutorial so when I changed, I just tossed the clothes in the other room. I wasn't expecting company."

His answer was completely plausible but that didn't bother Jessie. Her goal had been to get him on the defensive and it had worked. Moreover, she realized with a slight rush, he'd essentially admitted to wearing the outfit they'd seen on the person in the security footage outside the Lennox house.

"I'm sure you weren't," she replied, before veering sharply in another direction. "So you like to walk in the neighborhood."

He didn't seem troubled by the sudden topic change.

"Yes. Like I said before, I find it very relaxing with my stressful schedule these days."

"I know what you mean," she said. "I could use some relaxation time myself. By the way, I noticed you stopped at the Lennox house."

His eyebrows arched slightly, which she interpreted as him being truly surprised, perhaps for the first time that night. He recovered quickly.

"That's right. Did you know I did a House Cook for them once? It was the easiest commute I've ever had. Nice people too. Anyway, I pass by their place on lots of my walks. I think I was there around four forty-five today. How did you know about that?"

"Oh, I'm not talking about the earlier walk where you were wearing different clothes," Jessie told him, not specifically answering his question. "I'm talking about the more recent one when you were wearing the sweats, at least according to the security cameras at the Lennox house."

She let that last line linger for a second. Out of the corner of her eye, she saw Ryan stiffen slightly. They were entering a perilous stage now, when things could go sideways.

Sumner played it as if honestly perplexed.

"I'm not sure what you mean," he said softly.

"Yeah; I knew it was you both times even though you wore the hoodie on the second walk because you have this kind of halting gait," she said, cartoonishly reenacting his walking style. "It's like you're trying to protect an injured rib or something."

Curt Sumner's eyes narrowed involuntarily at that comment. He definitely didn't look cocky now. Before she could continue, both her phone and Ryan's pinged with a text. She recognized the tone as Jamil's.

"Hold on one second," she said, checking to make sure Ryan had noticed it too, and then standing up and moving to the corner of the room to read it. "I think this might be about the suspect we mentioned we were looking at."

She glanced down. Jamil's text was comprehensive. It read: *Reviewed CS's client list from the beginning. Fourth ever client was killed ten months ago. Her name was Chrissie Newton. Throat sliced—case never solved. Also, warrant for CS house was approved. Team en route now. Additionally, trying to confirm tutorials were auto uploads. Even if successful, might not be a smoking gun. By the way, found this additional security footage a half block from CS home at 5:59. Suggests CS was forwarding his calls from his phone to a burner to give false location. Hope it helps.*

It was a lot to process but Jessie kept her focus on the data that could actually help her in this room right now. Her fingers trembling slightly, she opened the list of Sumner's past clients and scrolled to the name Chrissie Newton. All it said was that the woman was married and lived in Marina del Rey.

Still, she was a client who was subsequently killed with a knife. That was huge. There was no way it was just a coincidence. It was clear that this woman was where the madness had started. Jessie didn't know how or why but it definitely all began with Chrissie Newton. Curt Sumner was unquestionably the man they were after. A thrill of certainty shot up her spine.

And yet she knew she'd never be able to connect him to Newton's death at this point. Too much time had passed. She had to move past it. Nonetheless, she committed the name to memory.

She waited for the rush of disillusion-tinged excitement to pass. Once it did, she opened the video clip that Jamil had included. It showed a man in black pants and a hoodie who was clearly Sumner. He dropped what looked like a cell phone on the ground next to a trash can at a residential intersection. Then he began smashing it with his foot. After that, he scooped up the pieces and threw most of them in the trash, then snapped the one remaining piece into two, tossed them in his mouth, and swallowed them. Jessie assumed it was the phone's SIM card. She looked over at Ryan, who had just finished reviewing the text as well.

She knew what he was thinking because she had come to the same conclusion. Even though the wheels were in motion, it wasn't enough.

They would soon have Sumner's clothes but they wouldn't be evidence of anything illegal. They might be able to show that he faked the time of tonight's tutorial but that did them little good. Proving he'd done the same thing the night Siobhan Pierson was killed was likely impossible. They knew he'd falsified his location for tonight's call with Cyndi but that wasn't a crime and confirming he'd done the same on the nights of the other murders was unfeasible in the time they had tonight, or maybe ever.

They didn't have enough to nail Sumner and they couldn't count on finding any evidence that would. The team going to his house would tear it upside down but unless he was foolish enough to keep the clothes he wore while committing his crimes—and he wasn't that foolish—that would be a dead end too.

Jessie glanced from Ryan to Sumner. The chef hadn't lost the apprehensive expression from when she'd needled him about walking oddly due to a possible rib injury. He was still off-balance. But if they let him leave this room now, he'd regain his equilibrium and likely never lose it again.

They couldn't let that happen.

CHAPTER THIRTY SIX

There was still a chance.

After all, Curt Sumner was here of his own accord. He hadn't invoked his right to remain silent. He hadn't asked for a lawyer, even though he had to know that she suspected the truth of what he'd done. Despite everything, he was still playing the game. He still wanted to beat her. He was still sure he could, and he was probably right.

That was why she had to keep going. He'd never be this vulnerable again. It was now or never. Jessie turned to face Sumner and flashed a big smile.

"We're making real progress," she said enthusiastically as she held up her phone, hoping she was as good a liar as Sumner.

That's great news," he replied, sounding as disingenuous as she felt.

She returned to the chair opposite him, sat down, and sighed loudly, as if she was losing interest in him. She did it intentionally to get under his skin. It was part of her plan, but it was a dicey choice to continue to goad a man like Sumner. He was unpredictable.

Once she started down this path, there was no way back. And if this went south, she'd be out of cards to play. But she had to do it. She needed a confession in case everything else fell through. Besides, something told her that he wanted to take credit for what he'd done. She sensed that he was proud of it.

She stared at his arrogant, overconfident smirk. His was the face of a man who was sure he was the cleverest person in the world. He wouldn't like it very much if she suggested otherwise. It was time undermine that aura of self-importance. She looked at Ryan one last time. He nodded imperceptibly. And with that, she dived in.

"I hate to do this again," she said reluctantly, "and I hope you don't take offense, but I really think you should reconsider asking for a lawyer. You genuinely seem like you might need one. You might be out of your depth here, Curt. No offense."

She smiled sympathetically, as if she was telling a hopeful job interviewee that she'd decided to go another way. He sneered back.

"I'm fine, thanks," he said. "I've got nothing to hide."

Relieved but not totally surprised, she played her first card.

"Okay then," she replied briskly. "So here's what's so confusing to me, Curt. You were on a walk at the same time that the clocks in your tutorial video say you were cooking. How is that possible?"

He nodded condescendingly.

"I could see why that might be confusing for you. But I'll clear it up. I keep having trouble with those clocks—batteries dying, electronics on the fritz. I never trust the accuracy of those clocks. I just use my watch."

Jessie pursed her lips as if pondering his words.

"Ah, thanks for clearing that up for me," she said. "But don't you find it odd that each screwed up clock had the exact same incorrect time as the other one throughout the whole video?"

It was Sumner's turn to wave dismissively.

"Who knows? I'm a chef, not a clockmaker. Honestly, I find even the most basic technology challenging. Figuring out how to put those videos together was a real bitch for me. I'm a bit of a Luddite."

Jessie looked at Curt Sumner, with his relaxed, untroubled smile, and suddenly a truth that she'd been fighting against this whole time became plain to her: she was going to lose.

As long as they were in this room and he thought there was any chance that he was at risk, Sumner would never let his guard down. And unless he did, she would never nail him. She had to change the dynamic, and in that moment, she could only think of one certain way to do it. She had to let him go.

"You know what, Curt?" she said, standing up, "I think we're wasting your time here."

"What?" both he and Ryan asked at the same time.

"Yeah," she said. "You're right—you're not a clockmaker. I think this is just one big misunderstanding. Detective Hernandez here is going to close out the paperwork and I'll give you a ride back home, okay?"

"Okay," Sumner said tentatively, standing up slowly. "So should we just go now?"

"Might as well," Jessie said, ignoring the hard stare Ryan was giving her as she opened the door and motioned for Sumner to step out. "Just give me one second to grab my coat from next door."

Ryan followed her into the observation room and closed the door.

"What the hell are you doing?" he demanded in an intense whisper.

"I'm shaking things up," she said as she turned on the voice memo function on her phone and shoved it in her coat pocket, before patting it for his benefit. "This will work short term but as soon as he and I are out of sight, get the tech folks to turn the wire I'm still wearing back on. I want multiple recording devices on this conversation."

"You're still trying to get a confession?" Ryan asked in disbelief.

"Give me your keys, sweetie," she said without answering. "Our guest is waiting."

"Be careful," he pleaded as he handed them over reluctantly.

She gave him a kiss on the cheek and stepped back outside, where Sumner was leaning against the wall.

"Ready?" she asked.

"I'm well past ready," he replied.

"Then let's go," she said, leading him down the hall in silence for a few seconds. Only once they were outside, in the cool air and away from anyone else, did she resume their conversation from the interrogation room as if it had never ended.

"I know what you meant back in there about being a Luddite. Hell, clocks *are* complicated," Jessie said, letting the sarcasm bleed through for a beat before adding, "And yet, despite your problems, you manage to get by, don't you?"

"I muddle through," Sumner replied, sounding equally smarmy as he walked along beside her, "although I'm not sure what you're referencing."

She'd played her first card back in the interrogation room. Now, as they left the sidewalk and moved into the station's exterior parking lot, she played her second one.

"Well, for starters, you somehow managed to figure out how to have your cell number forwarded to another phone so it looked like you were home when you were actually out of the house. That's pretty impressive for a Luddite."

Sumner's silence told her she'd hit a nerve. She kept going, talking in a singsong voice that she hoped he found annoying.

"I'm assuming you forwarded those calls to the burner phone you smashed into pieces with your foot and dumped in a trash can—all except for the SIM card, of course, which you swallowed. That was a weird choice."

"I thought you said this was all a big misunderstanding," he said, not amused.

"Oh, totally," she told him. "This is just me and my harebrained theorizing. Anyway, I think that trash can was on the corner of California Avenue and 11th Street, which is only half a block from your house. What a coincidence! Some people might wonder why you'd do something wacky like that, but not me. I don't like to pry."

"Of course you don't," he said archly.

"You sure you don't want that lawyer now?" she asked with a giggle, before adding, "Just kidding. Or am I? It doesn't really matter anyway. It's not like I'm a cop."

He looked less like he wanted legal representation and more like he wanted to slice her up. His eyes were blazing and he no longer had that relaxed, untroubled smile. Jessie saw Ryan's car in the distance and headed that way. As she walked, she noticed that there was no one else in the lot with them.

"I would never ask for a lawyer, Ms. Hunt," Sumner replied, still sounding even-keeled, though he didn't look it, "as that might mean an end to all this free entertainment."

"Yeah, you're right," she said, playing her third card. "We're having too much fun, aren't we? But I *do* think you're selling yourself short. You say you're a Luddite but you did also learn how to auto-upload those videos so it seemed like you were home when you were really out. I'm guessing you've done that at least once before, on the night that Siobhan Pierson died, so kudos to you."

She saw that he was about to respond but didn't want to give him the chance to lower his internal temperature with a snarky quip so she plowed through.

"One funny thing you'll learn, Curt, is that at the downtown station where we usually work, we have this researcher. He's the one who texted us back in the interrogation room. His name's Jamil and he's definitely *not* a Luddite. He's a real tech whiz kid, the kind of guy who can detect auto-uploads and track forwarded cell calls and access useful home security footage without even trying. I don't mean to compare you to him—that wouldn't be fair. But you're pretty good too."

Sumner exhaled deeply, much like Jessie often did when she was trying not to lose it with Hannah. His breath was visible in the crisp air.

"You give me too much credit," he said.

His voice was still calm but his eyes were shaky. This was as agitated as she'd seen him. To most people, he probably looked fine. But in her limited time spent with him, she knew otherwise. He was boiling inside. But if she wanted him to bubble over she had to push a little harder, even if she got burned.

"I think maybe I did give you too much credit," she said sincerely, her voice a whisper, "but not anymore."

"What?" he asked, confused. He'd clearly been expecting more sarcasm.

They had reached Ryan's car. Standing by the passenger door, Jessie turned to face Sumner directly. For the first time, she truly appreciated how big the man was. She was tall but he still towered over her by half a foot. It was hard not to be intimidated. But she did her best.

"I thought we were dealing with some evil genius," she said with what she hoped sounded like regret. "But you're not that. You're the guy who showed up on security video outside a potential victim's house. You're the guy who forgot to plan ahead and didn't realize that the new deck at the Carlisle house might mean other changes had been made too."

Sumner was squirming now, as if there was a creature inside him trying to get out. She kept going, hoping that either her phone or the wire was catching everything they said.

"You think you're so smart because you left your cell phone with its GPS at home to give yourself an alibi; because you picked victims within walking distance of both your home and the House Cooks you scheduled that night. That way, you didn't have to drive yourself or take a cab or a rideshare. That way, there were no witnesses and no digital record, no way to track your movements. You thought you were being so clever but you left bread crumbs everywhere. You think you're some architect of death but compared to the people I go up against, you're just an amateur."

Behind his tightly pursed lips, Sumner was grinding his teeth.

"You're wrong," he hissed quietly.

She was close. But she needed something more, something that would open the floodgates. And then she hit on it. He wanted to prove he was better than her. He wanted to prove she was wrong, that she had failed to judge him properly. She needed to let him have his moment of vindication, out here, alone, where there would be no consequences. And she had an idea how she would do it.

"*Am* I wrong, Curt?" she teased, leaning in toward him despite her thumping heart, trying to channel his arrogance. "I don't think so. All this is happening because you're weak. You just couldn't help but glance longingly at Sheena Lennox when we drove past her house, could you?"

She pressed on before he could respond.

"You think this was all some test of your mastery. You can gussy it up all you want, but you're deceiving yourself. Hell, that's what the Night Hunter did too. He thought he was an artist. But he was just like you and all the others, driven by desires he couldn't control. You're all consumed with the need to control others. But the irony is that you can't control yourself."

Sumner's eyes were fixed on the asphalt next to the car. His hands were balled into fists, pressing into his jacket. She could feel the fury radiating off him. Now it was time for the big lie.

"You had to look at Sheena," she spat victoriously, playing her final card, bluffing with all her might, "just like you had to have her. And if you couldn't have her, you were going to kill her. Just like you couldn't have Chrissie Newton, so you killed her."

That was what broke him. He took a step toward her, bumping into her with his chest, knocking her up against Ryan's car.

"You don't know what the hell you're talking about!" he snarled down at her.

Jessie tried not to flinch.

"What do you mean?' she asked, craning her neck back to make eye contact with him.

"I wasn't pining for Chrissie," he shouted, sticking his finger in her face. "It was the other way around. She practically threw herself at me!"

Jessie didn't know where he was going with this but it was her job to keep him riled up enough to get there. She couldn't stop now.

"Sure she did," she shot back skeptically, though she sensed that she was out on a limb that could break at any second, and when it did, Curt Sumner might break her.

"She did," he insisted, "during their House Cook. Hell, she wanted to go at it while her husband was in the bathroom. But I didn't do it, not until later. And then I found out she was frickin' crazy."

"Crazy, how?" Jessie asked.

She watched him seethe at the memory of it. He couldn't stop himself. He didn't even try.

"After a month of mediocre sex, she begs me to come over to her house. When I get there, she says she loves me and she's leaving her husband. I told her I wasn't interested. Then she starts threatening me, saying that she'll tell everyone that Chef Curt Sumner sleeps with wives who hire him. She was screaming at me, right up in my face, promising to ruin my career. I had to protect myself so I grabbed the closest thing I could find—a knife—and used it. I didn't have a choice."

He was standing in front of Jessie, his whole body shaking, the finger that was pointed at her quivering wildly. She worried that he might inadvertently poke her in the eye.

"I get it, Curt," she said, her voice now warm honey. "You didn't have a choice. She didn't leave you one."

"Right," he agreed, looking at her plaintively. "You understand."

Now that the dam had broken, he didn't seem to care about anything but making certain that she did. That was fine with her. Every second that he talked was another second for the cavalry to arrive.

Where the hell are they, by the way? Didn't they hear that confession?

"I do," Jessie assured him, putting her hand on his shoulder and easing him away from her. And she did understand. While she didn't buy his crap about not having a choice, now that she knew how this started, she could make an educated guess as to why it continued. "It happened so quickly, didn't it?"

He nodded that it did.

"But after it was over," she prodded gently, "once you knew you had gotten away with it, you couldn't stop reliving it, could you?"

Curt Sumner's eyes widened. He stared at her like she was literally reading his mind.

"I watched the life bleed out of her. I saw her last breath, the moment the light left her eyes. It was beautiful…and powerful…to know that this woman had been alive moments earlier and, because of me, that was all gone. To have that power in my hands—it was intoxicating."

"You wanted that feeling again," she nudged.

The second she said it, she knew she'd gone too far. The dreaminess in his eyes at the memory of killing Chrissie Newton disappeared, replaced by the cunning alertness that had defined him until a minute ago. He suddenly appeared to realize what he'd done, and how irreparable the damage was. Still, he tried.

"You bought all that?" he asked with forced nonchalance. "I was just messing with you. I can't believe you actually fell for it."

Though she knew she shouldn't, that she was baiting a hibernating bear, she gave him her own relaxed, untroubled smile.

"Too late for that, Curt," she said. "We got everything on the wire. You really should have asked for that lawyer."

She should have known better. Maybe she'd been lulled into complacency by his refined manner or her awareness that he was unarmed. Maybe it was just that he was such an unbelievably narcissistic bastard. But all that complacency vanished in a moment. Only the flare of his nostrils gave her any warning about what was coming.

He yanked his right fist, still balled up tight, back behind him and thrust it forward toward her face. With that brief second of preparation, Jessie ducked and dropped to her knees. Above her, she heard a loud shattering sound and felt pebbles of glass rain down on her neck.

She looked up to see that Sumner had smashed his fist through the front passenger window. He was staring at his hand, which was bloody and had bits of glass sticking out of it. For a moment, he seemed too shocked to scream.

Then he let out a howl that echoed through the parking lot. Jessie knew it was only a matter of time before his attention turned to her. As quickly as she could, she dropped her stomach and rolled under Ryan's car. Now on her back, the last thing she saw before she scuttled under were Sumner's eyes boring into hers.

She tried to scurry to the middle of the car but before she could, she felt his hands on her ankle. He hollered again at the pain that gripping her leg must have caused. But that didn't stop him from tugging at her furiously. She felt the asphalt scrape against the skin of her back as he yanked her out.

When she saw him again, he was standing over her, his bloody, glass-pocked right hand dripping down on her. He grimaced as he clenched it tight, oblivious to the blood that went from a trickle to a thin stream down the outside of his fist. Jessie wanted to kick at him but he was standing straddling her waist, making it impossible. All she could do was clench her knees into a ball and hope to drive her feet at him when he plunged his fist down.

He moved fast, dropping suddenly as she tried to tuck into a protective shell. Just as the gleaming fist picked up team, she saw something to the left out of the corner of her eye. Something slammed hard into Sumner. Before she could blink, he was gone.

She rolled over to find the chef sprawled out on the ground, gasping for breath. Just beyond him, Ryan was scrambling to his feet. With his eyes focused and clear, he took two steps forward and dropped to his knees, landing both squarely on Sumner's sternum. The man groaned. Then Ryan slid off, rolled him onto his back, and cuffed him.

"I'd read you your rights," he said, panting heavily, "but we've already been through all that. Besides, you've already confessed."

Sumner could only grunt in response. Jessie got to her feet, stumbled over to Ryan, and helped him up. He was clearly winded. But for a guy who'd been unable to walk seven months ago and had just made an open field tackle, he looked pretty good.

"You have no idea how pissed I am at you right now," he told her.

“You have no idea how hot you are right now,” she replied.

CHAPTER THIRTY SEVEN

"I just want to make sure that he's being kept on at least a twenty-four hour hold."

Ryan pulled into the driveway at home close to ten, just as Jessie finished up her conversation with the police psychiatrist evaluating Dr. Roland Gahan. He had been formally cleared of the murders, but considering that he had a gun in his mouth earlier this afternoon, it didn't seem advisable to just release him back into the world.

Ryan turned off the engine and waited while Jessie got her assurance that the surgeon was being transported to the hospital for a more formal evaluation.

"All good?" he asked when she hung up.

"I wouldn't go that far. The man lost his livelihood, his reputation, and his marriage. Now he may end up losing his medical license and his autonomy, so all in all, not a great day for him."

"At least he's not in jail, charged with murder," Ryan replied with strained enthusiasm.

"There is that," she conceded before looking at the door leading to the house and groaning. "I'm scared of what we're going to find in there."

"Hey, if there was bad news to share, Kat would have reached out by now. Sometimes no news really is good news."

"You really are a fount of positivity this evening," she noted warmly. "Between that and your heroic rescue earlier, it kind of makes a girl want to be around you, if you catch my drift."

"Your wish is my command," he said, trying to bow from the driver's seat.

Maybe it was the release of tension or the lack of sleep, but his goofy gesture was so endearing that she had half a mind to marry him right then and there. The idea filled her with equal parts giddiness and shame.

Why was she still insisting on holding off? She'd told herself that it was because of Hannah's issues, and because of the constant threats they faced. But there would always be threats.

Even if she gave up consulting for good and stuck to teaching at UCLA, as she was tempted to do, Ryan was still an LAPD detective.

And no matter how well therapy with Dr. Lemmon went for Hannah, she had a long road ahead of her to process what she'd done. Were those really reasons to hold off on getting married? Was she not allowed to be happy until *all* their issues were resolved? She knew better than most that such a day was unlikely to ever come. And like Ryan had told her the other day, the world couldn't just stop because things were hard right now.

"We should start telling people," she said.

"What?" Ryan asked, perplexed.

"About the engagement, we should start sharing the news."

"Okay," he said, his broad smile nearly blinding her, "Why the change of heart?"

"We have a source of joy in our lives. I'm tired of hiding it."

"That's what I like to hear, Hunt," he said loudly, slapping the steering wheel enthusiastically. "Who do you want to start with?"

Jessie opened the car door and got out.

"Considering that Kat already knows," she said, "I think there's only one logical choice: we have to tell Hannah."

Ryan gave her an apprehensive look as he got out.

"I'm all for it," he said. "But are you sure she's going to react well?"

"I'm not sure of anything with that girl," Jessie said as she opened the door to the house, "but if we don't tell her next, we'll never hear the end of it. So let's take the leap and hope for the best."

"Do I hear familiar voices?" Kat called out.

Jessie and Ryan rounded the corner to find her seated at the kitchen table, surrounded by scattered files.

"Oh no," Jessie said. "Are you still working on that crappy accounting case?"

"Just wrapping it up," Kat said, standing up and stretching. "That's why I'm smiling."

"How did it go?" Ryan asked.

"Turns out it wasn't all that different from the other cases I typically get. Remember how the head of the accounting firm thought an employee was siphoning off money in small amounts? He was partly right. Only it wasn't an employee, it was his partner, who also happens to be his wife. She was draining the funds to pay for her affair, which she conducted in various high-end downtown hotels."

"You look pretty satisfied about it," Jessie noted.

"It's just reassuring to know that no matter how technical a case seems, in my line of work it usually comes down to somebody screwing someone else or screwing *over* someone else. In this case it was both. And I partly have you to thank."

"Me?" Jessie said. "Why?"

"Because if I hadn't been holed up in this house, mostly at this table, I probably would have found some excuse to do unnecessary surveillance that would have kept me from seeing what was really going on, but being stuck here for two days kept me focused."

"So you're saying I shouldn't feel bad about imposing on you well beyond what should be asked of a reasonable person?" Jessie asked hopefully.

"Oh no, you should definitely feel bad," Kat assured her. "But considering the payday I'm getting from my extremely pissed off client, I'll let it go this once."

"I appreciate that," Jessie said, giving her a hug. "All the same, I can't thank you enough for doing this. You were a lifesaver."

"It wasn't so bad," Kat said. "When she wasn't in her room on a device, she was mostly pleasant, which is more than I expected."

"Is that where she is now?" Jessie asked.

"Yup, for the last hour," Kat answered, gathering up her files. "Oh hey, how did your case go? I assume well or you wouldn't be so chatty, or for that matter, home."

Jessie looked over at Ryan to see if he wanted to do the honors. But he had spent much of the drive home updating Captain Decker and she could tell he wasn't up to doing it again.

"Short version," she said. "We caught the guy, a chef who liked to cut a little too much. He was pretty good at it too. If he hadn't admitted his guilt, I don't think we could have nailed him."

"She's being modest," Ryan interjected. "That was a Jessie Hunt special. She bluffed her way into a confession."

"Wouldn't expect anything less," Kat said, dropping her files into a duffel bag. "Well, I'm headed out, you two lovebirds. Say goodbye to Hannah for me, will you?"

They promised they would and escorted her to the door. Once she left, Ryan turned to Jessie.

"Ready to break the news to your sister?" he asked.

Before she could answer, her phone rang. When she saw who it was, a cold shot of anxiety cut through her.

"It's Callum Reid," she said. "I better take it, just in case. We'll tell her after, okay?"

"That's fine," Ryan said, acting like there was nothing to worry about. "Gives me a chance to grab a drink."

While he went to kitchen, Jessie stepped into the living room to answer the call.

"Hey, Reid," she said. "Is everything okay?"

For a long second there was no answer and she feared the worst.

"Reid, are you there?"

After another second his familiar voice came on the line.

"Sorry about that," he said. "I dropped the phone."

"That's okay," she replied, relieved. "How are you feeling?"

"Pretty decent, all things considered," he told her, sounding like he meant it. "I'm on the couch, being catered to hand and foot. I should have had a myocardial infarction years ago."

"Don't push it!" Jessie heard Reid's wife shout in the background.

"Sorry, honey," he said, before returning to Jessie. "Are you alone?"

"That would be a no," Jessie said.

"Then I'll be quick," he said. "I just wanted to thank you for keeping my secret. I know you must have had second thoughts after things went sideways for me. But I'm glad I'm getting to end things on my own terms."

"Me too," Jessie said. "So how was the big news received?"

"Decker was disappointed but understanding. I think he could tell there was no changing my mind. And like you predicted, having a bigger budget and a new detective in the unit eased the pain for him. He's having a retirement party for me tomorrow. He wants to be the one to tell the whole HSS team. So when he makes the announcement, please act surprised."

"Not a problem," she promised.

"Thanks," he said. "And can I make one final request?"

"Of course."

"It's about Susannah Valentine."

"What about her?" Jessie asked warily.

"She's brand new and she's trying to impress everyone. Sometimes she might go a little overboard and I could see how it could rub someone the wrong way. But maybe you could take it easy on her?"

"Why are you telling me this?" Jessie asked. "Did she say something to you?"

"She didn't have to. I have very keen investigative instincts. After all, I'm a detective, or I was one until today."

"She didn't exactly present a winning first impression," Jessie admitted. "But for you, I'll try."

"Thanks, Hunt. And who knows, maybe you'll end up being besties, or whatever it is the kids call it these days."

"Goodbye, Reid," Jessie said.

"Goodbye, Hunt."

She hung up and started toward the kitchen for a drink when Ryan emerged with a glass of mineral water with a lime wedge, just the way she liked it.

"You are a prince among men," she said.

"I know," he said, handing her the drink. "How's Reid?"

"He's good," she said, "just wanted to check in on us."

It was a white lie, hopefully the last time she'd have to tell it.

"You ready to try this again?" he asked, looking at Hannah's door.

"Let's do it."

She knocked on the door. After a good five seconds, an irked voice yelled, "Yeah?"

"It's me and Ryan," she said. "We're home for the night. Can we come in?"

"It's not locked."

She opened the door and stepped in. Ryan followed close behind. Hannah was lying on her bed, scrolling through her phone. She must have sensed something was going on because she sat straight up.

"What is it?" she demanded. "Did someone die?"

"No," Jessie said, "at least not anyone you know."

"Then what is it? I can tell it's something big. Are you sending me away to boarding school?"

"Hannah, calm down," Jessie pleaded. "We do want to tell you something but it's nothing bad. Ryan asked me to marry him and I said yes. We're engaged."

She almost laughed as she watched her sister's defensive glower turn into slack-jawed astonishment.

"For real?" she asked.

"For real," Jessie said, showing her the ring on her hand.

"Wow, that's—congratulations," she said with real sincerity.

"Thank you," Jessie replied.

"When's the wedding?"

"Actually," Ryan said, "we haven't gotten that far yet. We've mostly kept it to ourselves until now."

"Okay," Hannah replied, mildly perplexed. "Well, whatever works for you. Congrats again."

It seemed like that was the end of the conversation as far as she was concerned.

"Did you have any other questions?" Jessie asked.

Hannah shrugged ambivalently.

"No, I'm good. I figure you'll fill me in when there's stuff worth sharing."

"Okay," Jessie said, trying not to take offense. It wasn't a stunning surprise that a seventeen-year-old might not be giddy to learn more details about her much old sister's engagement. Still, the coolness was palpable. She decided to change subjects.

"How did it go with Dr. Lemmon today?"

Hannah looked at Ryan and he got the message.

"I just remembered that I have a thing that I have to do in a room that's not this one," he said, before leaving and closing the door behind him.

"It was good," Hannah said once he was gone. "I know what you're wondering and the answer is no—I haven't told her about shooting the Night Hunter yet. But it was good to be back in therapy in person. I feel like I'm on the right track."

"That's great," Jessie said, deciding not to push the issue. "You can tell me more later if you like. For now, I'm going to get cleaned up and crash. I'm pretty wiped out. Don't stay up too late. You've got school tomorrow."

Hannah nodded and returned her attention to her phone. Jessie got up and moved to the door. Before she closed it, she took one last look at her sister. Hannah was immersed in her phone. To any casual observer, she looked like a normal teenager with normal problems. Maybe one day she really would be.

*

Hannah lay in bed. Her eyes were on the phone but her mind was elsewhere.

She kept thinking back to Dr. Lemmon's request in therapy: "Tell me what you were thinking about just now."

She had wanted to. But some part of her knew that if she had said what she was really thinking out loud to another person, even a therapist, it would change everything. How could she admit to Dr. Lemmon what she could barely admit to herself?

Yes, she had shot the Night Hunter because he was a monster who would always be a threat to herself and the people she loved as long as he lived. But that wasn't the main reason: she had killed the unarmed, handcuffed, elderly man because she wanted to.

And now, weeks later, she could admit something else: she liked it. More than that, she missed it.

EPILOGUE

The hulking, sweaty woman was crying uncontrollably.

It was all Andy Robinson could do not to throw up as she hugged her. But she gulped hard and squeezed her back. When they finally separated, Andy looked down at her prison uniform. It was damp but she wasn't sure whether the liquid was tears or perspiration.

"I ruined your clothes," Livia said apologetically as she wiped her wet nose with the back her massive forearm.

It was true. Not only was the unflattering, yellow shirt wet, it now stunk of Livia's body odor. Livia wasn't big on showers.

"Don't worry about it," Andy said, smiling broadly and ignoring Livia's matted black hair. "It's not like I'm going to be walking the red carpet in this outfit anytime soon. Besides, the guards have another one just like it waiting for me."

"Yeah, I guess," Livia agreed, looking despondent.

"Hey," Andy said encouragingly, "let's focus on you. You're getting out of here. Pretty soon you'll be lying in a park under a tree, eating bonbons."

"I'm going to miss you, Andy," Livia said, her bulging cheeks threatening to jiggle again as she fought back more tears.

"Me too," Andy said, clutching the giant's hand and pretending not to notice the mucus where Livia had used it as a tissue. "But remember, it going to be okay. We've talked about this. If you start to doubt yourself, just follow the principles we discussed."

"I still think I should write them down," Livia said.

"No, they're more powerful if you just keep them in your mind. When you feel like you're getting into trouble, just follow those principles. Remember, your mind is your strongest tool. It can take you anywhere if you let it."

"Uh-huh," Livia said, starting to blubber again.

"Livia Bucco, time to go," shouted a guard from down the hall.

Livia looked back at Andy with panic in her eyes.

"I'm scared," she whispered, "I don't think I can do it."

"Sure you can," Andy promised. "I know it's scary to be out in the world again. But I believe in you."

Livia took a deep breath and shook her head hard, like she was trying to force demons out of it.

"Thank you, Andy," she said softly. "If it wasn't for you, I'd probably be behind bars in this nuthouse forever. It's only because of you that I'm going free. I won't let you down."

Livia gave Andy one last squishy, gag-inducing hug and headed off to the waiting guard, who would process her out of the Female Forensic In-Patient Psychiatric Unit at the Twin Towers Correctional Facility Medical Services Building. She didn't look back for fear of losing it again, but if she had, she might have been surprised by the devilish twinkle in Andy Robinson's bright blue eyes.

THE PERFECT VEIL
(A Jessie Hunt Psychological Suspense Thriller—Book Seventeen)

"A masterpiece of thriller and mystery. Blake Pierce did a magnificent job developing characters with a psychological side so well described that we feel inside their minds, follow their fears and cheer for their success. Full of twists, this book will keep you awake until the turn of the last page."
--Books and Movie Reviews, Roberto Mattos (re *Once Gone*)

THE PERFECT VEIL is book #17 in a new psychological suspense series by bestselling author Blake Pierce, which begins with *The Perfect Wife*, a #1 bestseller (and free download) with over 5,000 five-star ratings and 900 five-star reviews.

Women are found murdered in Los Angeles, all connected to a powerful cult. As Jessie unearths secret after secret about their inside relationships, she soon realizes she is up against forces more powerful than she can imagine. With her investigation seemingly shut down and a killer out there with an active agenda, will Jessie be able to save the next victim before it's too late?

A fast-paced psychological suspense thriller with unforgettable characters and heart-pounding suspense, THE JESSIE HUNT series is a riveting new series that will leave you turning pages late into the night.

Books #18 (THE PERFECT INDISCRETION) and #19 (THE PERFECT RUMOR) are now also available.

Blake Pierce

Blake Pierce is the USA Today bestselling author of the RILEY PAGE mystery series, which includes seventeen books. Blake Pierce is also the author of the MACKENZIE WHITE mystery series, comprising fourteen books; of the AVERY BLACK mystery series, comprising six books; of the KERI LOCKE mystery series, comprising five books; of the MAKING OF RILEY PAIGE mystery series, comprising six books; of the KATE WISE mystery series, comprising seven books; of the CHLOE FINE psychological suspense mystery, comprising six books; of the JESSE HUNT psychological suspense thriller series, comprising nineteen books; of the AU PAIR psychological suspense thriller series, comprising three books; of the ZOE PRIME mystery series, comprising six books; of the ADELE SHARP mystery series, comprising thirteen books, of the EUROPEAN VOYAGE cozy mystery series, comprising six books (and counting); of the new LAURA FROST FBI suspense thriller, comprising four books (and counting); of the new ELLA DARK FBI suspense thriller, comprising six books (and counting); of the A YEAR IN EUROPE cozy mystery series, comprising nine books, of the AVA GOLD mystery series, comprising three books (and counting); and of the RACHEL GIFT mystery series, comprising three books (and counting).

An avid reader and lifelong fan of the mystery and thriller genres, Blake loves to hear from you, so please feel free to visit www.blakepierceauthor.com to learn more and stay in touch.

BOOKS BY BLAKE PIERCE

RACHEL GIFT MYSTERY SERIES
HER LAST WISH (Book #1)
HER LAST CHANCE (Book #2)
HER LAST HOPE (Book #3)

AVA GOLD MYSTERY SERIES
CITY OF PREY (Book #1)
CITY OF FEAR (Book #2)
CITY OF BONES (Book #3)

A YEAR IN EUROPE
A MURDER IN PARIS (Book #1)
DEATH IN FLORENCE (Book #2)
VENGEANCE IN VIENNA (Book #3)
A FATALITY IN SPAIN (Book #4)
SCANDAL IN LONDON (Book #5)
AN IMPOSTOR IN DUBLIN (Book #6)
SEDUCTION IN BORDEAUX (Book #7)
JEALOUSY IN SWITZERLAND (Book #8)
A DEBACLE IN PRAGUE (Book #9)

ELLA DARK FBI SUSPENSE THRILLER
GIRL, ALONE (Book #1)
GIRL, TAKEN (Book #2)
GIRL, HUNTED (Book #3)
GIRL, SILENCED (Book #4)
GIRL, VANISHED (Book 5)
GIRL ERASED (Book #6)

LAURA FROST FBI SUSPENSE THRILLER
ALREADY GONE (Book #1)
ALREADY SEEN (Book #2)
ALREADY TRAPPED (Book #3)
ALREADY MISSING (Book #4)
ALREADY DEAD (Book #5)

EUROPEAN VOYAGE COZY MYSTERY SERIES
MURDER (AND BAKLAVA) (Book #1)

DEATH (AND APPLE STRUDEL) (Book #2)
CRIME (AND LAGER) (Book #3)
MISFORTUNE (AND GOUDA) (Book #4)
CALAMITY (AND A DANISH) (Book #5)
MAYHEM (AND HERRING) (Book #6)

ADELE SHARP MYSTERY SERIES
LEFT TO DIE (Book #1)
LEFT TO RUN (Book #2)
LEFT TO HIDE (Book #3)
LEFT TO KILL (Book #4)
LEFT TO MURDER (Book #5)
LEFT TO ENVY (Book #6)
LEFT TO LAPSE (Book #7)
LEFT TO VANISH (Book #8)
LEFT TO HUNT (Book #9)
LEFT TO FEAR (Book #10)
LEFT TO PREY (Book #11)
LEFT TO LURE (Book #12)
LEFT TO CRAVE (Book #13)

THE AU PAIR SERIES
ALMOST GONE (Book#1)
ALMOST LOST (Book #2)
ALMOST DEAD (Book #3)

ZOE PRIME MYSTERY SERIES
FACE OF DEATH (Book#1)
FACE OF MURDER (Book #2)
FACE OF FEAR (Book #3)
FACE OF MADNESS (Book #4)
FACE OF FURY (Book #5)
FACE OF DARKNESS (Book #6)

A JESSIE HUNT PSYCHOLOGICAL SUSPENSE SERIES
THE PERFECT WIFE (Book #1)
THE PERFECT BLOCK (Book #2)
THE PERFECT HOUSE (Book #3)
THE PERFECT SMILE (Book #4)
THE PERFECT LIE (Book #5)

THE PERFECT LOOK (Book #6)
THE PERFECT AFFAIR (Book #7)
THE PERFECT ALIBI (Book #8)
THE PERFECT NEIGHBOR (Book #9)
THE PERFECT DISGUISE (Book #10)
THE PERFECT SECRET (Book #11)
THE PERFECT FAÇADE (Book #12)
THE PERFECT IMPRESSION (Book #13)
THE PERFECT DECEIT (Book #14)
THE PERFECT MISTRESS (Book #15)
THE PERFECT IMAGE (Book #16)
THE PERFECT VEIL (Book #17)
THE PERFECT INDISCRETION (Book #18)
THE PERFECT RUMOR (Book #19)

CHLOE FINE PSYCHOLOGICAL SUSPENSE SERIES
NEXT DOOR (Book #1)
A NEIGHBOR'S LIE (Book #2)
CUL DE SAC (Book #3)
SILENT NEIGHBOR (Book #4)
HOMECOMING (Book #5)
TINTED WINDOWS (Book #6)

KATE WISE MYSTERY SERIES
IF SHE KNEW (Book #1)
IF SHE SAW (Book #2)
IF SHE RAN (Book #3)
IF SHE HID (Book #4)
IF SHE FLED (Book #5)
IF SHE FEARED (Book #6)
IF SHE HEARD (Book #7)

THE MAKING OF RILEY PAIGE SERIES
WATCHING (Book #1)
WAITING (Book #2)
LURING (Book #3)
TAKING (Book #4)
STALKING (Book #5)
KILLING (Book #6)

RILEY PAIGE MYSTERY SERIES
ONCE GONE (Book #1)
ONCE TAKEN (Book #2)
ONCE CRAVED (Book #3)
ONCE LURED (Book #4)
ONCE HUNTED (Book #5)
ONCE PINED (Book #6)
ONCE FORSAKEN (Book #7)
ONCE COLD (Book #8)
ONCE STALKED (Book #9)
ONCE LOST (Book #10)
ONCE BURIED (Book #11)
ONCE BOUND (Book #12)
ONCE TRAPPED (Book #13)
ONCE DORMANT (Book #14)
ONCE SHUNNED (Book #15)
ONCE MISSED (Book #16)
ONCE CHOSEN (Book #17)

MACKENZIE WHITE MYSTERY SERIES
BEFORE HE KILLS (Book #1)
BEFORE HE SEES (Book #2)
BEFORE HE COVETS (Book #3)
BEFORE HE TAKES (Book #4)
BEFORE HE NEEDS (Book #5)
BEFORE HE FEELS (Book #6)
BEFORE HE SINS (Book #7)
BEFORE HE HUNTS (Book #8)
BEFORE HE PREYS (Book #9)
BEFORE HE LONGS (Book #10)
BEFORE HE LAPSES (Book #11)
BEFORE HE ENVIES (Book #12)
BEFORE HE STALKS (Book #13)
BEFORE HE HARMS (Book #14)

AVERY BLACK MYSTERY SERIES
CAUSE TO KILL (Book #1)
CAUSE TO RUN (Book #2)
CAUSE TO HIDE (Book #3)
CAUSE TO FEAR (Book #4)

CAUSE TO SAVE (Book #5)
CAUSE TO DREAD (Book #6)

KERI LOCKE MYSTERY SERIES
A TRACE OF DEATH (Book #1)
A TRACE OF MURDER (Book #2)
A TRACE OF VICE (Book #3)
A TRACE OF CRIME (Book #4)
A TRACE OF HOPE (Book #5)

CPSIA information can be obtained
at www.ICGtesting.com
Printed in the USA
LVHW111309180922
728624LV00024B/433